EMPIRE BORN

When Michael Hope is murdered in a robbery in upcountry Kenya, the Minister of Tourism takes the matter most seriously. The Special Branch is called in; the culprits must be found. It is of only passing interest to the authorities that Michael has been killed in the country where he was born and brought up before returning to England with his family at the time of independence. But for Michael's widow Juliet and a British journalist sent to cover the story, the killing leads to new discoveries about the secretive Michael, whose work in the slums of Brixton had led him into a severe personal crisis.

EMPIRE BORN is a highly evocative novel ranging from the last days of colonial Africa to the barricades of Brixton.

'The novel succeeds, where many "Empire" novels fail, in braving the myriad complications and subtleties of the legacy of colonialism and showing that there is no easy comfort available for Michael or anyone else'

New Statesman

'A gripping story and a fascinating one for our time . . . a vivid and important book'

Catholic Herald

**Also by the same author,
and available from Coronet**

Upperdown

About the author

Stephen Cook, who spent part of his
childhood in East Africa, is a journalist on *The
Guardian*. His one previous novel,
UPPERDOWN, was highly praised. He lives
with his wife and son in London.

Empire Born

Stephen Cook

CORONET BOOKS
Hodder and Stoughton

First published in Great Britain in 1986
by Hodder & Stoughton Limited

Coronet edition 1987

British Library C.I.P.

Cook, Stephen, *1949–*
 Empire born.
 I. Title
 823'.914[F]   PR6053.0524/

ISBN 0 340 41722 6

Printed and bound in Great Britain
for Hodder and Stoughton
Paperbacks, a division of Hodder and
Stoughton Ltd., Mill Road,
Dunton Green, Sevenoaks, Kent
TN13 2YA.
(Editorial Office: 47 Bedford Square,
London WC1B 3DP) by
Cox & Wyman Ltd., Reading

Chronology

1952	Hope family emigrates to Kenya
1952–5	Mau Mau uprising
1954	Michael Hope born
1963	Kenya's independence under President Kenyatta Hope family returns to England
1963–75	Michael Hope educated at various schools and Exeter University
1978	Death of Kenyatta Michael Hope starts working in Brixton
1981	April: First riots in Brixton July: Michael and Juliet Hope are married
1982	July: Michael and Juliet visit Kenya August: Unsuccessful coup attempt in Kenya Juliet returns to England

GLOSSARY

Swahili Words

posho:	ground maize (a staple food)
uhuru:	freedom (used with capital 'U' to mean Independence for Kenya in 1963)
kazi:	work
bwana:	Sir, master
kiboko:	hippopotamus; hence 'hippo-hide whip'
panga:	long agricultural knife
shenzi:	mongrel; bastard
wabenzi:	modern Swahili slang for rich men driving Mercedes-Benz cars.

Other Words

KANU:	Kenya African National Union, now the ruling party
munt:	derogatory South African expression for blacks
yarpie:	derogatory English colonial word for South Africans
Cavirondo:	the crested crane (national bird of Uganda)
pongo:	colonial slang for newcomer from Britain
mzungu:	European, white person
(pl. *wazungu*)	
jembe:	agricultural digging implement, shaped like an adze
ayah:	nanny, nurse
syce:	groom (horses)
rondavel:	round, mud-and-wattle building with thatched roof

PART ONE: AFRICA

One

The ambush happened at one end of the long, narrow bridge over the Noigameget river. It had been prepared by men who had evidently done this sort of thing before, and it worked faultlessly: this was 1982, when such attacks were almost familiar in the African highlands of Kenya, whose wealthy few are beset by the growing tribe of the poor.

One of the gang was waiting in scrubby bushes beside the red dirt road where it began its descent into the river valley. When he had seen that the car was worth having – it was a Peugeot 504, the very best – he gave two slow blinks on his dim torch to the other three waiting at the far side of the bridge. Before the light of the headlamps reached them, they swiftly pulled on the ropes attached to the fifteen-foot thorn tree they had felled, and dragged it across the road ten yards beyond the bridge – leaving space for the car to get off the bridge itself, but not enough for it to negotiate a path around the trunk or the bushy top at the edges of the steeply cambered road. The white car, braking steadily all down the two-hundred-yard incline, moved into second gear with a blip in the hum of the engine, and slowly began to cross the bridge, its lights playing patterns through the sloping metal rails which guarded the sides. The driver now caught sight of the tree blocking his way beyond the twenty-yard slab which spanned the dark water, and the note of the engine gurgled and hesitated as he eased indecisively off the accelerator.

There was no choice, however: he had to stop. As he wound down the window to peer into the warm darkness, the men were swiftly there, at both sides of the car, tugging the doors open, pulling at the arms of the two passengers and shouting at them to get out. The fact that the couple in the car were white did not cause any hesitation in the attackers; the young men of modern Kenya who had fallen into the criminal life suffered from none of the reluctance of their fathers and grandfathers about laying hands on white flesh. It was no longer taboo, and it usually meant better spoils. As they were bundled from their seats and round to the front of the car, Michael Hope and his wife Juliet noticed in their shock and dismay that the men were armed, two of them with the two-foot-long farm knives called *pangas*, and one with a large, clumsy-looking pistol.

'What do you want, what do you want?' gasped Juliet repeatedly, speaking in English because she knew no Swahili, but receiving no reply she could understand. She tried to move closer to her husband, her terror increasing, but one of the men held her firmly by the arms at one side of the car while the others dragged Michael further from her.

Seeing his wife appealing to him as she struggled and slipped on the loose dirt beneath her feet, Michael Hope made a sudden, convulsive, ducking effort to free himself. It succeeded temporarily, and he moved towards the man holding Juliet, opening his arms as if in a prelude to an appeal for her release. But one of his own captors, half by reflex at Michael's escape, struck out at him with his *panga*, and the long, newly honed blade carved hard across his shoulder and down his back. He fell slowly forward and on to his face, his pale shirt swiftly sucking up the blood from a red cleft where the bone showed in the harsh light of the headlamps. He began a curiously muted choking and gasping, paddling his hands and feet across the loose surface of the road, as if having some eccentric little squabble with himself. His wife stopped struggling, and screamed loudly at the sight of her felled husband, and the robbers began shouting angrily at each other, as if suddenly aware that the stakes were now much higher.

The man who had struck out with his *panga* threw a thin rope across to the one holding Juliet; he had been going to use it to tie up her husband, but there was no need now. As the man tried to attach the rope to one of her wrists, she half-escaped from him, and he had to drop the rope and drag her to the ground to stop her escaping. One of the other two, who had started to drag the tree out of the path of the car, came over to help in the binding of her hands behind her. She began to scream differently now, in great intermittent gusts of noise which only stopped when one of the men took a dirty piece of cloth from his pocket and pushed it roughly into her mouth to gag her. The man with the gun had managed to finish pulling the tree aside by himself and was now in the car, revving the engine, shouting for the other two. The fourth man, panting from his run down the hill and across the bridge, arrived and climbed into the back of the car. Juliet's captors pushed her, wrists bound, towards her bleeding and slowly writhing husband, and she staggered and fell at his side. All the men were now in the car, and with a metallic grinding of the gears and a roar of the engine, it began to pull away.

10

It immediately stopped again, however, and Juliet looked up to see three of them climb out of the car again and come towards her. She tried to get up and run, fearing rape or death, but she was grabbed and held while hands were thrust roughly into the pockets of her bush shirt: they had forgotten to search them for valuables. They unbuckled the watch from her wrist, then turned their attention to Michael. They pulled him over on to his back to go through his pockets; his face was white, his eyes closed and his limbs unresisting. They came up with several hundred-shilling notes and a crushed packet of American cigarettes. As they were moving back to the car, one of them hesitated, gesturing and nodding at the figure below them on the ground, now mumbling and moaning with pain under the eyes of his helpless wife. Another hurried, anxious argument took place; and then the man who had been at the wheel took a step towards Michael, pointed the heavy gun, and shot him through the breastbone.

When Juliet opened her eyes again after the blinding, booming detonation a foot from her face, the car was pulling away violently, its rear wheels skidding and throwing up earth. After the shot, the sound of the engine was very small and quickly distant as the car climbed up out of the river valley. Michael was quiet and still now, and the bright night sky of Africa showed up a small, expanding dark mark on his chest. She leaned close to his face, and heard a bubbling sound in his open mouth, like water in an obstructed drain. Her shoulders heaved and she tried to wrestle her hands free of the rope holding them tightly behind her back. Failing, she suddenly got to her feet and began to run clumsily up the road after the car, but after twenty yards she faltered, stopped, and stumbled back to the body in the road. Michael's eyes were closed now, and blood was flowing from his mouth, but his chest beneath the now-soaked shirt was still rising and falling. She dropped to her knees beside his head and tried, in a grotesque maternal pantomime, to shuffle forward to bring his head on to her lap. But without hands to lift him, she could not do it, and the dying man could offer no help. She gave up, and instead lowered herself slowly, guided by some confused instinct, to the ground beside him, and pushed herself, helpless and defeated, against the length of his blood-wet body. When the people from the nearby village arrived, alerted by the screaming and the shot, she had not moved again, and Michael was dead.

This violent murder of a British tourist was a serious business in a

11

country which needed all the foreign wealth it could get, which depended heavily on its reputation in the West as the safest and most stable country in black Africa. There would be consternation at the highest levels, anxious and discreet diplomatic contacts, angry exchanges in Parliament, a determination that something would be done. And in due course a most painful irony would come to light: Michael Hope had not only died in their country, but had also been born there twenty-eight years before.

Two

Ten miles beyond the Noigameget river lies the small town of Kitale, an administrative and agricultural centre for the district. Its most impressive feature is the main road, a straight avenue shaded by the dark green leaves of fine podo trees, and which seems to sweep on past the shabby town centre as if hurrying disdainfully to the wilder untouched country further north. There is a hotel, a post office, a bank, a police station, two streets of boxy concrete buildings behind cracked, dusty pavements, a few bougainvillea bushes; on the more spacious fringes of town stand those vital institutions of highland colonial life – the church, the showground and the Kitale Club with its golf course. It was here, nearly thirty years before the ambush at the river bridge, that Mr and Mrs Hope, restless expatriates from the industrial Midlands, had arrived to run a small business selling agricultural machinery to the surrounding farms. They realised almost as soon as they arrived that they were too late, that the time of white domination was drawing to a close, but they determined to stay and make the most of the remaining years. Their business did well, and their son Michael, who was to be their only child, was born at the local hospital.

Soon afterwards they moved out of the town, away from the boxy cement buildings and the nearby black township which made them feel uncomfortable, and rented a place on Mount View Farm. The owner of the farm had moved to Nairobi, leaving in charge a young English manager who lived in a couple of *rondavels* near the milking sheds, and the Hopes took the main bungalow; they became addicted to its peace and beauty before they appreciated its isolation, six miles outside Kitale on the way towards Mount Elgon and the Uganda border. Built in a brick which was the orange-red of the local soil, with a roof of cedar tiles decked with flowering creepers, it sat snugly on one of the mountain's more prominent foothills, and its long verandahs looked down the gentle, golden-brown slopes of the farm to the wooded river valley. And then the eye would be carried up, up to the blue and green slopes of Elgon itself, the mysterious triple-humped mountain with its high bamboo forests, its elusive elephant herds, and the great, secret caves which ran far into its body. The Hopes would sit silently with their gin in the brief, intense

13

twilight after they returned from work, gazing at this heart-stopping country, silently amazed to be there, amazed that any of this could ever have happened, anxious about their future, bewitched on their verandah.

With their uneasiness about Africans, it took them a long time and much hesitation to commit Michael to the care of a native, but they saw how the long-established settlers casually handed over their offspring to black women as soon as they were born, and when Mary was recommended to them by the Northrops after their own children were sent away to boarding school, the Hopes 'took the plunge', as they put it. They were assured by the Northrops, their nearest neighbours at Twiga Farm who fell into the trusty category of 'old Kenya hands', that Mary was reliable and that her own baby would not interfere with her duties. As the first uneasy weeks went by, they discovered that Mary was indeed a paragon: she wore a green cotton dress cut like a nurse's uniform, kept her eyes averted when spoken to, never failed in her attention to the treasured Michael, and went to church on Sundays in the missionary centre a few miles away. The Hope parents did not enquire or speculate too much about what Mary might do with the rest of her meagre time off, but their minds dwelt at times on the origins of her little boy, Kimutei.

'I do hope Mary is, well . . . respectable,' Mrs Hope would say, looking anxiously across at her husband. He would sigh and reply with a wry smile born of white contempt for black morality: 'Even if she's not, I don't know what we can do about it, dear. Besides, everything seems to be working out very well.'

Because Kimutei was a house servant's son, and lived with Mary in one brick-built room behind the house rather than in one of the mud-and-wattle huts down on the farm, he had few black friends. His mother always dressed him carefully in clean shorts and shirt, and the rag-clad farm boys would either stare at him, unsure of his identity, or jeer at him, sometimes throwing stones. And so it came about that Michael and Kimutei were thrown together for the first time, and were scarcely conscious of their difference during their earliest years. They would wander the garden and farm together, ever further from Mary's vigilance. Michael would walk freely into their small, smoky home, and he and Kimutei would argue and squirm on the rickety, rope-strung bed while Mary cooked maize meal above a few scraps of charcoal between three stones at the back door. There were scenes, however, when the food was cooked and

14

placed before Kimutei; Michael wanted some, and was occasionally allowed to sample the glutinous, grainy *posho*. But soon he would be taken off to the main house for his bath, so he would be neat and clean and ready for his meal when his parents came home from work.

Kimutei never entered the main house, although Michael sometimes brought him on the verandah, under the uneasy eye of his parents, to play with his model cars. Mary would take Michael alone into the bathroom, sometimes screaming with fury at being parted from his friend, and bathe him carefully in the orange-stained water which had left a ladder of tidemarks on the once-white enamel. Kimutei was washed in the mornings, under a tap behind the servants' block, with the water running away into an evil-smelling puddle. Michael, shining and subdued after his bath, would be fed by his doting, pretty mother – chicken, or meat, and sweet puddings.

As the two boys grew older and became more adventurous, they were harder for Mary to control. They would escape from her and break into the forbidden maize-crib down in the farmyard, a tall building whose eerie, shadowed interior exerted a strong pull on them. The farm manager, the young, embarrassed Mr Bryant, heard childish laughter from inside the crib one day and pulled open the door to find the two three-year-olds sliding down the mounds of maize cobs, which moved beneath them and dumped them in a small avalanche on the wire-mesh floor, the dust from the grain hanging and swimming in the sun shafting through the cracks in the walls. Bryant shouted angrily, thinking at first, in the gloom, that they were both black children. He stamped in closer, his boots turning and slipping on the cobs, and realised that one was Michael. His voice softened.

'Michael!' It was that half-admonishing, half-approving tone used by adults when boys were being boys. 'What *are* you doing here? This is out of bounds, you know.'

Ignoring the motionless and silent Kimutei, Bryant bent down to lift Michael gently and hold him against his chest, where the child glared into his slightly spotty face, panting from his illegal exertions.

'Put me *down*!' he yelled suddenly. Bryant's face clouded; he strode unsteadily out into the sunlight, his grip tighter now on the struggling boy, and looked angrily about for Mary. Her finely tuned ear had picked up Michael's shout, however, and she was already running anxiously over from the milking sheds where she had been gossiping with some of the farmhands.

'Mary!' he shouted. 'What d'you think you're doing? Eh? Come here!'

He thrust Michael, now sobbing, into her arms and disappeared into the crib again. When he emerged, he was holding Kimutei by the arm with one hand while slapping wildly at the boy's bottom with the other. Then he half-threw him on to the dusty farm track with a grunted: 'And *don't* come back!' and walked over to Mary, dusting off his hands.

Kimutei picked himself up, glancing reproachfully over his shoulder at Bryant. He had taken punishment, unlike Michael, but was making no noise. His small face was hard and tight, his eyes shining. First he looked at Mary, engaged with calming Michael, but her glance told him she was no refuge for him just now, his own mother. So he turned and walked slowly away, in his waddling, little boy's walk, turning occasionally to watch developments behind him.

'Sorry, *bwana*, sorry,' Mary was saying to Bryant. 'They run away all the time, they are very bad boys. Sorry, *bwana*.' Her forehead was creased with anxiety, her body bobbing in obeisance.

Bryant's anger had ebbed and he stood frowning, gangling with inexperience and embarrassment.

'Yes,' he said hesitantly, running each hand down the thick blond hairs on the opposite forearm to clear the remaining dust. 'Well, I shall have to tell *bwana* Hope about this.'

'No, *bwana*, please.' Mary's bobbing had become a grotesque kind of curtsey. 'Do not tell *bwana* Hope. Sack for me!'

Michael was now quiet, his face streaked by tears, looking at Bryant who grunted and looked away. The milk herd, black and white with swaying udders, was ambling towards them now from the pastures down near the river. He looked again at Mary. He had not yet learnt the even, weary curtness which the bulk of whites used with Africans in this country, and his behaviour tended to swing from harshness to the kind of politeness with which he would treat fellow countrymen at home in England.

'All right,' he grunted, setting off towards the milking shed, readjusting his khaki felt hat. 'Don't let it happen again, now, will you?'

It was inevitable that the activities of the two boys would one day cause serious trouble with Michael's parents. It was usually Michael who took the initiative in any bad behaviour, while Kimutei later took the blame. This state of affairs encouraged Michael to become bolder, and it was he who suggested that they should go swimming in the water tank up behind the house – something that had been specifically and repeatedly forbidden by adults anxious about drownings. It was an object of fear and challenge for the boys: a round, cemented tank with walls four feet high and a brown surface, smooth and opaque as mud, across which the water scorpions would flick and skid, barely touching the surface. There were steps leading into the water, next to the huge ball cock which would occasionally allow a violent gush of new water into the tank. It was here that Michael, already aware that it was white who gave orders to black, urged the fearful Kimutei, stripped to his shorts, to pioneer the stone steps, invisible beneath the brown water.

Kimutei looked round doubtfully, teeth bared and eyes wide in a mixture of fear and delight. Michael had a stick in his hand, and prodded his friend imperiously in the buttocks.

'Go on, fool,' he urged in Swahili, a bullying note in his voice. 'In, in, in.'

'No!' squealed Kimutei. 'It's too deep, the scorpions will get me!'

'They can't bite,' jeered Michael. 'My dad told me they couldn't. Go on, swim!'

Kimutei took another hesitant step down, and was now up to his waist, shivering and bouncing a little on his toes, arms extended.

'They've got those long spikes on their tails,' shouted Kimutei, voice trembling with fright and the chill of the brown water which lapped at his darker midriff. Suddenly, as if to frighten off the threatening insects, he began to beat the water around him. The splashing excited him and he began to laugh and squeal. Michael, hands up to protect his face from the flying water, joined in the laughter. The noise was such that they did not hear the angry shouts of Michael's father, running up the little path towards them from the house.

The boys had considered themselves safe, for the early hours of Saturday afternoon were usually a dead time when the Hope parents slept off a lunchtime in the club and the heavy sun seemed to cast a blanket of silence and stillness over the farm. But Michael's father had woken in a sudden sweat, with an instinctive feeling that something was wrong, and had then heard the shouts and splashings through the drawn curtains.

His fearsome appearance – stripped to the waist, hair sticking up from the pillow, his face puffed with alcohol and sleep – silenced

17

the boys instantly, and they cowered. Since Kimutei was actually in the water, he was the first target. No black man in this country would have dared to lay hands on a white child, but Kimutei was now struck without hesitation, and there would be no later apology or justification to Mary. Michael was almost grinning as he watched his father put Kimutei over his knee; he knew that it meant less pain for him. And so the equality of their friendship would drain away. Michael was carried roughly, but not too roughly, back to the house, while Kimutei squatted in the dust by the tank, rubbing his bottom, with silent tears again marking his dusty face.

'I caught that little bugger Kimutei halfway into the tank this afternoon, with Michael following behind, of course,' said Michael's father to his mother that evening, as they sat on the verandah, the sky falling to crimson and gold behind Elgon.

'Ah!' said his mother, taking a sip of her gin and tonic. 'I wondered what the kerfuffle was, but I'm afraid I just went straight back to sleep.'

'Made me think, though, we ought to teach Michael to swim properly. Then if he does fall into the tank or the dam or something, he'll be OK.'

'Well, we could take him to the pool in town – perhaps on Saturdays. We could take him there at lunchtime instead of going to the club. 'Course' – here she grinned and flicked a fingernail, clicking, against her glass – 'it'll mean less of this . . .'

'Hmm. Mind you, it might be no bad thing.'

They fell to silence again in the familiar magic of the sundown. The crickets were starting up, in their tireless, whirring rhythm, and a few pigeons were cooing gently from the branches of the big cork tree halfway down the farm. Michael came running round the corner of the house to find his parents transfixed in their obscure adult communion like living statues, and he came to a sudden halt and retreated quietly. The instinct for innocence warned him to keep away from his parents at such times.

'Right,' said Mr Hope eventually. 'We'll do that. It'll help him to start mixing a bit more with other white kids. I get less happy with that boy Kimutei as time goes by, I'm afraid. Not a good influence. The sooner Michael gets off to school, the better.'

He called the houseboy, a wrinkled man of fifty who came padding round from the kitchen in bare feet, his long white cotton gown luminous in the failing light, his face eager and anxious to please.

18

Neither of the two whites looked at him. They placed their glasses on the tray he proffered.

'Same again, Joshua,' said Mr Hope.

From their classrooms, the boys and girls of Kitale School could hear the band of the King's African Rifles strike up the tunes of British military history half a mile away in the town. It began with 'The Dam Busters' March', and then slipped into the slow dignity of 'Scipio'. Michael stared at the sun spilling through the windows into warm, square pools on the red cement floor as the music of Handel's Europe seeped through his mind. He was a solid, freckled child now, with pale blue eyes and blond hair bleached almost white by the sun; his regular, slightly rounded features had developed a serious, almost melancholy set, and there was a hesitancy in the way he carried himself. He was now in his first year at school and he was still not resigned to the discipline of the classroom. He wanted to be outside, playing in bare feet beneath the jacaranda trees in the garden at home. Today, however, there was a legitimate escape. It was Empire Day, and the Queen Mother, on her tour of East Africa, was passing through the town. The children were all going down to watch the spectacle and greet the royal visitor. It was a high point of the colonial year; there had been a rehearsal the day before.

'And now, children,' chirruped Miss Maynard. 'I'm going to hand you out your flags, and I want you to wave like mad and cheer when Her Majesty comes past. And *not* before, if you please. Jan de Fries, come up here, will you, and hand out the flags for me.'

Ma Maynard, as she was universally called, carried a faint tang of mothballs and a missionary air, inspiring both derision and awe in her charges. They had recently put several drawing pins on her chair in a half-terrified attempt to crack her serenity and provoke her temper but, protected by formidable corsetry beyond the knowledge and experience of these four- to six-year-olds, she had felt nothing. They had believed her to be superhuman until Susie Short, whose mother wore similar garments to contain her own billows of flesh, put the real explanation about.

Jan de Fries had not been selected at random to hand out the tiny cloth Union flags on sticks, which had first been acquired by the school during the last war and lay in cupboards in the corridor between patriotic occasions. Ma Maynard knew that Empire Day had been inaugurated as the celebration of the aid given by the

19

British colonies to the imperial subjugation of the Transvaal and the Orange Free State in the second Boer War in 1902. In her view the South Africans – the bloody *yarpies* as they were known among British settlers here in their more relaxed moments – had always been rebels, and if they and their offspring were going to come and live in a loyal colony under the protection of the Queen, they could bloody well kiss the flag. Ma Maynard was a deep believer in the benefits the world had taken from the spread of British civilisation – she had been in India before coming over here – and its symbolic cadences gave deep emotional joy to her. Jan de Fries, however, was almost certainly unaware of his ritual humiliation as he stumped up and down the rows of pale yellow plywood desks, awkwardly handing out the flags, dropping one here and there. He was another square, blond child, and his mind was also on the afternoon's half-holiday – a chance to get out on the farm with his air rifle and shoot a few birds.

Jan and Michael chose each other when the class formed up in the corridor in twos to walk into town where the band was playing and the Queen Mother would pass. As they emerged in the sun and set off between the tall gum trees which lined the school drive, they began scuffing their shoes in the loose gravel and chanting under their breath the latest rude rhyme about Ma Maynard. The two girls in front of them, persuaded of the dignity of the occasion, turned round and shushed them piously.

'Ach, shut up, goody-goody,' said Jan in his thick accent, failing in his lunge to catch the dark ponytail of one of the girls. He was trying instead to trip her, encouraged by Michael, when he received a sudden strong push in the back from the boy behind. He turned angrily to find it was Christopher Austin.

Jan hesitated, because Christopher was the tallest and strongest boy in the class; he was also joyless and unpopular, and never joined in the fun of classroom disobedience. Evidently he had seized this opportunity of defending the girls in order to ingratiate himself, make friends. He was staring threateningly at the two in front of him.

'Shut up yourself, *yarpie*.' Christopher waved his Union flag at Jan, an admonishing weapon. 'And don't hit girls.'

'Make me shut up,' said Jan automatically, but with a tone of doubt. 'Bloody *pongo*.'

'*Pongo*' was the contemptuous word for people with white knees

20

who had just arrived from Britain, or who never adjusted to Africa. 'Bloody' was ultimately daring for boys of this age. Chris was not going to take such talk, and reached forward with the long, strong arms that had earned him the nickname 'Chimpy'. But this confrontation had slowed and disrupted the crocodile, and the voice of Ma Maynard shrilled from the back.

'Behave yourselves, you boys, and keep *moving*! We don't want to miss the Queen Mother, now, do we?'

'Yes,' said Michael, but he said it quietly and fell back into step. He and Jan giggled.

'I'll get you later,' hissed Chris. Jan and Michael exchanged silent glances of solidarity and contempt for their rival; they were the pirates, the rebels, and all the others were soft and boring, sucking up to the teachers. It would take more than *him* to bring them into line.

But now they were moving out of the school grounds and along the main road, a thin strip of black tarmac at the centre of a wide dirt highway. A little further along, before the podo trees began, several KAR platoons were drawn up on an open space in front of the showground. The band was coming strutting and glittering straight down the road towards the children, and Ma Maynard clucked and fluttered, moving them to the side. As it passed them, Michael was suddenly captivated by the splendour of the blaring music and display. The band leader, marching out in front with his tall red fez and gleaming white outsize gloves, just then hurled his mace in the air, where it spun and glinted in the sun. His head tilted back, his teeth standing out whitely as he squinted upward, and then the mace was safely, miraculously, back in the huge glove which now thrust it forward and back again, cockily, in time to the music. The bandsman with the big drum balanced on the vivid red-edged leopard skin covering his torso gave a sudden complex of heavy beats, and the marching players began to turn, silkily, and melt back through their own ranks. The force of the music, which seemed to move charged waves of air against the children's faces, receded again. The band broke into 'Colonel Bogey'.

Michael's class, cowed by the noise and grandeur, filed to their place behind a white rope which marked off the crowds from the royal path. All they had to look at for the moment, as they stood silently fingering their flags and waiting for the grand arrival, were the children on the opposite side of the road: the black children,

21

raggle-taggle in contrast to their own uniformed neatness of khaki shorts, blue shirts, and blue dresses, but nevertheless dragooned into tidy lines by half a dozen black police wielding canes. Further along were a few Asian children, a splash of coloured turbans and saris. Everyone was in their appointed place; there were some, but not many, Union flags on the black side of the road.

Another multiple thudding on the drums, and the music stopped. There was a great hush over the waiting crowds, as if a huge congregation were waiting for the small voice of the priest to follow the booming of the organ and bells which had summoned them. Then suddenly, far to the right where the road led out of town into the shimmering-hot farmlands, there was movement. 'Here she comes!' came a little cry. It was not the voice of an over-excited schoolgirl unable to contain herself, but that of Ma Maynard, breaking her own rules of decorum in the heat of the moment. An army Land-Rover, its tyres humming slightly on the hot tarmac, came into view first. Behind it were several large black limousines flying coloured pennants from little spikes on their bonnets. With a drum roll which echoed and swished like a rainstorm sweeping in from the hills, the band broke into 'God Save the Queen'. Up went the childish flags and cheers.

But the climax was momentary: a glittering window in the black paintwork, a glimpse, for some, of the pink hat above the bulldoggy face, of a benevolent, fixed smile cracking its uncolonial pallor. Then came two or three more large vehicles bearing men in dark clothes, more Land-Rovers of the military escort – all white soldiers for this task – and that was it. For a second Africa had been suspended in a high British vision: black men contained and belted in the pressed khaki uniform of the Crown, drawn up meekly in ranks, responding to orders, playing European music with passable skill. The filed teeth of the grinning savage which haunted the white man's mind were blunted and drawn. And yet only a few years before, there had been the Mau Mau 'emergency', with its dark rituals and horrible murders, and the questions hung uneasily in the minds of the white adults: is all this really still true? How long can it last? Necks craned after the procession, the music struck up bravely again; otherwise there was only the sun, the dusty road, and the high blue sky.

The children were solemn as they filed back to school to collect their books and bags. They too had felt a shiver, the breathing of change. It had come to them, perhaps, through the blank stare of one of the bandsmen snapping impassively through his routine; through the reluctance of some school servant to meet their eye, maybe, or the defiant glance of one of the town-dwelling Africans on the other side of the road – a young one, below the age of deference.

When Jan and Michael were walking down to the main road again where they would be picked up by their parents, they came across a gaggle of older pupils among the trees beside the drive. Little roars and shouts were escaping from this crowd, and it moved in a mass back and forth, as if accommodating some moving thing in its middle. Jan guessed first.

'It's a fight,' he shouted, running over to push in among the spectators. Michael followed.

Two of the biggest boys in the school, both about thirteen, were rolling on the ground in a grimmer struggle than most playground scraps. They were John Cockerell, big-boned and blond, and Martin Ehlers, another South African, swarthy and wiry, a farmer's son like Jan. The usual restraints of schoolboy skirmishes had already been cast aside, and the two were going for each other's eyes, ears and hair. Cockerell's breath was bubbling through a cluster of blood and snot beneath his nostrils, and their clothes were caked with the reddish dust. The crowd was partisan, the few South African children rooting wildly for Ehlers while the British majority supported the losing Cockerell. Where did this place Jan and Michael, their friendship?

'Kick him in the balls, Ehlers! Finish him off!' The eyes of the ten-year-old South African were shining with bloodlust.

'Get up and box!' came a hesitant voice from the rival camp, evidently parroting the exhortations of the school's rather pukka sports master.

But the affair was beyond boxing now. Ehlers had wrestled himself astride Cockerell, pinning his arms to the ground with his knees. Cockerell's bucking and heaving was ineffectual and exhausted, and Jan and Michael no longer looked at each other as Ehlers, in what seemed like slow motion, began dropping methodical, heavy punches into the other boy's face. Michael had never seen violence like it. The noise was like when they twisted up wet towels on swimming days and swung them against the wall. More blood was blotching Cockerell's face, running deep red from his nose. Michael felt a panic, wanted to run forward and intervene; but suddenly the victorious South African camp moved forward and lifted their champion from the defeated body, cheering and ruffling his dusty hair and banging him on the back. And Jan suddenly ran from Michael's side and joined in the group mobbing the hero of his persecuted race.

As Cockerell became conscious that the blows had stopped, he began to cry, in the pitiful, heaving fashion of a much younger child. He climbed to his feet, unaided by his supporters who now drifted off, and shuffled away. He was alongside Michael, who was about to say something to show his sympathy and confusion, when he suddenly turned in a fit of defiance and screamed at Ehlers.

'You bastard, Ehlers! You fucking smelly *yarpie* bastard!'

His voice had slipped upwards and was thin and shrill, like a girl's. It contained the outrage of one who had not believed defeat to be possible by a bloody *yarpie*, by one of this rough, crude bunch of semi-blacks who had infiltrated this prized colony of the officer class. He turned away and shuffled off, sobbing.

Michael was sitting on the whitewashed culvert by the main road when his mother drew up in her Ford Anglia. She stepped out, wearing a cotton dress which showed off her pretty legs, and came smiling towards him. But he avoided her, fearing she was going to embrace him in the sight of his schoolfriends, and climbed silently into the car. She looked at him with concern as they started along the road out of town, towards their bungalow on the hill six miles away where they had their horses, their servants, their long, cool verandah.

'Well, darling, did you see the Queen Mother?'

'No.'

'Oh dear, couldn't you see? Daddy and I saw her from the club. Did somebody get in your way?'

'Not really, but there were so many cars and they went past so fast.'

'Oh dear, what a pity. Is anything the matter, dear?'

He shook his head, not knowing what to say. She reached over and rested a hand on his arm.

'Come on, tell Mummy.'

The magic worked.

'There was a fight and Cockerell got beaten . . . by a *yarpie*.'

'Who's Cockerell?'

'He's the biggest boy in the school. He was meant to be the toughest.'

'But he got beaten by a *yarpie*?'

'Yes. He had blood all over his face.'

His mother's pert, pretty features tightened. She looked straight ahead, eyes narrowing in the glare bouncing from the car bonnet. Then she spoke again with new anxiety in her voice.

'I don't know what they're up to at that school of yours sometimes. What was it about? Why didn't the teachers stop it? I don't want you involved in anything like that, d'you hear?'

'My best friend's a *yarpie*,' blurted Michael, as if it were a guilty secret.

'You're not to use that word!' snapped his mother, all the brisker for the fact that she had just used it herself. 'And anyway, I know Jan, he's a very nice boy, in spite of . . . well, oh, I don't know. Sometimes I don't know what to make of this blasted country.'

She glanced at Michael, who was looking intently out of the window at a group of black people on the road ahead.

'We'll have to see about getting you into a school in England,' she said quietly. Michael did not hear as he screwed round in his seat to wave at the group as they passed.

'Stop, Mummy, stop! It's Kimutei! We could give him a lift!'

Mrs Hope did not raise her foot even slightly from the accelerator. It was not a habit of white settlers of this country to give lifts to the children of their servants; in the back of a pick-up, perhaps, but certainly not in a car.

'We're nearly home, darling,' she said brightly. 'And besides, he's got lots of friends with him. I expect they all went down to see the Queen Mother as well. We can't give them all a lift.'

'Please, Mummy, can't we stop?'

Her voice was firmer now: 'No, darling, we're nearly home and . . .'

Michael's mind suddenly threw up a phrase he had heard one day when he was standing near two farmers' wives and peering into the jars of sweets at J. M. Patel's. The words came out quietly, as a piece of knowledge gained.

'It's because they smell, isn't it?'

His mother changed down, crashing the gears a little, and turned into the dusty track which led to their house. 'Now, darling, don't

25

talk like that. They're just different. I expect we smell a bit funny to them, too.'

Michael had an instinct for insincerity in his mother, and when he detected it, it disturbed him so unpleasantly that his usual solution was to put the subject aside. He did not want to grow up too fast, to confront the issues he saw clouding his parents' faces, leading them to use violent language and call rudely for more gin.

'Can I go riding this afternoon?'

'Of course, darling.' She smiled at him with relief. The pleasant things about this country still outweighed the problems. The pressure lifted from her wide brow, slightly freckled by the sun.

Three

The dark blue Land-Rover drew up outside Kitale main police station just before midnight. A spattering of rain had blown down from Elgon, and the wipers mixed it to a muddy paste with the dust on the windscreen. Juliet Hope, sitting chilled and uncomfortable in the back of the vehicle with Michael's dead body, peered over the driver's khaki shoulder and made out a stone-built colonial building, with a green corrugated-iron roof sweeping down low over a balus-traded verandah. Such buildings, dotted all over this and other continents, had reassured her several times during this, her first visit to Africa: the old hotels, the houses of friends they had visited, even the more modern lodges in the game parks – all had this comforting style which promised safety and familiarity in a country of mud-hut villages and shanty towns. But the safety had come too late this time, and she sat unmoving as the two policemen opened the back door and beckoned to her.

Reluctantly, she edged towards the rear and stepped down. But as one of the officers half-put an arm around her shoulder to steer her towards the wooden steps leading into the station, she suddenly turned round with a small cry, not wanting to leave Michael, this loose shape under stained pieces of sacking on the floor of the Land-Rover. The officer anticipated her question.

'Hospital,' he said. 'Morgue.'

It was not intended brutally, but his unfamiliarity with English made the words coarse and stark. Juliet's delicate features, already blotched and twisted by her distress, wound up still further, making her ugly, and for a second it seemed she would spit at him, scratch his face. Then her muscles sagged into hopelessness, and she slowly turned her back on the Land-Rover.

'See the chief inspector, Madam, in CID.' The officer stood back respectfully, his eyes inscrutable. He had been gentle towards her ever since stepping out of the vehicle and finding her there squatting on the road. Until he was close enough to see her blonde hair in the brightness of the night sky, he had thought from her attitude that she was a black woman.

Juliet stepped up on to the verandah and into the front office where a dim, unshaded bulb hung from the ceiling. She winced up

27

at it, noting with a familiar irritation which pushed aside her state of shock for a moment that here was another example of modern primitiveness. There were taps, but they leaked or ran dry, there were machines, but they were usually broken, and a light bulb, if it worked, was never shaded. She had once watched with prissy Western exasperation as a hotel servant had pushed two naked bristling wires from an electric fire directly into the holes of a wall socket. Michael was able – had been able – to tolerate such things.

An officer with sergeant's stripes half-rose behind a large, battered table and motioned her to go through a door at the rear; the curiosity in his eyes was poorly masked and he peered after her, noting the jeans frayed at the bottoms, the dusty feet in leather sandals. These Europeans, these *wazungu*, never wore the wealth they all had.

Juliet faltered and almost took a step back when she entered a room across the yard and saw the huge form of Chief Inspector Kariuke rising to his feet behind the desk. Another bare overhead bulb glinted on his big cheeks and nose, but his eyes were in shadow. He gave a slight bow and motioned her towards a wooden chair.

'Please, Madam, sit down.' His voice was full and confident, suggesting a man who knew his work. He watched her walk, frail and shrunken-looking, across the room, allowing enough silence for her to settle, but not so much she would feel threatened. She was a type familiar to him over the last ten years: the white woman tourist struggling with an inward revulsion at the heat, dust and dirt of Africa, and only really overcoming it in those rare moments when her surroundings, artificially and temporarily, gave her all the conveniences of home. A very different woman from the old colonial types, and far harder to handle.

'This is a very bad business, Madam . . .' he began. But her eyes flashed at him, and he understood that she was not going to take sympathy from a black man, not at the moment, anyway. He was inwardly relieved: he was happier to drop the gallantry. He paused to let things settle again, then made a small gesture of helplessness with his big hand.

'We will just do the most essential things tonight, and then you must go and get some sleep. Do you have a place to stay?'

Juliet nodded dully, and brushed the dusty loop of blonde hair from her cheek.

'Yes, the Northrops. It was their car – we were taking it back to them, we'd borrowed it.'

Her voice was flat, without feeling. She studied Kariuke now, trying to take the measure of him. His size intimidated her, though his eyes were kind, but it was his voice, she realised, which she found most confusing. His English seemed perfectly composed, but old-fashioned in its idiom and unpredictably accented. She recalled the broadcast voices of African statesmen – Nyerere, or Kenneth Kaunda.

Kariuke knew the Northrops well, but saw no use now in social chat. They had a big farm off the Endebess road, looking over towards Elgon: one of the few white families locally who had hung on for the nineteen years since independence. Their children had gone elsewhere, one to Australia, one back 'home' to England, but the old couple were still there, an established and largely accepted part of the landscape. They often had visitors from Britain.

'In that case I will drive you there myself.'

'What will they do with my husband?' She was staring at him fiercely.

'They will put him in a hospital morgue where a doctor will carry out a post mortem,' said Kariuke. 'I have told four officers to check the activities of known criminals and robbers and in the morning there will be a full-scale investigation. I must assure you, Mrs Hope, that we will do everything we can.'

Kariuke drummed his fingers lightly on the tatty blotter, looked round the room ruminatively and added, with a sudden warmth: 'It is a stain on our country.'

Juliet looked at him without expression, unmoved by his patriotic emotion, perhaps unable to believe in it. He picked up her scepticism, and brought himself back to business.

'I will have to send a telex to headquarters in Nairobi,' he said. 'So I must ask you to tell me brief details of what happened.'

She looked puzzled: surely everyone knew, surely the whole world knew of the violence done to her, of her loss.

'Don't you *know*?'

'You were the only witness,' said Kariuke gently. She looked at him, realising she was going to have to describe it, and slowly she lowered her face into her hands and began a noiseless, heaving weeping. Kariuke looked at the lightly tanned hands, with prominent tendons; the wedding ring, still shiny and ill-fitting, could not have been there long. Then he suddenly stood up, as if to break off his own sentimentality. There was murder of one kind or another in his

29

district every few weeks. Lots of black girls were widowed; why should this be different?

He turned and looked at the beads of rain on the window, waiting for her to be able to talk again. The orange-red earth would steam slightly in the morning sun, and the crops would push strongly upwards. He liked it here, in the fertile up-country highlands, removed from the politics and increasing viciousness of Nairobi. And now he was being dragged back into it; he had known as soon as the duty officer had woken him – 'A man's been killed, Chief Inspector, sir – a *white* man' – that a hornet's nest was stirring around his ears. Would they have woken him for a black man's death? Well, if a 504 was involved, and the man had money or influence, perhaps. But who was Mrs Hope and her nuisance of a dead husband? Two tourists among thousands who did the game parks and coast – maybe also sampled the black prostitute boys and girls at Malindi. There was going to be publicity, most of it bad. The Minister of Tourism, foreign journalists nosing around, a lot of kids picked up and knocked about to convince the world that every stone was being turned . . . He checked his slide into pessimism. Feelings were too fluid, too unpredictable in these small hours. Perhaps they would have a lucky break. He could see that Mrs Hope's reflection in the rainy window was calm again, and he turned round.

'They'd pulled a tree across the road . . . I didn't like the look of it, I told Michael not to stop, to drive round it . . . we'd heard about this kind of thing. But he couldn't. They had the doors open in no time and pulled us out. Michael got away from two of them, and that's when they, they . . .' She lowered her head to one hand and rubbed her brow savagely to keep back the tears.

'How many men?'

'Three,' she continued, grateful for the question to nudge her on. 'One had a gun, a big revolver-type thing . . .'

Her control then dissolved, and she spread her arms and opened her tear-stained face to Kariuke and shouted at him, shaking her head as she threw her pain and outrage at him.

'They didn't have to shoot him! They didn't have to kill him! He loved this bloody filthy country, do you know that? He grew up here!'

Kariuke raised his eyebrows. The picture was filling out.

'Did you see them well? Can you describe them?'

She was calm again now, and lifted her head just high enough to spit a gleeful little dart at him. 'No, I didn't – and anyway, they all look the same to me.'

Kariuke nodded, blinking to absorb the insult. He was a man, however, who knew when not to be provoked. He said nothing, and waited.

'I'd recognise the two who tied me up.' She was suddenly humble at his turning of the cheek. 'One of them had a kind of scar on his face, some kind of tribal markings.'

Kariuke nodded again, impassive.

'Anything else? Any clothing you noticed? So we can put out a description?'

She shook her head wearily.

'I don't know – maybe tomorrow . . . I must let the Northrops know what's happened. God knows what they're going to say. And Michael's parents back home, what about them . . .?'

She stared at him again, this time with eyes exhausted at the nightmare to which she was condemned, which was now her reality. He nodded with sympathy.

'I know. We will finish soon, Mrs Hope. Perhaps tomorrow when you are feeling better we can go through it again. But I must ask you one more thing. Apart from the murder of your husband and the theft of the car and belongings, was there any other crime? Did they assault you?'

Juliet pushed back her hair again, her eyes widening. Then she closed them for a moment and spoke in a hiss.

'Oh, you'd love that, wouldn't you? That would really complete the picture, wouldn't it, if they'd raped me as well? Well, bad luck, Mr big black policeman, they didn't, so you'll have to think of something else to get off on. All right? No rape, just murder. But the murder's something to be getting on with, isn't it?'

Kariuke looked down at his folded hands, remembering how white women had spoken to him in the first ten years of his police service, under the colonial regime. These tourists were different, there was no doubt, but scratch the surface and they all knew how to be memsahibs. Perhaps it was passed on, inherited from two hundred years of empire. Hard to drop the habit. And why so very fierce at the suggestion of sexual attack by black men? He stood up, tapping the table with two large, plump fingers to close the interview.

'Please excuse me, Mrs Hope, but it was my duty to ask. I am happy the answer is no.'

31

The country was still damp from the overnight rain when Kariuke drove out for the second time to the Northrops' farm under a clear morning sky. He had been there only seven hours before to deliver Juliet to the anxious old couple, waiting up in the shadowy farmhouse lit by a single Tilley lamp. In their solicitous company Juliet's shock and grief had poured out with no restraint, and Kariuke had quietly told Bill Northrop he would be back first thing. He had slammed the car door and revved the engine loudly to shut out the tortured sounds from the house.

As the old Peugeot rattled down the dirt road this morning Kariuke felt the disbelief familiar to him, over the years, on the day after a crime. With the sun shining benignly on a calm world, it seemed impossible that only a few hours ago there had been cruelty and violence. His mind flashed for a second to the great carved wound in the white back of that body on the dirty morgue table. He felt very tired as he turned off the main road where an old plough disc bolted to a post read, in faded blue letters, 'Twiga Farm'. Bill and Marjorie Northrop had been here nearly fifty years, made the country their home and taken out citizenship at independence. They had learnt fluent Swahili and even used the language to name their farm after the giraffe which had lived here in great numbers when they first arrived to claim it from the bush. They had always treated their workers well. Kariuke was glad to be dealing with a family like this rather than the kind of whites who came out here on temporary contracts with naive notions about the country, about what could and could not be done.

The driveway took him through the farmyard, where men were busy in the dairy and tractor shed. The house, wood and stone with its faded red tile roof, stood among lawns and flowerbeds which Marjorie Northrop had created and nurtured over the years. When Kariuke drew up and switched off the engine, a peaceful silence invaded the car through the open window, broken only by a few gentle farmyard noises behind him – a man shouting at a cow, the rattling of a chain on some piece of machinery. The normality appalled him.

He caught sight of Bill Northrop at the bottom of the sloping garden, standing under a huge, dark green avocado tree. Even from this distance his tall, grey figure, slightly stooped anyway, seemed to be listing and sagging under a new weight. He must have heard the

32

engine but he did not turn until Kariuke was out of the car and had begun to walk towards him. His step was slow and reluctant. They met beside a bed of canna lilies whose pendulous red and yellow petals still glistened with drops of dew. Northrop, although his eyes were reproachful, took his right hand out of his worn cavalry twill trousers and held it out towards Kariuke.

'Good morning, sir,' said Kariuke, taking his hand. 'How is Mrs Hope?'

Northrop turned away as if he did not want Kariuke to see his distress. After a short silence he shrugged his bony shoulders.

'She's been in a terrible state all night, of course. Couldn't expect otherwise. Marjorie gave her some fairly hefty tranquillisers in the end, so at least she's asleep now. I suppose you want to talk to her?'

He turned round towards Kariuke again, who nodded. Northrop's face had the reddish-brown tinge of many long-established settlers, whose flesh seemed to have absorbed some of the red earth and hot sun. It made a stark contrast with his near-white hair, still thick and bushy over his ears. He grimaced now, and the skin wrinkled up the sides of his prominent, beaked nose.

'I doubt if she's awake yet, poor kid. We'll have to ask Marjorie about it and take her advice. She used to be a nurse, you know, which is fortunate. Hasn't done any for years, of course, but you don't forget that sort of thing, do you? I expect she'll look after me when I turn senile.'

He stopped, aware that he was rambling to avoid the point, and faced Kariuke. The two men had often found their views were similar. They even spoke a 1950s brand of English which would make them fogeys in present-day England – although Kariuke's accent and occasional misuse of phrases marked him out.

'Look here, Kariuke,' said Northrop. 'Is there the faintest chance of catching the bastards who did this? They'd only been married less than a year, you know, come out here almost on their blasted honeymoon, and then' – he waved an old arm about, helplessly – 'this happens.'

The question had been turning over in Kariuke's mind and disturbing his sleep. He was grateful for a chance to put his fears and feelings into words. He screwed up his round features, narrowing his eyes at the mountain on the near horizon.

'That is hard to say. It depends on many things. I have sent men

33

out there now, where it happened at the Noigameget bridge . . . why were they on that road, do you know?'

'They'd been down to the coast and to one or two other places to visit friends, and they'd been to Lake Baringo on the way back. They told us in advance they were using the back way to come home, through Kabarnet and Tambach. I couldn't see anything wrong with the plan – after all, there's plenty of traffic on that road and nothing like this has ever happened before along there. God Almighty, that sort of thing hardly ever happens even down in Nairobi. What's it all coming to?'

'I'm afraid that Nairobi is beginning to export its criminals to other parts of the country,' said Kariuke. 'Things have been getting worse in Kisumu and Eldoret. But I have the men out there searching and questioning the villagers. The criminals must have been there a long time, setting up the road block, and there are some huts about half a mile away. But I want to ask you – can you identify the car again?'

Northrop nodded. 'Yes, and the chassis and window glass are marked,' he said, with hope and triumph in his voice. 'I thought twice about having it done, I can tell you – quite a costly business. And I didn't think it necessary up here. But in the end I decided to do it – bloody good thing, as it turns out.'

'You must give me the details and they can be circulated immediately. And we must find out what belongings were stolen, and keep a look-out for them. And do not worry about political backing – I had a phone call from the Minister of Tourism this morning. He is only concerned about trade and foreign exchange, of course, but it means we can have a full-scale enquiry. And what we need most, of course, is a stroke of luck.'

Northrop was nodding, a little curl at the ends of his lips as if turning over some private irony.

'Political backing, eh? Perhaps the President himself will take an interest, put the heat on? And I suppose it means that when you fail to find the culprits, some poor ignorant bloody peasants are picked out and get it stuck on them, eh? After all, what's a little matter of innocence when a multi-million-dollar industry's in danger? Eh? Not that it would make much difference if they caught someone – the damage is done, either way. It wouldn't make much difference to us, or to Juliet. Even if they got the right men, it wouldn't bring the boy back, would it? And would an execution really help, a good old-fashioned hanging? And if you got the wrong men, of course, and hung them, it would just make everything worse. Christ, Kariuke, I know I'm carrying on a bit, but I feel, I feel' – his balled fists were deep in his pockets, his arms rigid – 'oh, I don't know, completely helpless.'

Kariuke picked a leaf from a bougainvillea bush and rolled it in his fingers, feeling the slight dampness as he crushed it. For the tenth time already in this case, it seemed, he was having to keep his own counsel in the face of strong words – racially loaded words. In fact he agreed with Northrop's sarcastic analysis, but he wanted to remind him who had set up the political system in this country, and tell him that things were essentially no different in Britain; it was just that *they* had it all tuned and refined to the last detail, so that everything looked like high principle and morality, or tradition at least. The real reason they hated and sneered at African politics, he thought, was because it reminded them in its crudeness of the foundations of their own system – sleight of hand, manoeuvres behind the scenes, the bending of the rules, the sacrificial lambs. He sighed; better change the subject.

'Mrs Hope told me her husband grew up in this country.' He jettisoned the leaf and examined the stain on his fingers. 'So he must have known the place well?'

Northrop began talking eagerly, as if also grateful to put aside politics and the endless underlying arguments about decolonisation.

'Yes, he did. Left with his family when he was nine or ten – they weren't too keen on the prospect of *Uhuru*, not that any of us were, and back they went to that freezing, miserable country they called home. But Michael had been here long enough to get the place into his blood.'

He paused, looking at Kariuke for a moment, trying but failing to hold back what was in his mind.

'Of course, you don't know what this is, do you? To get bitten by another country which is not originally your own, and to want never to leave it. You think we're here, and all the rest *were* here, just because we're greedy and want to have servants and order them about and knock our notions of civilisation into them. That might play a part, I grant you, but by itself it wouldn't have made Marjorie and me stay on, with all the political uncertainty, and stick with it in spite of what Amin's been up to a few miles to the west – *and* what might happen here. It's just that after a while you don't *belong* anywhere else, and all *this*' – he pulled one hand out of his pocket and waved it at the sky, the mountain, the trees – 'just gets inside you and won't leave.'

He looked at Kariuke, wondering if he had got through, but knew that he had heard this tune before and was not impressed. Northrop closed his eyes and clamped his mouth for a moment: he could never convey to people his deep emotional attachment to this country.

'You've never been to England, have you?' he asked. Kariuke shook his head, smiling.

'That explains it. That's why you don't understand. You have to know what a wet November is like on a London pavement before you know what I'm on about. I'm sorry, last night's put me in a bit of a state. You want to know about Michael. Well, his family was here for nearly ten years. Michael's father, nice enough bloke, sold machinery – firm closed down before you arrived, of course – and his wife did the paperwork. Quite a successful little team. They sold me quite a lot of stuff, of course, which is how we got to know them. They lived just down there at Mount View, and they'd come over in the evening sometimes when Michael was a kid – carry him out of the car in his pyjamas and put him in our back bedroom while we hit the bottle and told dirty jokes. Poor old Michael. So he died in the country he thought of as his home. He told me that, you know, in this garden a couple of weeks ago, before they borrowed the car for a final trip round the country. Said that he couldn't settle down in England, even after nineteen years. Mind you, he seemed to have a talent for getting into trouble, through no particular fault of his own, probably, but he sort of attracted it. It happened a couple of times out here, in fact, and there's been something rather more serious in England just recently. Not that it matters now – Juliet can tell you all that, if you want to know. Yet he always seemed such a serious kid, with a slightly puzzled look, as if there was something he didn't understand, and he had that funny little scar on his upper lip which made him look like one of life's victims.'

Northrop gave a wincing little smile, the product of whimsical memory and present pain.

'Apparently he picked it up on some illicit jaunt up the mountain with a friend of his – one of the bits of trouble I mentioned just now. A black friend, believe it or not, Kariuke, the son of his *ayah*. Not that the friendship was allowed to last. His parents put a stop to it in the end, I seem to remember. His parents were very worried about that sort of thing – rather over-anxious about the racial question. That's why they quit at independence, of course.'

'And your children, Mr Northrop, did they have black friends?' The irony was masked by the gentleness of his tone. 'Did they go to mixed schools, maybe?'

Northrop's answer was to look reproachfully at the other man, as if to suggest it was unfair of him to score little points at a time like this. But he also remembered that he too had taunted Kariuke that day.

'All right, old boy,' he said. 'Let's call it a draw. We'd better not waste time reminiscing and getting into sparring matches. But just for the record, my kids did have some black friends, yes. They went to all-white boarding schools in Nairobi, I grant you, but they kept some sort of relationship with a few of the local boys. We're talking about a matter of degree, really – ours were about halfway along the scale, but the Hopes prevented Michael from making any progress at all.'

'And at the end of the scale, I presume, white man meets black man on equal terms,' said Kariuke, seeming to study a few Jersey cattle grazing in the field next to the garden. 'Do you think white people will ever allow that, Mr Northrop?'

Abruptly, Northrop stopped walking. The gesture hinted that he was going to play *bwana*, rebuke the cheeky native; but he had long ago dropped such habits and learnt to think more deeply. Kariuke met his worried stare with brown, sceptical eyes.

'Do you think black people can wait for them to do it, Mr Kariuke?'

The tension held a moment, then they smiled wryly and began walking towards the house again, each watching the last of the dew brush up on to his shoes. As they clumped up the three wooden steps to the verandah, Marjorie Northrop appeared at the front door in her faded red dressing gown. Her hair, normally piled up, was falling round her face as if she wanted it to disguise the tiredness.

'Morning, Mr Kariuke,' she said quietly. 'Juliet's ready to talk to you again now.'

The two men stepped, blinking, into the sudden cool shade of the house. The smell of woodsmoke from the previous night's fire sweetened the air. Kariuke walked on slowly into the sitting room, where a milky shaft of sunlight fell through the gap in the still-drawn curtains at the far end of the room. Juliet was huddled in one of the armchairs next to the ash-filled fireplace, her small hands clasped tightly as she waited for her next ordeal.

Six thousand miles away in Fleet Street the foreign editor of the *Daily Post* re-read the brief Reuters' story as he waited to go in to the editor's office for the morning conference.

> Nairobi, Tuesday. A British tourist was killed in a robbery on a remote road near Kenya's border with Uganda, according to unconfirmed reports here today. The man's wife is said to have survived and is staying with friends in the town of Kitale. Kenya Police have promised a statement later today.

He felt sure the editor would go for it. If they sent a good operator out there fast, they could get to the wife, the friends, the full details. He envisaged a good centre spread with pictures; the woman might even have been raped – poor wretch. He noticed as he shuffled in with the other department heads that the editor had a bored look: so much the better, he thought, sitting down at the table. He would be looking for something to get worked up about.

As he waited his turn to submit his list, his confidence grew. After all, it was very much the kind of thing they were going for these days – what you might call black crime, at home and abroad. As if to confirm his thought, the voice of the news editor at that moment droned out something about an 'epidemic of street crime' somewhere. Two years ago when the Zimbabwe independence agreement had been signed, the *Post* had bitten its tongue and printed editorials of hollow praise as the last patch of black Africa slipped from white control; but now it was carrying stories of corruption, intimidation and tribal violence there, pointing the gleeful finger at savages killing each other again. At home, the previous year had seen the riots, and now the police had put together figures to show that half of London's muggings were done by blacks. Oh, yes, it was their kind of story all right. He read the Reuters' summary to the conference, and the editor peered at him with interest over the half-moon glasses which gave him a misleading air of academic refinement.

'Mm,' he said, 'we'd better have a word about that one afterwards.' Cynics in the newsroom said that the editor was only interested in racial stories because he lived in Dulwich and saw his wife and children as the next target for the muggers and rapists of neighbouring Brixton.

As the others trooped out of the office the editor went to the window and stared silently down at the crocodile of gaudy delivery vans in the side street below.

'I don't know, Mike. Stories like that are a nightmare, aren't they? The nightmare of every man who's ever lain beneath a mosquito net listening to the drums down in the village – or walked through the streets of a modern African capital, for that matter. London will be no better than a third-world city, the rate we're going. I suppose the race relations industry will tell us it's all the legacy of slavery or colonialism or some such crap – it's the social deprivation and multiple disadvantage, you see, which forces these black muggers to pad around dark alleys in rubber-soled shoes, holding flick-knives against old ladies' throats.'

He's hooked all right, thought the foreign editor with satisfaction, squaring up his papers and suppressing his impatience.

'They're not content just to get their own back in Africa, it seems; they've got to cross the water and do it here too. I don't know, sometimes I'd like to see the army round up the lot at bayonet point and put them back on banana boats to the West Indies, or whatever starving flyblown country they came from.'

He turned to look wryly at the foreign editor and walked over to his lavishly furnished desk. 'Not that one can say that, of course, these days – so much for free speech, eh? All this mealy-mouthed stuff about a welcome if they behave themselves . . .'

'And no quotas.' The foreign editor parroted the *Post*'s editorial line with a grin of sympathy.

'Absolutely no quotas,' laughed the editor.

The foreign editor tapped the Reuters' story with the back of two fingers.

'Do we send, d'you think?'

'Yes, send. And make sure it's someone who won't piss around finding excuses for those murdering fucking coons.'

Four

'Jan's a very nice boy, in spite of . . . Well, I don't know.'

These words from his mother made their mark on Michael. Her disapproval of South Africans and the memory of Cockerell screaming like a girl out of his bloodied face undermined the friendship. Other differences developed: Michael's father taught him how to use a .22 rifle, part of a family collection of firearms which included a little pistol for Mrs Hope to keep under her pillow when her husband was away or she had a row with servants. But Jan's father only had a shabby .303 which was still too heavy for the boy to handle. Michael's parents bought him a pony, but there were only donkeys and an ageing mule on the de Fries farm. Michael regretted the growing gulf, but was also glad, since it pleased his parents. He acquiesced as they steered him towards English friends.

Eventually the tension brought cruelty at school. Michael was playing marbles with two other boys in the morning break, telling them how he was going to win prizes at horse shows, when Jan stumped towards them on his sunburned legs. He took his best marble out of his pocket and threw it down to form the prize of the next game. It was an inch across, with beautiful creamy swirls inside, and was nobly chipped from past conflicts.

'Can I play, man?' he asked, looking only at Michael, who was taller than him now. Michael stared at him as if he were a stranger, and Jan's freckled face began to redden. He jerked his thumb at his marble, lying in the playground dust, a sacrificial offering.

'Can I play?' he repeated.

A peculiar silence developed. Then Michael stepped close to the marble, his eyes fixed on Jan's crestfallen face, and kicked it away in a puff of dust. It glittered through the air and landed among small stones and bits of paper under some bushes.

'You can take your rotten marble and get lost. Who d'you think you are, butting in to our game? We were quite happy till you came along and stuck your horrid little *yarpie* nose in. Just because Ehlers beat Cockerell doesn't mean you can start getting too big for your boots. And any case, Ehlers is just a big monkey.'

Michael tucked his thumbs in his armpits, shoved his tongue behind his lower lip, and made hooting noises. Jan stood there blinking. Christopher Austin had appeared to watch the drama with a little twisted smile.

'What are you standing there for, de Fries?' Christopher intervened. 'Going to start a scrap, or something?'

Michael looked round at him, surprised. Then he remembered that Chris had been looking for a chance to give Jan a thumping ever since Empire Day. Perhaps Jan was going to get a thick ear or a twisted arm – Chris specialised in various schoolboy tortures.

But Jan shuffled off silently to the hedge where he stood kicking the paper and stones around, hands in pockets. His eyes were too wet to look for the marble, and he thought about his big, clumsy father, his thin, red-skinned mother, the little dusty farm with no car, no guns, no horses. But by the time Ma Maynard appeared in front of the school to peer serenely into the distances of the British Empire and ring the small brass handbell, he had his tears under control. As the class sat through a lesson about trawling and drifting in the North Sea, he could hear Michael and Chris whispering together at the back, palling up. When the others went in for lunch, he went alone to the playground and got to his knees among the bushes, searching for his scrap of glittering glass.

Michael knew there were caves on Elgon, huge caves reaching miles into the mountain. He had heard his parents and their friends talking about them, about the giant fruit bats which lived there, covering the floors with a thick and stinking carpet of droppings, about the mystery of their origins. But most intriguing of all to him was the story of how the elephants would sometimes make their way into the caves at dusk in great, silent, slow-treading convoys, lured by some mystery in the mountain's interior. His imagination was primed by the works of Rider Haggard, of which there was a large stock in the school library, and he would look up at the mountain, at its green and purple slopes, deciphering where the entrances might be, and he would lie in bed at night working out fantasies of daring expeditions to the bowels of the earth.

'When are we going up to the caves?' he kept asking his parents. His father would laugh and look down at him, ruffling his hair, and Michael would feel angry and patronised. They refused to understand his urgent, seven-year-old excitements, and fobbed him off with promises of 'one day'.

'Yes, but when is one day?' he persisted.

'Just . . . one day.'

Sulks and persistence paid off, however, and the expedition was set for a Sunday. Mr Hope arranged to exchange his Standard Vanguard for a friend's Land-Rover for the weekend, to make sure they would not get bogged down on the mountain's slippery tracks if it were to rain. Michael was in high spirits, telling everyone of the adventure before him; and two days before, he encountered Kimutei, for the first time for many months.

Since Michael had started at school, his friendship with Kimutei, as his parents planned, had gradually withered. Mary and Kimutei still lived on the farm, so there was some opportunity for the two boys to meet, but Kimutei was going to school too, and the difference in their experience drove a wedge between them. Michael's school had a swimming pool, and well-furnished classroom blocks, and a school hall decorated with gold-painted wooden plaques where the children sang hymns about heathen countries, calling them to 'deliver their land from error's chain'. Kimutei's school was a single large wooden hut with a cracked concrete floor, a leaky red corrugated-iron roof, and rickety backless benches; there was no piano to accompany the singing, and the children swam in the river, risking bilharzia. Michael had a pile of sturdy, hardbacked textbooks, specially ordered from Nairobi, while Kimutei carried one or two dog-eared and battered exercise books. He had, nevertheless, learned enough to converse with Michael in English.

'We're going to the caves on Sunday,' Michael said, gesturing vaguely at the ever-present shape of the mountain, dominating the farm.

'Have you never been there?' Kimutei seemed amazed that these *wazungu*, with their cars and big well-fed bodies, had not yet reached so far into their surroundings. 'I have been many times.'

Michael studied him resentfully. How could Kimutei, by himself, have gone up there, all those miles along the forest tracks?

'Oh yes? How?'

'How? Walking, of course.'

Kimutei's smile was wider now.

'You never.'

'It's not far – the caves are not at the top, you know.'

'Of course I know. So who took you?'

'Some friends. Older boys.'

42

'No grown-ups?'

Kimutei shook his head. Michael kicked at a stone in the farm track. A great ambition to him was apparently a mundane event to Kimutei. So what of the wisdom received from parents and school and culture, that the African was inferior, especially in matters needing courage and intelligence?

'What did you see, then?' Michael was resentful at being cast as supplicant.

'They are just big, high holes in the mountain. Our people have always known of them. At one time they lived in there.'

Michael leapt on this, evidence after all of the primitiveness of the Africans. His sudden smile was mocking as his mind filled with images from books of ape-men with receding foreheads dragging carcasses into rocky caverns.

'They *lived* there? In caves? Ugh! Just like in the Stone Age.'

'Have the *wazungu* never lived in caves?' Kimutei was impassive.

'No, never,' said Michael with newfound confidence. 'And I suppose you saw the elephants up there, did you?'

'Many times. There are some caves where the elephants come every night to eat the rock.'

Michael laughed.

'*Eat* the rock? What d'you mean? Elephants don't eat rock, stupid.'

'They do, in the caves,' asserted Kimutei, face closed and serious, refusing to be mocked. 'There is salt in the rock. And *you* will not see the elephants, because you will not find the right place and will be afraid to stay until dark.'

'Did you walk back in the dark?'

'Yes.'

They came to a halt by the gatepost of the Hopes' garden. Michael looked down at his dusty shoes in silence, struggling with his pride.

'Will you show me where the elephants are? If my parents let you come?'

They looked at each other from close range, each studying a face known since babyhood but less familiar as the years went by.

'*Please*, Kimutei.'

Kimutei turned his eyes away, looking at the mountain. Did he really want to share its secrets with a *mzungu*, a foreigner whom he was beginning to see, now that he was at school and growing up, as an oppressor and an enemy of his people?

'All right,' he said eventually, the habit of pleasing the white man prevailing. 'But will your father let me come?'

Michael nodded emphatically. He would use any means – tears, tantrums – to overcome the expected reluctance. The elephants were stalking through his imagination like great, grey ghosts.

'And just you and me will go off and see the elephants,' he said.

They suddenly smiled at each other, delighted in their secret complicity. With a little whoop, Michael turned and ran off to the house, then turned and jumped in the air to wave. Kimutei waved back.

There was little conversation in the Land-Rover as it crossed the river at the bottom of the farm and began grinding up the track beyond, ever deeper into the dark green shade of the forest. There had been an argument about Kimutei and the atmosphere was tense: the gloomy afternoon, with its low cloud and threat of rain, added to a feeling that things had started badly and could easily get worse. In the back, between the feet of Michael and Kimutei, there was a great pile of chain which could be attached to a tree so that the Land-Rover could winch itself out of the mud if the four-wheel drive failed.

The two boys leaned forward over the shoulders of Mr and Mrs Hope to watch the progress of the vehicle as it crawled in low gear through muddy streams and round slippery hairpins, upwards to the secrets of the mountain, green-canopied by forest. Mr Hope had a map on the seat beside him, and some notes and sketches given to him by a friend who knew the area well. After half an hour the note of the engine slowed as he pulled the Land-Rover to the very side of the track, squeezed against a moist, moss-covered bank.

'Are we there?' asked Michael breathlessly.

'We are.' His father switched off the engine.

Michael grabbed the handle and threw the back door open. The air was cooler and moister up here, and he could see nothing but the green forest pressing in on all sides. Great vines and creepers trailed from the higher branches, and strange clicking and cracking and whooping noises echoed from invisible places: the forest and its denizens talking to themselves and each other. Of the caves there was no sign, and Michael ran round to the driver's door and confronted his father with a worried, resentful face.

'Where are they? The caves?' he asked, thinking he was being deceived.

'Up there,' replied his father, amused at the boy's impatience and pointing to a stony slope between ragged-barked trees a few yards in front. Michael and Kimutei started up it without waiting for the adults.

'I suppose there was no real harm in Kimutei coming along,' said Mrs Hope, pulling on a sweater, her voice sceptical.

'I suppose not,' agreed her husband. 'The kid's well behaved enough. Perhaps we were wrong to object.'

'I don't want it becoming a habit again, that's all,' said Mrs Hope, tidying her hair in the driving mirror.

'Don't worry,' said Mr Hope as they climbed out and slammed the doors. 'When the Austins move out to the farm he'll spend all his time with young Christopher, just you wait.'

'Mmm. I've heard some funny tales about that family, mind you. That Austin man's got a reputation of being very rough with his labour.'

Fifty feet above them, Michael stood staring at the great ragged mouth of the cave, and Kimutei stood watching his reactions. Michael had expected something smaller and neater, more finely dramatic, and this great black wound in the side of the mountain, sixty yards wide and a hundred feet high, somehow disappointed him. He looked at Kimutei accusingly.

'Is this the biggest?'

Kimutei nodded. 'The other ones are smaller,' he said. 'The ones where the elephants go.'

Michael suddenly regained his enthusiasm, and turned back to the top of the slope to urge his parents upward.

'Come on,' he shouted. 'It's really huge.'

The white family and the one black boy drew together in a protective knot before walking slowly under the great overhang and into the shadows of the cave. Mr Hope carried a powerful torch, but when he flashed it upward it failed to show the roof in any detail, so high was it still. A foul smell of bat dung rose from the dusty softness beneath their feet, and their laughs and chokings of disgust echoed in the unseen spaces around them. Suddenly, the patch of daylight dimming behind them and the torch beam taking a stronger outline, there was a loud flapping and swooshing, and the great dark bats were wheeling and fluttering round their ears, giving eerie little baby's squeaks. The torch beam lurched and swept back and forth in the darkness ahead as Mr Hope ducked by reflex, grabbing for his wife and son.

'What's *that?*' yelled Michael.

'Only bats, you fool,' said Mr Hope, failing to cover the tremor in his voice as the winged, foot-wide creatures swept over them blindly, brushing them with wind like the devil. 'They won't hurt you.'

Kimutei had told Michael about the bats, but even he had jumped. They all laughed nervously and their pace slowed as they moved further in. The daylight was a loaf-sized glow fifty yards behind them when they stopped to look and listen. The torch now picked out muddy walls and a rock ceiling like solid lava.

'D'you think this is where the elephants come?' asked Michael, testing his parents against what Kimutei had told him.

'That's what they say,' said Mr Hope. 'Wouldn't be surprised if it's just a tall story from the natives, myself. But either way, I think we ought to be heading back soon.'

Michael and Kimutei nudged each other, hugging their secret as the party filed back to the daylight, blinking. The Hopes had brought the tea basket up with them, and set themselves on a large, flat rock with sandwiches and Thermos flasks. The boys gained permission to scout around by themselves for half an hour, and made off together with the spare torch and a promise that Michael's tea would be kept for him. It was left unclear what Kimutei would eat and drink.

'Can't quite understand it,' remarked Mr Hope huffily, biting into a chicken sandwich. 'Those two haven't seen each other for ages, but they're sticking together like glue.'

Mrs Hope poured tea thoughtfully. 'I hope they're not up to something.'

Kimutei and Michael had already reached the corner of the big cave's mouth and were clambering over sharp volcanic boulders, making their way downwards round the shoulder of the mountain. The forest was sparser here, the prospect more open because of the steepness. For ten minutes they followed a track Kimutei had picked up, saying nothing in their haste.

'D'you think we'll see the elephants, then?' Michael panted eventually, pushing a springy bush out of his face.

'I don't think so,' said Kimutei. 'They don't come until it is dark. But we can see the place where they go. It is not far now, but we will have to hurry.'

They reached the second cave at the top of its upper lip and were confronted with a thirty-foot drop beneath their feet. Rather than waste time making a slow, safe loop to bring them down to the lower lip, they began to edge along the top, teetering and slipping on loose rocks, stumbling over bushes and trailing vines. Haste and excitement caused their downfall. They were only twenty yards from flat ground when Michael tripped, grabbed at Kimutei, and they both fell in a clattering of loose stones down a steep slope. Michael came to rest first, his face hitting a rock, and Kimutei slid into him, also hurt.

The silence of the forest closed around them, and the clouds above were darker. Michael's face was numb, and his hand came up to touch it and find the wetness of blood. His leg was beginning to hurt badly round the ankle, and looking at the redness on his hand brought the panicky thought that his parents had no idea where he was. He saw Kimutei immobile on his hands and knees, with blood on his face as well.

'Kimutei,' he said, hearing that his voice was thick and clotted. 'Are you all right?'

Kimutei put his hand to the side of his face and touched the cut there, gingerly.

'I am bleeding,' he said slowly, as if he could not believe it. 'And so are you.'

He reached out as if to touch Michael's face, but Michael shrank away and lay back, covering his eyes with his arm, wanting to cry. If only he hadn't come on this stupid walk with this bloody African, he would be safe and with his parents. He didn't want to be touched by this bloody fool black, and his leg was beginning to hurt more than he could bear. The familiar phrases of anger and insult slipped into his mind to shift the blame.

Kimutei had managed to rise to his feet and was trying to take hold of Michael under both arms to pull him up as well.

'Don't!' screamed Michael. 'Can't you see I've broken my leg, you stupid wog? I can't stand up!'

Kimutei knelt down and felt Michael's ankle, provoking more screamed accusations of black incompetence. Kimutei dropped the leg and began scrabbling and searching among the rocks around them.

'What are you doing?' mumbled Michael. It was hurting him to talk now, and his voice felt stiff and lumpy.

'I am looking for the torch.'

'But aren't you going back to get them – tell my father?' asked

Michael. Kimutei shook his head, finding the torch and switching it on. The fierceness of the beam emphasised how dark it was already; the louring skies and encroaching trees brought the dusk earlier than out in the plains.

'It is best if I stay with you,' said Kimutei. 'Then we can flash the torch and they will find us. If I go, you will be frightened, and they will be angry with me. There are leopards on the mountain.'

Michael was silent, looking at Kimutei squatting beside him, bleeding from the head. The earlier insults forgotten, he was beginning to feel grudgingly grateful for the other boy's presence of mind. He admitted to himself that he would be frightened if left alone. He raised his knee to put his foot on the ground and test his ankle, but winced with pain: he could definitely not walk. They would have to wait here, the two of them, and when it was dark and his parents would begin to get worried and look for them, they could flash the torch in their direction.

'How far is it? Can we shout?' he asked. His racial pride was dissipated, and he threw himself on Kimutei's judgment. They sat close together on the rocky ground, their faces bloody, as if of the same race.

'Yes, we can shout,' said Kimutei. 'But first we should do something for our cuts. Have you got a handkerchief?'

'Yes.' Michael pulled one out of his pocket; it was clean that morning – one of his mother's fetishes. Kimutei grinned as he took it.

'White boys always have clean handkerchiefs,' he said. 'We blow our noses on the ground, and you think it is dirty. But you carry the dirt around with you afterwards.'

Michael did not argue; instead he yelped as Kimutei leaned forward and touched his cut mouth with the handkerchief, trying to clean it and stop the blood.

'Aaa . . . cha,' hissed Kimutei, showing his strong even teeth. 'It is a deep cut.'

Michael felt soothed by the attention, and slipped into feeling that he was cared for and there was no real danger. He looked up at the brooding clouds and the leaning trees. Then the ideals of the books he had read, of Kipling and John Buchan and Rider Haggard, suddenly flowed back to him, and he took the bloody cloth away from his mouth and sat up. Kimutei was fiddling with the torch.

'What about you? You should have a bandage too.'

Kimutei patted the side of his head, looked at his hand: still fresh blood, although the fading light made it hard to see. He tutted.

'It is not so bad,' he said. But Michael ripped the soiled piece of cloth in half and offered the cleaner piece; Kimutei hesitated, then took it and began to dab the side of his face. He made little sounds of pain which were quite foreign to Michael – strange crooning, breathy sounds which no white person would make – and which Michael found comforting as he lay back again and looked at the darkening sky, the moving clouds. He found it hard to move his lips at all now, and the throbbing in his ankle was like hammer blows falling in the same place every second. He tried to tell himself that they were heroes in an adventure, and would be recognised as such after their rescue. But he knew it was not true.

'I will shout now,' said Kimutei. 'And it is dark enough to use the torch.'

He flashed the torch twice, back over the steep wooded valley they had crossed. His voice sounded awkward, raised so high that it trembled, shouting 'Help.' Michael closed his eyes to shut out his fear and wait. They would be here soon, his mother to comfort him and his father to carry him back to light and safety; but the shouts seemed to grow more puny, and the ground beneath him felt damp and chilly. He began to shiver.

'I'm frightened,' he mumbled through the pain in his mouth. 'Why don't they come?'

Kimutei did not reply, but his next shout seemed still weaker. Then Michael heard an answering shout, very faint; he recognised the voice of his father and sat up. As they both stared into the gloom, they saw the beam of a torch, tiny under the huge, shadowy bulk of the mountain, flashing and waving. Kimutei dropped on his haunches beside Michael, grabbing his hand, eyes glittering in the remaining light. They smiled in delight at each other.

'They are coming! They can see the torch!'

Michael looked around him, his pain receding now that rescue was near, no longer frightened of the black forest pressing and rustling so near to them. It was then that he saw the great shadows, his heart jumping suddenly as he realised what they were; he blinked to improve his vision, but they remained dim shapes. His eyes watered with straining as he stared at the elephants.

'Kimutei!' It came as a hoarse mumble.

The other boy immediately saw them, fifty yards away. Together they watched as the huge, grey wraiths wound out of the trees in a lugubrious slow-march, undeterred by the recent shouting. The tusks of the leading males seemed to glow in the final light, and the dignified, mysterious procession of great beasts moved into the mouth of the cave, heads hung low, to seek its mineral-laden rock. In a whisper, Kimutei counted twelve, including two calves which scuttled and stumbled beneath the legs of their mothers. Then the cave had swallowed them, and nothing moved.

The two boys sat in a silence of veneration: a time of ordeal had coincided with the witness of a longed-for mystery, and they had no words for the fellowship between them. They did not look at each other for fear of acknowledging it, of making their lives more difficult. Another shout came from Michael's father, close this time.

Kimutei stumbled to his feet again, flashing the torch and calling. Within a few minutes Michael's parents, their torch beam swinging wildly against the sky, were scrambling down the slope above them, nearly falling themselves. Kimutei sat by Michael again for the last few moments.

Michael's father, panting and sweating, came straight to the ground at Michael's side, shining the torch on him, feeling his body to test for injuries, almost weeping.

'Daddy, we saw the elephants!' blurted Michael through his cut mouth.

'Bugger the elephants,' gasped his father. 'Are you all right? Where are you hurt?'

His mother was leaning over him as well, and Kimutei stood up and moved to one side, a black, isolated figure with no place in this tableau. Michael pointed out his ankle, and his mother felt it gently. There was a tear in her cotton trousers and her pretty face was dirty.

'Just a sprain, with any luck,' she said, brushing the hair out of her face. 'What's the cut like?'

'Looks quite nasty,' murmured Mr Hope. 'Right across his upper lip – probably need a couple of stitches. Hope it doesn't leave a scar.'

He stood up, leaving the nursing to his wife, his mind turning in its relief to other things. He looked angrily at Kimutei.

'Whose damn-fool idea was this anyway, taking off across the mountain like this in the bloody dark? Yours, eh, boy?'

'No, bwana,' said Kimutei timidly.

'No, bwana, no bwana,' mimicked the white man bitterly. 'And when did you last tell the truth, you little black bastard? What you

50

need is a dose of the *kiboko* across your backside. Then we'll have a bit less of your "no, *bwana*".'

Michael started an attempt to defend his friend; but to his surprise his mother suddenly got to her feet and pushed past her husband towards Kimutei.

'Don't talk to the kid like that,' she said, yielding like her husband to the anger which follows anxiety. 'He might be hurt as well, or hasn't that occurred to you?'

Mr Hope seemed taken aback, and made no reply while his wife gently took the torch from Kimutei's hand and shone it on his face, which was still wet with blood from the cut running down his cheek in front of his ear.

'He *is* hurt,' she said solicitously. 'Give me your handkerchief, will you? He's got to have a bandage, it's a very nasty cut.'

Mr Hope silently handed over his handkerchief, clean like Michael's, and Kimutei submitted to the *memsahib*. Then Michael was hoisted on his father's back and they set off on the path, stumbling on stones and roots, hurrying to leave the mountain and its caves to all the moving, rustling, clicking noises of the African night. As they eventually reached the Land-Rover, great gouts of rain began to fall.

The elephants were not mentioned again that night.

Five

'Even when I first met Michael, when we were both at university, he was worried about black people. Concerned.'

As the white races had done in the tropics for more than a century, Juliet was unburdening herself over a strong drink at dusk. She took another sip of her gin and tonic, and elaborated.

'He specialised in British imperial history for his degree, he was interested in the origins of slavery, he knew about the politics of independent Africa, about black immigration into Britain – everything. And he took it all very personally, as if he was responsible for it all. We used to tease him about his *bwana* complex and call him the district commissioner, but he didn't find it very funny. And why should he? It all came from his early experience out here, which was very important to him, there's no doubt about that. And he seemed to want to understand and redeem all the sins of his fathers against the black race. And that public school he went to, with some kind of tradition for educating the Indian civil service, probably didn't help matters. So he became a social worker, choosing to work in Brixton, getting involved in what they call anti-racist work.'

It was nearly two days after the attack now, and Juliet was beginning to come out of the shock, to be able to talk freely. She sat with her legs folded underneath her on the battered, wood-framed sofa on the Northrops' verandah, wearing an old woollen cardigan of Marjorie's. Her hand, with its delicate print of blue veins at the wrist, trembled slightly as she raised the glass of gin and tonic. The sun was lowering itself, reddening, towards the dark flank of the mountain.

'But his approach was always a bit Victorian, I'm afraid – visions of Lady Bountiful condescending to the poor. He'd been forced by his own experience to think hard about racial conflict – like the incident we were discussing at dinner a couple of weeks ago, d'you remember, when he got beaten up? At the age of eight or whatever it was. But because he'd thought about it and changed his colonial spots and was on their side now, I think he expected them all to love him and got rather confused when they didn't. That's why he was so fascinated by this bloke Everett – don't you remember him being mentioned by Michael, soon after we arrived? And about him being a Rastafarian and everything?'

Marjorie Northrop nodded. She was impressed by Juliet's resilience – reliving every detail of the attack in the long interview with Kariuke the previous day, enduring the enervating phone calls to Michael's parents on a crackling line, and now examining her memories and feelings. Her eyes seemed black in the failing light.

'Well, Everett told him where to get off, most of the time. But Michael wouldn't accept that and was always trying to win him over, to gain acceptance. He'd go to some of the black clubs where Everett and his friends would go, cellars in condemned houses mostly, with illegal gambling and drugs on sale, but he was usually asked to leave. I think they always thought he was a policeman. Occasionally they'd let him in and harangue him about Rasta philosophy and white oppression and Babylon and the return to Ethiopia and that sort of thing, and Michael would come back glowing with it. It was as if he loved being told what complete shits all white people are – they can be real racists, you know, the Rastas, they actually believe whites are inferior, just the sort of thing we're not allowed to believe about blacks. He said he only did it because it was useful for his job, with a lot of his clients round there being black. He needed the background and so on, didn't take it all too personally.

'But he did, I could tell. Too much guilt. He acted as if blacks could do no wrong, as if anything they might do wrong was really the fault of white people and what they'd done to blacks in the past. In a way, that meant he didn't treat them as people, as individuals. Maybe they picked up that feeling, that in the end all he noticed and cared about was their skin colour – just like the police, in a way, but from a different angle. And mostly they either rejected him like Everett, or took him for a ride, got what they could out of it. And they could tell a sucker when they saw one, some of those young black kids he dealt with. Sharp as a razor. They have to survive on the streets, after all.'

Bill Northrop appeared on the verandah and looked cautiously at Juliet. 'What about a refill, you two?' he asked cheerily, ringing the small bell from the table.

His wife asked him if pay night at the farm office had gone smoothly, and Juliet gazed thoughtfully out into the dusk, where the crickets were working up a solid, whirring rhythm.

'Same as usual – few minor disputes about this and that. But, er, the headman took me aside and said I should pass on how sorry everyone was – everyone on the farm, that is, the workers. They've all heard, naturally, and they know Juliet's involved.'

He paused, looking at Juliet and rubbing his big nose in his embarrassment. She did not move.

'I, er, wondered whether or not to tell you.'

'D'you think they're genuinely upset? That they really care?' She turned to him suddenly.

'Oh, yes, I think so, in their way they . . .'

'Or,' she cut in, voice like a chisel, 'do you think they're secretly very happy, very pleased indeed? After all, it must have been a dream they've inherited for generations now, ever since the soldiers and settlers and magistrates arrived and started *civilising* things, don't you think? Kill a white man? The secret fantasy of every African who's had his land taken, been forced away from his home, been sworn at or had his face slapped or his wages cut by a white man?'

She turned her head back abruptly to contemplation of the gathering night. Bad mistake, thought Northrop; couldn't blame the poor girl for thinking every black was a mortal enemy just now. He hoped Marjorie would field this one. She glanced at him with a little nod, and he picked up the glasses gratefully to fetch the drinks himself.

When he returned, carrying a tray gingerly in unpractised hands, Juliet was talking about Michael's time in prison in England. Michael had explained it briefly to the Northrops in one of his letters before he and Juliet arrived, but during the visit itself everyone had fought shy of the subject, unsure of Michael's feelings, how well he had got over it all.

'Looking back, it seems like an inevitable chain of events, really. Deciding to live in south London, then choosing Brixton because Michael got a job there. And then the riots, just down the road from where we live, and him getting caught up in them, which was so stupid and avoidable. I could hear it all from the front window, and I saw the flames of the buildings going up. Michael insisted on going down there, but I stayed at home. The whole thing was really quite a shock.'

'It shocked us too, I can tell you,' murmured Northrop, unable to check the feelings of a man whose vision of England had been frozen somewhere between the two world wars. The overseas editions of the *Daily Telegraph* had brought news which made the vision waver: the growth of crime and television, the 'permissive' 1960s, the power of the unions, the recession and political hatreds of the 1970s. But the riots had shattered it finally. He was sure Moscow had some kind of a hand in it. The golden mist had disappeared, leaving broken and decaying cities in harsh black and white: another reason never to go 'home'.

'It probably shocked you more than us,' said Juliet. 'After all, we'd been living close to it, we must have been aware at one level that things were building up, without actually realising it or expecting it. And out here it must have been inconceivable.'

She sighed heavily, and fiddled with her wedding ring.

'Anyway, I'm sure if it hadn't been for the business with Everett, his guilt about blacks and the need to help them, he'd never have got involved in the riots. He said he only went to watch, of course, to check on police behaviour and so on. But I think he was really there to prove himself, show solidarity, go through fire and win acceptance, that sort of thing. As for the police, well, I'm sure they lied at his trial, about the brick and everything – some of them are quite unscrupulous about that sort of thing down there, even I say that and I'm normally quite pro-police.

'But I think Michael thought the rioters were right to be burning buildings and attacking the police, because he sympathised so much with the blacks, their conditions and the prejudices against them. And then the police gave him a very bad time when they arrested him, and he was locked in the cells overnight. He wasn't badly hurt or anything, just a few cuts and scratches he could have picked up without being actually beaten up deliberately by them, but *something* very nasty happened to him, I know that. But he refused to talk about it. The only thing he ever said to me about it was that he'd had a long conversation with a certain copper – he said it with an ironic grin, as if he was speaking in code and I was meant to understand it. Typical Michael, all secretive and symbolic. Anyway, he really detested the police afterwards, while he was waiting for his case.

'And then the sentence. Well, that was another awful shock to me, I thought it was impossible they'd send someone like that to prison – you know, middle-class, professional, never been in trouble before. But I think he expected it. He said the magistrates were out to make examples, to encourage the others and all that. And the council at the advice centre were unexpectedly difficult about it all and suspended him and everything – but you know all that. That's the reason why we came, isn't it? So he could forget it all and have a bit of a rest and decide what he was going to do from now on. I think he hoped to give himself a new lease of life by returning to his roots and rethinking things. Strange, isn't it, a white man comes to Africa to find his roots? So he comes back here, he comes home, and look what happens.'

She shook her head slowly and raised her glass. The others could hear the gentle clunking of the ice cubes as she took a slow, sad drink.

'And you got married, what, after he was arrested but before the trial?' said Marjorie gently; it was half question, half statement.

'Yes, we got married. Not that I could really say why. We'd known each other for about ten years, so we had no romantic illusions. We'd seen each other's worse side often enough, had plenty of rows, moved out on each other, but at the time of the riots we'd been living together for a couple of years. Things weren't going too well, in fact. There was a sort of limbo – nothing seemed to happen, and neither of us had the energy or decisiveness to make anything happen, do anything dramatic.

'And then the drama suddenly arrived from outside, and it prompted us into deciding to do something positive about our relationship. When Mike didn't come home that night, I thought he'd been killed or was injured. I was ringing round the hospitals next day when he walked in. The police hadn't let him phone me, of course: all part of the unofficial punishment they dish out. Still, at least he didn't get worked over like some of those black kids. And then, well, the experience of thinking I'd lost him, although it was only brief, made me focus on whether I'd be happier without him. And I found that I wanted to stay. And Michael seemed to feel the same. It was strange, he became much more fond of me during that time, while he was suspended from work. He would cook little suppers for me when I got home from the office. I think having a stable home suddenly became very important because it was a traumatic time for him.

'He expected to be considered something of a hero, I think, by Everett and the boys, but down on the Front Line they weren't particularly impressed. There were hundreds of others on similar charges for similar things, and he wasn't the only white. He was perhaps the most middle-class person, but that probably made him a sucker rather than a hero. I think he felt his sacrifice was being rejected, and they still wouldn't let him into the clubs. It made him even more quiet and difficult to talk to, but at the same time he was very affectionate. I think I was his stability and he needed me.'

Juliet turned towards them, and in the silence and the trace of light from the house windows behind her, they noticed that she was weeping. Marjorie moved to her side on the sofa, and Bill got up and moved to the rail of the verandah. Looking out over his darkened farm, his life's work, he thought and felt nothing; he breathed the scents from the flowerbed below him, noticed the first shiver of chill in the air. Michael had loved it all too. Then the telephone broke through the muted sounds of grief behind him.

His first thought was that it was Michael's parents again, asking more painful, unanswerable questions. As he moved into the house, he heard the houseboy answer it.

'Who is it, Sangali?' He took the receiver.

'*Bwana* Delvers, *bwana*.'

'And who the hell is *bwana* Delvers?'

'I was asking him when you took the phone, *bwana*. He said urgent.'

'OK, Sangali. And let's have dinner soon.'

'Yes, *bwana*. Dinner up.'

Several hours afterwards, Marjorie and Bill lay in the semi-darkness staring up into the vague white dome of their double mosquito net.

'That phone call, you know,' said Bill. 'It wasn't farm business as I said. It was a newspaper reporter. They've sent him all the way out from London.'

'Good God!' Marjorie propped herself on an elbow to stare at him. 'What on earth for?'

'Cover the story properly, from the human angle. That's how he put it, anyway.' Bill's voice was flat, as if he were reserving judgment.

'Human angle indeed! Sounds more to me like pushing his nose into people's private affairs. What did you tell him?'

'Well, I told him it was out of the question tonight, of course – he wanted Juliet to come to the phone, you see. And I said I didn't think it would be a good idea any time. Mind you – he was a very plausible sort of chap.'

'Yes, I'm sure they're specially trained in smarming their way into people's good books when they want to get something out of them.

57

I wouldn't trust reporters, Bill, and I don't think you should. How did you leave it?'

'He's going to ring again tomorrow. I said I'd ask Juliet if she was prepared to talk to him when she felt in a fit state.'

'What? Why didn't you just give him a flat no and tell him to get on the first plane home?'

Marjorie saw the silhouette of her husband's nose disappear as he turned his face to hers. She could see the shine of his eyes.

'My dear, it wasn't my decision – it's hers. She is an adult, you know.'

Marjorie was quiet for a moment, her breathing heavy with indignation. Down near the river, a hyaena laughed madly.

'Well, I suppose so,' she sighed.

Chief Inspector Kariuke walked slowly towards the cells, his shoes clopping on the worn, springy boards: it was time to find out what was happening to the two men he'd had arrested – petty local criminals trying to go straight, and useful sources of information, therefore, when a little judicious pressure was applied. But the Special Branch officers who had arrived from Nairobi in sunglasses and brightly coloured shirts had more or less taken over the enquiry and contrived so far to keep him away from his own suspects. They had been in custody for nearly thirty-six hours now, and only the big shots had seen them. He pushed open the door, and the constable in the outer office stood up behind his table.

'Where are they?' asked Kariuke.

'End cell, sir.' The constable unhooked the keys from a board.

'Come in there with me,' said Kariuke, walking down the steps into the cell corridor. The place smelt of urine and fear. The constable stepped in front to open the door.

The two men were sitting on the concrete ledge in the dimness at the back, their heads sunk to their chests and their handcuffed hands hanging between their knees. The constable locked the door behind them.

'Stand up, you two.' The prisoners' heads jerked up at a voice they recognised. They got to their feet, the movement evidently painful, and stood slackly. Blood had joined the other stains on their shabby T-shirts and had dried in black patches. Moving close and staring with feigned belligerence into their faces, Kariuke recognised the puffiness, the burst lips, the caked blood in the nostrils, which come from slapping and punching.

'Any complaints?'

One of them looked up at Kariuke, a spurt of defiance in his eyes. 'Why are you picking on us, sir? We didn't do it.'

'And we don't know who did,' chimed the other man wearily. His speech was slow and clumsy, and Kariuke saw now that the side of his jaw was swollen in a large and gleaming bruise. He tried to swallow his anger at this stupid brutality. It reminded him of his earliest days in the police, under the British, working with the special army-led teams against the Mau Mau.

'You expect me to believe that? The last time I saw you two, you were saying how you always know what's going on in town. Now, suddenly, you are blind and you have seen nothing. Why this change? I warn you, I am expecting some information from you, good information. Constable, get me a chair.'

Kariuke studied the two while he waited: a couple of small-time thieves who worked now and then in shabby garages in the back streets, drank in the bus station bar, and had done time in prison for burgling the houses of government officials and breaking bottles in the faces of their own kind. Just the sort of people a visiting gang would use for a little local information about the lie of the land, this and that. He sat cautiously on the rickety chair which the constable put behind him. He would give it a last try – they could be holding out because they'd been cut in on the proceeds, or threatened with death if they talked.

'Sit down,' he said softly. 'And let us think about the problem.'

The two sat on the concrete shelf. The high barred window at one side showed that the light was now falling to dusk. Out at Twiga Farm the purple shadows would be moving up from the river valley and the Northrops and their guest would probably be pouring gin over their sorrows. Kariuke felt he could do with a strong drink himself. He felt he was being pulled, like a leaf into an eddy, into something he could neither avoid nor control.

'We have here the worst crime in the area for some years,' he said. 'This is not a feud or a dowry killing – it is more the kind of thing which happens over the border. But we are not in Uganda, we are in Kenya, which is not run by some criminal or madman. Not yet, anyway. So when a gang of robbers holds up a car and kills someone, it is a very serious affair. And when the person they kill is a tourist, a white man, it becomes a very special murder. The government is interested and becomes involved. The country depends on tourists coming here and spending money. Some people may not like that. They say they do not see any of the money and that anyway it is a bit too much like old times, when the whites ruled the country. But I am not interested in that – I am employed to catch criminals and the men who did this crime are very serious criminals indeed. And I think all people who are patriotic will do their best to help me. And when I talk about patriotic citizens, I hope I am also talking about you.'

He raised his eyebrows in threatening interrogation.

'Yes, sir,' they intoned wearily. Their manner made it clear this angle had already been used. It was probably the stock-in-trade of these city slickers with their large stomachs and flashy clothes; a mixture of violence and righteous patriotism as they dealt with 'state security' – a concept which, in his experience, was more often than not confused with the interests and whims of powerful men in government and industry. Kariuke exhaled a long sigh and stood up. It was too much like old times. Suddenly he had had enough of the foul atmosphere, the dirty stained walls, the grubbiness of police work.

'OK, you two. I think you had better spend another night or two here, just in case you change your minds. And here is something to think about: did you know there is a reward for information in this case?'

'How much?' asked the bruised one, his voice suddenly less heavy.

'It depends on the information. If it leads to an arrest, maybe ten thousand shillings.'

They were looking speculatively at each other as he walked out. He thought, if there was another telex from headquarters wanting to know of any developments, he would pass it straight over to the big shots. If they were running the show, beating up his usual suspects, they could also take the responsibility.

'See that those two get some food and blankets,' he told the constable. 'We'll let them out in the morning – if our two friends have finished with them, that is.'

'I think they've got everything they want out of it, sir.'

Kariuke grinned at the constable in a moment of understanding: he wasn't alone in his resentments. As he walked over the yard, looking forward to home and a good night's rest, a Land-Rover came noisily through the gates and two constables jumped out. One of them went to the back of the vehicle while the other ran over to him.

'Sir, we've brought in a man from one of the villages. He says he saw the gang, but he's worried he'll be killed if he talks. He wants us to promise protection.'

Kariuke saw the evening at home, the dinner, recede and vanish. Still, he wasn't going to let the goons have first go at this particular witness. He ran a hand down hard over his face, feeling the grease and grime.

'OK,' he said, trying to brace himself. 'Bring him round to my office straight away.'

Bob Delvers was in a foul temper. This trip was just what he needed, but it had got off to a bad start. The moment he'd stepped off the plane to the heady remembered smells of dust and cow dung and woodsmoke, things had begun to go wrong, starting with the half-hour wait for the passport check. He'd managed to control his anger at that stage by forcing himself to think about the queues of black and Asian people at Heathrow; but when he'd found his hire-car booking had gone awry, he'd lost control and used some undiplomatic language. 'A car is not available, sah,' he mimicked viciously under his breath, rolling his eyes like the sweating young white-shirted man behind the rental desk and harbouring deeply prejudiced thoughts about Africans and inefficiency. And then there were no taxis. He glowered out at the Nairobi game park, his square, pock-marked face framed in the cracked window of the green corporation bus as it rattled over the high, sunlit plain towards the city.

His mood improved, however, as the bus began swaying and diving through the dense city traffic and he caught sight of the brilliant, many-coloured bougainvillea bushes spilling off the first roundabout. At the roadside men sat or slept in the shade of jacarandas, and women in gaudy dresses swayed past with baskets or tins on their heads. He remembered he was away from his wife and family, who had been driving him batty recently, that the story out here was a doddle, that the beer was very drinkable and that some very attractive local girls tended to put themselves in the way of foreigners with money.

He got out by the post office in Kenyatta Avenue and walked

down towards the New Stanley Hotel, a blue-eyed compact figure suggesting clumsy strength: the kind of man who was not fast enough to duck, but who would still be on his feet after the last punch had been thrown. He walked round the legless smiling beggar he remembered from a previous trip and went into the smart hotel lobby where a man in uniform hurried to take his case.

The hotel booking, at least, had worked. In his room he lit the first of his duty-free cigarettes and booked a call to the office – their ideas could change from one hour to the next. He went into the bathroom for a toothmug for his duty-free Scotch, then strolled round the parquet-floored room in stockinged feet, looking down at the Nairobi office workers making their way home. Ants, he thought, just like the London crowds, only here they were a more convincing and consistent colour for ants. Delvers did not have a particularly high opinion of black people, wherever they were. His views about the recent riots at home included a good measure of racial fear and hatred: like the editor, he lived in Dulwich, the most desirable suburb near to Brixton, and he had two teenage daughters about whom he felt strongly, even if he did not see very much of them these days. The phone rang.

'Your call to the UK, sir.'

Delvers lay on the bed with receiver in one hand and glass in the other, wiggling his toes as he talked.

'Hello, this is Bob Delvers in Nairobi. Remember me?'

'Of course, Bob.'

The foreign editor's voice was flat: he was not excited by the skipping of continents and the impact of a new culture.

'Well, I'm here. It's nice to be back. Just thought I'd find out if there's anything new your end.'

'There has been something, in fact. Turns out this bloke who was killed out there was that social worker who was done for chucking bricks at the police during the riots. Anyway, the *Standard* are splashing on it today. "Gun Victim was Rioter" – usual 72-point stuff.'

'Christ,' broke in Delvers, his toes going like eels. 'That's a bit bloody ironic, isn't it? Throwing bricks for the darkies, then they clobber him. That'll teach the little bugger.'

'Hang on, Bob. There's a bit of difference between the Rastas down in Brixton and the armed robbers of the Kenya highlands. Not the same lot at all.'

'Oh, no? You try telling that to the editor – I've had several lectures on race from him. Talking of the editor, doesn't this rather knock the story down for him? What I'm doing out here, I mean?'

'It might – I haven't seen him yet. But you just carry on as planned for the moment. The *Standard* have got a picture of Hope, by the way. Funny-looking sod.'

'What was he like?' Delvers, more reflective, put the glass to his mouth, allowing the Scotch to dribble over his tongue.

'Short fair hair, serious-looking – but then they are these days, aren't they, the lefties? He's got a mark on his top lip, like a harelip or possibly a deep scar. Anyway, Bob, I'll leave you to it. You've got the number of that stringer out there, haven't you?'

'Yeah, Schmidt. I'm going to ring him now.'

Delvers got up, slugged another inch of whisky into his glass and padded over to the window. The sunset had come suddenly, and the streets were quiet and shadowy. The city's night watchmen were already taking up positions outside the smart shops with their blankets and braziers and cudgels. A group of children in rags ran laughing and shouting across the traffic lights below, causing a Mercedes to hoot and swerve. A black fist on an impeccably suited arm waved at them through the car window.

Delvers thought desultorily about the black man and the white man. He remembered the Soweto riots six years earlier, where the first victim was a white social worker; stoned and burned for his pains. The foreign editor wanted a distinction between blacks in Africa and blacks in the West Indies or Brixton: not really the same bunch of people. But Delvers inclined to the editor's view – all of a tribe; and there were plenty of blacks these days who would argue the same. The Rastafarian dream of the return to Ethiopia was getting stronger all the time among the young blacks in south London. Then there was the pan-African movement – there'd been something recently about some nutcase from the States visiting Britain with propaganda about how unemployed black kids in Birmingham would never be free until the continent of Africa had thrown off capitalism and imperialism.

He sighed and walked over to the phone, glad of tasks to curtail such riddles which were not his business anyway. He phoned Mike Schmidt and arranged to meet him in the bar, had a shower and change, and went down to see if the blasted rental firm had delivered his car yet.

Schmidt was a short American with fawning eyes and a small moustache who veered between sycophancy and prickliness. Delvers, at the bar buying drinks, sighed again: it was a movie he had been through before. Local stringer, resentful at big star sent out from London, rubs in newcomer's ignorance of local conditions and politics; but stringer is flattered at being sought out, and doesn't dare get too rude in case it harms his prospects. Stringer knows local ropes, but can't write himself out of a paper bag – not in the *Post*'s style, anyway. Delvers picked up the two glasses and bottles of Tusker in his big, short hands, and carried them to the table where Schmidt sat looking indecipherable and stroking the ends of his moustache.

'Cheers,' said Delvers, watching the moustache trail in the froth. They exchanged news about a mutual acquaintance, and Schmidt complained at the difficulty of getting his stories into British papers.

'Why don't you do a piece about the crime rate out here?' suggested Delvers. Schmidt snorted, and the froth blew off his moustache.

'Yeah,' he said bitterly. 'That's about the only sort of crap they'll take. If you'll excuse me calling it crap – it's only a small part of the picture, you see. What I'm trying to write about is the internal politics of the place, and the strategic implications . . .'

'The strategic implications of the sex life of the royal family is about as far as the *Post* goes down that road,' cut in Delvers.

'Yeah, yeah,' said Schmidt wearily. 'Well, that's how they sell papers, I suppose. But they might start to think differently when there's trouble – real trouble – out here.'

He looked challengingly at Delvers, who decided on a hard line.

'Every stringer likes to think his neck of the woods is the world's next trouble spot,' he said evenly. 'They all reckon that President Canaan Banana, or Chile con Carne, or whoever, is the most significant politician since John F. Kennedy.'

Schmidt threw his hands up and his head down.

'OK,' he said. 'OK. But if there's a coup in three months' time, don't say I didn't tell you. You can forget all that stuff about the most stable country in Africa.'

Delvers summoned one of the white-robed waiters in red fezzes and ordered two more Tuskers. It was Schmidt's turn, but never mind.

'What *about* the crime rate, then?' He grinned to secure a truce.

Schmidt stared sullenly for a moment, then relaxed and fawned, holding up a warning finger:

'OK, you win. But if you write about it, I want a large tip fee, OK? I'm a struggling freelance, you work for a profitable paper.'

Delvers nodded and leaned back on the leather cushions.

'Well, it's bad, as you obviously know. There are a lot of very rich people, both Kenyan and foreign, in this town, surrounded by a growing number of very poor people. Rocketing population, land hunger, flight to the towns, unemployment, corruption: the perfect recipe for producing bold and violent criminals, as in many other third-world countries. And some of the criminals have got guns now.'

'And they use them.'

'Sure they use them. There's a shooting every few weeks. Comes and goes a bit, but there've been some pretty far-out cases. Couple of years back, a white couple – Kenyan citizens, retired, living on the outskirts of town – were woken in the night by noises, someone trying to get into the place. He gets his shotgun down, goes to the window, and tells them to get lost before he shoots them. They just open up at him through the window, bullet through the chest. Then they break the window down and shoot the wife as well before they clear the place out. She survived, he didn't. Probably didn't make the UK papers because they weren't Brits. They'd lived here all their lives. You should have a look at some of these rich Nairobi suburbs – like fortresses, some of them. High walls, steel gates like it was Hollywood, dogs, night watchmen, bars, alarms. And then you should go round one of the shanties – I'll take you if you've got a free afternoon. Mathari Valley, that'll open your eyes.'

'No thanks,' said Delvers, swigging beer, needling. 'If I have a spare afternoon I'll spend it on the beach at Malindi.'

'Malindi! Huh! You couldn't get on the beach at Malindi these days without being mobbed out by touts and prostitutes of all shapes and sexes.'

'Can't be bad.' Delvers grinned provocatively.

'I think even you might find it too much – unless you like eight-year-old kids begging to sell you their arse.'

Schmidt suddenly laughed and shook his head.

'It's funny, you know. The word got around in the hotels that it wasn't safe to leave your valuables in the room. So people took things down to the beach – money, watches, rings, what have you. So the gangs stopped breaking in and just worked the beaches instead. They'd look for a place with just two or three people lying

65

about and walk up to them with *pangas* and say, "give". Give us the lot or we'll chop your fucking head open. Simple – you ever seen one of these *pangas*?'

'Big, heavy, about two foot long . . .'

'Designed for chopping sisal. Hone a razor edge on one of those and, boy, do you have a lethal weapon. Anyway, they had a big police operation down at the coast and that kind of thing more or less came to a halt. The tourist industry matters a great deal to this country.'

'What about this Hope case? Have the gangs operated that far up the country before?'

'Not as far as I know. Government's very worried about it – tourism again. The Minister of Tourism and the Foreign Minister held a press conference today, with all the foreign press corps practically dragged in there by the police. Got a copy of the statement, if you like. Usual stuff about no stone unturned, every reassurance to foreign visitors, extra police vigilance, determination at the highest level, you know the sort of thing.'

He fished in his chest pocket and brought out a crumpled piece of paper. Delvers glanced at it: ten paragraphs of eyewash, and the Kenyan lions clutching their red, black and green shield at the top. He pocketed it.

'Thanks.'

'I was chatting to some of the guys at police headquarters,' said Schmidt casually. 'They were telling me they've sent a Special Branch team up there.'

'Oh yes? And who's the copper in charge of it all?'

'Well, interesting you should ask. The top man locally is called Kariuke, who used to be going places down here but was shifted to the sticks for reasons which weren't entirely clear. The rumour was he was going to blow the whistle on some big-time political corruption, but they managed to persuade him not to – how, I don't know, but methods can be pretty rough round here – and he was shipped out of harm's way.'

'Any idea where Mrs Hope is?'

'The local papers were saying this morning that she's staying with some friends, old settler-type farmers just outside Kitale. Name of Northrop.'

'On the phone, d'you think?'

'I haven't tried, myself.'

Delvers gave him a withering look.

'No, I thought you wouldn't have.'

'It's not my kind of story, Bob. I leave this kind of thing to the hyaenas.'

Delvers drained his beer and stood up: he had what he needed. But Schmidt, truculent now, was going to have his say.

'The thing that gets me about you guys is your fucking confidence. You just breeze into some place – any place – use a few lowdown tricks and wave the greenbacks around until you get what you want, which is usually pretty disreputable, and then get the hell out of there. Don't give a damn, do you?'

Delvers was looking round the bar: tourists with sunburned noses, a few large businessmen laughing too loudly, a black girl with a lovely figure on a bar stool. He turned back to Schmidt, suppressing a desire to smack him in the face.

'No,' he said. 'Complete professional. Not my job to carry the sorrows of the world. I'll leave that to the nice guys like you.'

He held out his hand.

'See you, Mike, thanks.'

Schmidt was anxious again.

'See you. Say, can I buy you a beer back tomorrow?'

'Tomorrow, old boy, I confidently expect to be sitting on the Northrops' verandah with a lunchtime gin in my hand. So long.'

Schmidt signalled glumly for the waiter and studied the backside of the girl at the bar, who was deep in negotiation with one of the laughing businessmen. That was what he was, he told himself: a whore. And Delvers had just screwed him.

Upstairs Delvers was going through the Kenya telephone directory, Scotch in hand, muttering under his breath: 'Northrop, Northrop . . . ah, here we are. Twiga Farm, that sounds like it.'

He lifted the receiver with his spare hand and told the operator: 'Please get me Kitale 313. And don't take all night, it's urgent.'

Six

The Austin family moved out to Mount View Farm when Michael and Christopher were both seven years old. Mr Austin, an aggressive and bad-tempered man with a blond toothbrush moustache, had been appointed by the absentee owner as the latest of many farm managers, and the family took over a newly built brick house down near the farmyard. The episode at the caves had created a bond between Michael and Kimutei, but it had also made Michael's parents more determined than ever that the two should not meet. Christopher soon filled the gap.

The first time Michael went round to the Austins' house for tea, he became aware of a sinister presence in the sitting room – a piece of grey rubber hosepipe, with a loop of twine through a hole in one end of it, hung on a hook. It was the only object on one wall in a generally stark room, and the family referred to it as if it were another person. When Christopher was sent away from the table to wash his hands more thoroughly, he was warned by his father that 'the hose would be after him'. As he left the room he cast a terrified look over his shoulder, as if it might really leap down and pursue him. Michael looked fearfully at the bristling Mr Austin, afraid to reach for the thinly spread bread and butter lest the grubbiness of his own hands be noticed. Mrs Austin, who had an elaborate, piled-up hairstyle, seemed as much in fear of her husband as Christopher. Her eyes seemed to cringe.

A few weeks later, during the school holidays, Michael saw the hose go into action. He was running through the farmyard after lunch to persuade Christopher to come down to the dam for a swim. He was about to pass the gateposts of the Austins' newly laid-out garden when he heard a yelling commotion and halted; he retreated and peered cautiously round the tractor shed.

Mr Austin was pulling a protesting, pleading Christopher towards the house. The boy's legs were dragging and bumping across the ground, his body a dead weight, and he was pouring out a fluent stream of words, rising occasionally to a little scream.

'No, Daddy, no, I'll never do it again, Daddy, please don't, I'm sorry, Daddy, don't give me the hose, PLEASE, it's not my fault, Daddy, NO . . .'

The pleading and repentance were having no effect on the striding, khaki-clad father, and the noise became fainter as the two mounted the verandah, Christopher's legs bumping inertly against the steps. Michael's heart was beating so fast his senses were clouding: this snivelling creature was not the Christopher he knew, the tall, strong boy who ruled the class and dispensed summary justice – why didn't he fight, resist?

Michael found a strange appetite coming over him: he wanted to witness the beating of the stiff, vindictive Christopher, watch the biter being bitten. With a boldness which excited and frightened him, he walked quickly in the afternoon heat up the dusty drive to the house.

He stepped lightly across the pale new boards of the verandah and peered through the crack in the French doors: the hose was missing from its hook. From Christopher's bedroom at the back came the sounds of punishment – an intermittent swish, accompanied by a heavy grunt, and followed by a scream. Christopher's protesting monologue still flowed between the screams, but among the pleading and self-abasement there now came extraordinary flurries of hatred and obscenity. Michael had never heard such words at home.

'No, Daddy, stop, Daddy, AAAGH, you fucking bastard, Daddy, OWWW, please Daddy, I'm sorry, you shitbag, Daddy, you fucking arsehole, I hate you, Daddy, let me go, Daddy, stop . . .'

Michael moved off the verandah to the side of the house, letting his ears lead him to the open bedroom window: the lowest pane was just above his head. In a kind of exaltation, he found himself putting the sides of his feet on a little ledge a foot above the ground and pulling himself up so he could see inside.

Mr Austin was flailing at his son with the hose, not caring where he struck him; Christopher would escape occasionally and run for the door, or try to climb beneath the bed. But the wiry strength which ensured his dominance at school was no use to him now: his father would catch him, pull him back, and deliver more of the wild, swishing blows, giving little grunts of satisfied exertion, his little blue eyes like steel points in his reddened face. A chair in the room was overturned, the bedclothes had been pulled aside, and to his amazement Michael saw the legs of a small teddy bear underneath the pillow. Christopher, the persecutor of sissies, had a teddy bear!

Michael suddenly became aware, through some subtle change of the light and shadows surrounding him, that someone else was there.

69

He looked sideways and saw Mrs Austin standing at the corner of the house looking at him silently, her arms folded across her chest. There was a gleam in her dog-like eyes, and a little slack smile on her painted lips. Michael froze in a confusion of reactions: was she going to seize and submit him next for her husband's beating? Or was she just listening and observing too, participating passively in some savage family ritual? Her expression told him that here was deep water, and his immobility exploded in flight. He dropped from his perch and ran, kicking through the piles of soil in the still-unplanted garden. When he reached the safety of his own bedroom two hundred yards away up the hill, he locked the door and lay panting on the bed.

What had Christopher done? The only time he, Michael, had been beaten – briefly, and with more a twig than a stick – was when he was caught impaling frogs on sticks down at the dam. In the next two days he walked past the Austins' house several times, warily, scaring himself with the thought that a fleet-footed Mr Austin might at any moment sweep down and drag him off to the torture chamber. But he never saw Christopher, and even wondered if he might be dead, and buried in the loose red soil of the unfinished garden.

Then, next morning, he was there at the Hopes' door, his white towel rolled neatly and tucked under his arm, asking if Michael could come swimming. Michael was amazed how normal he seemed. Christopher looked calmly back at him, his face serious, his body tense. At the dam, he was slow in changing, and Michael swam ahead of him across the orange-red sheet of water. When they had clambered through the reeds and were sitting on the dam, panting, Michael's curiosity tumbled out.

'Why did your dad give you the hose?'

Christopher looked away, taking his hands from round his drawn-up knees and clasping them again lower down, behind his thighs. The movement was intended to conceal, but Michael's eyes followed it. He now saw the marks, red and blue and slightly raised, across the back of Christopher's legs, where most of the blows had landed.

'Gor, is that what it did?' Michael leaned over in fascination, forefinger extended to touch the wounded places. Christopher flinched and moved out of reach.

'Does it hurt?'

Christopher nodded briefly, picking up a black stick and chipping

70

rapidly with it at the stony earth of the dam. Then he stopped chipping and turned to Michael.

'No, not really,' he said defiantly. 'It did for a bit, but it doesn't any more.'

He hurled the stick suddenly into the water. Michael watched it spin and splash, his eyes half closed against the silver light glancing off the surface. A slight wind was raising small waves, and a group of crested cranes were wading on stiletto legs through the shallows at the far end. Chris must have driven his dad's car into the ditch, or drunk some whisky, or broken something that cost hundreds of pounds. And now he was so calm about the punishment!

'Gosh, Chris, what did you do wrong?' he asked wonderingly.

'I pinched some chocolate biscuits.'

Michael stared at him, slack-mouthed and disbelieving.

' 'Strue. I was playing in the farmyard where I'm not supposed to, and Dad caught me and made me go without any lunch. I was really hungry, so I waited till Dad was down in the farm office and Mum was asleep, and I got into the store through the window and there was this packet of chocolate biscuits. I only took a few so they wouldn't miss them. Then I was scoffing them in the garage when Dad came in and caught me. I dunno how he knew – I reckon Mum must have told him. Anyway, I got the hose.'

'Gor. I wouldn't have got that just for pinching biscuits.'

The two looked at each other for a second, contemplating the stark differences between their families. Christopher looked away first, and his voice was defensive and angry.

'Anyway, how d'you know about it? I never told you.'

' 'Cos I saw the marks on your legs,' said Michael. Christopher would probably thump him if he ever found out that he'd watched the beating.

'It must have really hurt,' he added, trying to be placatory.

'Yeah, well, one day it might happen to you,' muttered Christopher.

'D'you think your dad would do it to me?'

'He'd do it to anyone if he got the chance,' said Christopher bitterly, standing up without any attempt now to hide his marked legs from Michael, who studied the bruises with horror, a foot from his face. They stood proud of the surface, with little clots of yellow among the red and blue.

'I've got my penknife with me,' said Christopher bloodthirstily.

'C'mon, let's swim down the other end and creep up on those Cavirondos.'

They stumbled their way down through the rushes, the mud squirting up through their toes in smooth, red sausages, and began to doggy-paddle towards the shallow end, stalking the beautiful, gold-crested birds.

The barking and yelping of a troop of baboons raiding the maize crop woke Michael on his first morning at the Northrops'. He lay without moving in the desolate purple half-light, watching it spread and glow round the curtains, cold and alone in a strange bed. His parents had gone on holiday, leaving him on the neighbouring farm with other adults who were hardly known to him; even the smells were strange – the sweetness of the cedar wood in the floors and roof, a trace of mothballs in the blankets on his bed, a hint of an unfamiliar woman's perfume. He turned over and buried his face in the pillow.

There was a tap at the door and he sat suddenly upright, fearing invasion. He remembered how his mother had reacted one evening recently when there had been a knock at the house door, holding her husband's arm, warning him that someone might be waiting there with a *panga*. The light in the bedroom had changed, making everything grainy, like a black and white photograph. Mr Northrop's voice came through the door.

'Michael? Are you coming milking?'

He had said in the bravado of the previous evening that he wanted to; he didn't want to any more, but felt he had to. Away from home, you could never do what you wanted. He wished his mother was breezing prettily into the room, drawing his curtains, getting his clothes.

'Oh, yes,' he called, his voice tired and small. 'I'll get up then.'

The door opened a crack; Mr Northrop's face, with its large bony nose, wore a kindly smile and his hair was standing up at the back like the crest of a hoopoe bird.

'You'll have to be pretty brisk,' he warned. 'Out of the house in five minutes, OK?'

Michael climbed, shivering, out of bed and pulled on his crumpled clothes. A cock crowed outside and he pulled back the curtains: a flock of cranes was beating its way across a pale sky ribbed with milky strips of cloud. When he had splashed water on his face and made his way to the warm, smoky kitchen, the melancholy of dawn had evaporated. Northrop was leaning against the rickety wooden table with a cup of tea and the houseboy was busy with the crackling stove.

'Hello, young man.' Northrop was hearty and welcoming. 'Well done – I thought you were set for another hour or two. Cup of tea?'

Michael took the tea, feeling grown-up, with a part to play. Outside, the milking gong sounded, its shock waves seeming to move the air. As they left the house, they saw a farmhand, his legs like thin sticks below the tatters of an old raincoat, beating steadily with an iron bar on the old plough blade suspended from the thatched eaves of the machinery shed. The cows were being driven up from the misty further reaches of the farm by herdsmen loping around their charges in sandals made of old car tyres, whistling and delivering smacking blows with their supple sticks.

'They're a bit late,' said Northrop, rubbing his hands against the lingering chill. 'We've got a long round in the township today, too.'

Michael watched the milkers forcing the cows' heads into the stalls, then pinging the thin jets of milk into the metal pails with agile black fingers. Northrop came and stood beside him, leaning over to pull a large grey tic off the cow's flank. To Michael's horror, he burst the insect's taut body between his fingers, and idly wiped the gouts of black blood on the rough post next to them.

'Want to have a go?' asked Northrop.

'Ugh, no thanks.'

Northrop looked at Michael's screwed-up face and laughed: he was staring at the post.

'Not with the tics – with the milking, I mean.'

'Oh – all right.'

Michael blushed. The farmhand yielded his stool, and he gingerly took the long teats, mottled pink and blue-black, in his hands, finding them much harder than he expected. He pulled and squeezed with no result. The farmhand, laughing, squatted at his side and took the two other teats in demonstration.

'Like this,' he said. His skin smelt of sweat and animals, and his eyes were gentle and brown-curdled.

But Michael brushed his arm away petulantly and went on vainly as before. The man backed off, hurt. Northrop made a placatory gesture at him and laid an arm on Michael's shoulder.

'Have another go tomorrow,' he said soothingly. 'It's not as easy as it looks, and we're in a bit of a hurry today. Better let the chap get on with it.'

Michael rose from the stool, red with anger and frustration, and the farmhand took over with a reproachful look. Michael glared at him.

Loaded with churns of milk, the old Peugeot pick-up ground off down the long farm drive between the tall gum trees. Michael sulked, gazing out of the window at the dusty roadside. The heat of the day was rising as they drove into Kitale and turned off into the little African township. Northrop waved at customers and people he knew as he drove slowly through the narrow streets, choked with dogs, bicycles, old women carrying yard-high bundles of sticks on their bent backs. After several deliveries, Northrop noticed Michael looking pale and anxious.

'What's the matter?'

'Nothing.' Michael swallowed hard.

Northrop suddenly realised that the boy had never been in a place like this. He looked around: there was a naked child squatting in the fetid gutter, noise and clouds of flies everywhere. Most whites chose never to see these places, he remembered, and confined themselves to the wide streets and swept pavements and Indian-run shops of the main town, with its bougainvillea and occasional jacarandas.

'Don't worry,' he said with a smile. 'They all know me.'

Just then a man lurched towards them and as the pick-up passed him he leaned over and banged his fist on the bonnet.

'*Uhuru!*' he shouted. Northrop's face at the window received the gust of his breath, laden with the sweetish fumes of home-brewed maize beer. His eyes were bloodshot, his face moist.

'Damn fool!' he muttered, glancing at Michael and trying to laugh. 'Drunk as a lord, of course, and obviously not very keen on the second part of the slogan – the *kazi* bit.'

'It means freedom and work, doesn't it?' asked Michael quickly. '*Uhuru na kazi*. That's what they were all shouting in town one day after school, loads of people and police and everything, and Dad turned round and went home a different way.'

'Yes, that KANU rally. Bloody politicians, leading the natives astray. They'll promise the earth, of course, if only they get *Uhuru*, and there'll be work and a farm and a full belly for everyone; and

74

when it happens, of course, it won't be like that. It'll be worse, I'm afraid. Bloody fools.'

'*Is* it going to happen?' asked Michael. 'My dad says they won't let it.'

Northrop looked at him: the political education of this child was not his business. If that was the official line in the Hope family, fair enough. But everyone knew it *was* going to happen, and was speculating fearfully whether it would be 'another Congo'. The murder and rape and mutilation there were fresh in the minds of the white colonists of Africa.

'Well, maybe they won't,' he said with false lightness. 'Here we are at Kamau's: biggest delivery of the lot. Don't worry when three or four blokes jump on the back to take off the churns. I'm going inside to get the account settled, OK? You'd better just stay here.'

He disappeared into a shop where tin signs advertised Aspro and flykillers. A few people were sitting in home-made chairs on a concrete verandah, watching Michael and flicking flies away from their faces. Michael sat still, trying to look casual, his arm resting on the wound-down window. The vehicle bucked as the men, with bangs and shouts, dragged the churns off the back. A few passers-by stopped to watch, and soon there was a little knot of people round the pick-up. Michael glanced at them, but looked away quickly, anxiously trying to preserve aloofness and indifference. A boy of about his own age seemed to be trying to catch his attention, and even as he stared straight ahead Michael could see him out of the corner of his eye, gesticulating, pointing and laughing. The sun was halfway up the sky now; the metal of the pick-up door felt hot on the soft underside of his arm, and he blinked against the steely reflections off the bonnet. The boy was now walking slowly round the front of the pick-up, grinning at him, his bony limbs very long and loose. Now he was at the window; Michael sat immobile, his mind clouding.

'What are you looking at?' The boy's voice was strangely low and throaty, and still he was grinning. Michael said nothing, swallowing the thick saliva which had gathered in his mouth; then the boy nudged hard at his arm, and repeated the question more aggressively.

'What are you staring at, *shenzi?*'

The word was an insult Michael had often directed at the farm-hands, the houseboy, his *syce*: 'mongrel', it meant, 'ill-begotten'. It had never been turned back at him before.

'Nothing,' he said, still not moving. More than one word, he felt, and his voice would quaver.

'Get out,' ordered the boy. Michael looked at him: he was dressed in a ragged shirt and shorts, and his face had high cheekbones and slack lips pulled into a strained and twisted smile. His eyes had a deep, dark light in them.

Scared, Michael turned away, saying nothing, trying to gauge how to get out of this trap. He could shuffle along the bench seat, jump out of the driver's door, and run into the shop. But the crowd was larger now, blocking the space between the pick-up and the shop. The boy nudged his arm again, harder.

'You're scared,' he challenged.

Michael felt himself moving, as if he had no choice. Slowly, like a sleepwalker, he pulled open the door and stepped out. Then he saw something coming towards him very fast, flinched too late, and found himself on his back, face numb and ears singing, blinking at the blue, impassive sky.

A noise rose up, great shouts of triumph and glee. A circle of black faces appeared, looking down at him, grinning and laughing. As he climbed to his feet, he put one hand to his mouth and looked at the blood on it, surprised. He touched his face again, feeling for his lips, his teeth.

His hand broke the force of the second punch. The boy had long arms and stony knuckles, and behind them his eyes hovered like hornets. Michael moved backwards, but knew he was encircled by the crowd. Another punch came; he ducked, and the blow glanced off his temple. He managed to draw his fists up, like the other boy.

The next blow smashed through them and landed painfully on his nose. A roar went up again, and he covered his face with his palms in panic and fear. Another blow, another shout. Through his splaying fingers he saw the face of an old woman with beads in her hair and wooden roundels in her ear lobes; her face was lit up with excitement, her pink mouth open in delight.

'*Shenzi!*' came the voice of his opponent, low and hoarse.

Michael put his head down and rushed blindly forward. His hands slid round the boy's washboard ribs, gripped him round the waist. His face was against the thin chest, safe at last from the knobby fists, and the smell of sweat and dust scoured his nostrils. He pushed, and the boy collapsed beneath his better-nourished, better-padded white body. The shout this time was one of rage and disappointment.

76

Michael wrestled one of the boy's wrists to the ground and settled his weight on the bucking body. The boy was swearing and spitting as Michael pinned the other hand as well. Then a new note entered the hubbub around them, a single raised voice. Michael lifted his fist and smashed it down into the boy's face. It was a blow which had haunted and fascinated him ever since he saw Ehlers use it on Cockerell on Empire Day; its cruelty, the helplessness of the victim, had shocked him then, but now he needed it to fulfil and satisfy him. He felt his fist flattening the flesh, his knuckles sliding on to the teeth. When he lifted his fist for a second blow, the face beneath him was contorted and bleeding, a bubble of thick snot at one nostril. Blood for blood: Michael rejoiced.

Then the intruding voice was nearer, and he suddenly felt himself seized from behind and lifted off his prey. It was Northrop: at first the spectators had obstructed him, but now they let him through to save the black child. He picked Michael up and stuffed him urgently into the pick-up where he sat, dazed, dusty and bleeding, his chest heaving. The crowd closed round the black boy.

As Northrop went quickly round to the driver's door, some of the crowd moved to Michael's window to laugh, shout and point. He looked straight ahead, afraid to look at any of them and confront their hatred. Northrop started the engine and let the clutch out too sharply in his agitation; the pick-up lurched forward and stalled. One or two people now banged on the bonnet and wings, shouting 'Uhuru!'

'God Almighty,' cursed Northrop, restarting the engine, fearing real danger. 'What's got into this lot today?'

Michael said nothing, and Northrop looked over at him; he was a mess, with blood and dust all over his clothes.

'Are you all right?' he asked anxiously. 'Nothing broken?'

Michael shook his head and turned his face to the open window to hide the swelling tears. He found himself staring again, this time at closer range, into the face of the old woman. She was trotting beside the pick-up, holding the door handle, and her mouth now opened, revealing a few dirty peg teeth, and poured out a long, high squeal of derision; her little bright eyes were fixed implacably on his face. He snatched at the window winder and turned up the pane as quickly as he could.

As they turned out of the township on to the main road, Michael's silent crying turned to large, shaking sobs. Northrop frowned, and

77

the skin seemed tighter than usual over his bony nose. The boy was in his charge, he was doing his best to amuse him, and this happened. There could have been a full-scale riot, both of them beaten up or worse. Awkwardly, he leaned over and took hold of Michael's upper arm; his own children were much older, and away at boarding school, and he had forgotten the rules about comforting boys of this age.

'There, there,' he muttered. 'It's all over now. We'll soon get you home and cleaned up. How on earth did it all begin?'

Michael had to wait for a trough between the waves of sobs. The blood on his face was drying now.

'It wasn't my fault.' His voice lurched out between the convulsions in his chest. 'He just came over and started a fight.'

'What? Just like that? What did he say?'

'Called me sh . . . sh . . . shenzi.'

Northrop turned his eyes back to the hot road and took a firmer grip on the wheel. Things were changing in this country all right, he thought: even during the Mau Mau you never got this amount of political and racial feeling – not this far up-country, anyway. And down in Nairobi the whites were getting in on the act as well these days. Only yesterday there'd been a picture in the *Kenya Weekly News* of a demonstration at Government House by people giving notice that they weren't going to stand by and let the Colonial Office in London hand the country over to Jomo and his gang without a fight. Northrop was not sure which he disliked more – the ranting and false promises of the African parties, or the whites on that demonstration, the men with trilby hats and crazy eyes, the stone-faced women in dark sunglasses carrying banners. He looked again at Michael, who was silent now, gazing blankly ahead.

'I don't know what this bloody country's coming to,' muttered Northrop in his confusion as they swung on to the drive to Twiga Farm. It was a phrase often uttered in these times by white settlers who had reached the end of patience and understanding and could no longer see what the future held for them.

Seven

Delvers left for Kitale at seven in the morning. He remembered the
road from an earlier trip to Uganda, where he had interviewed Idi
Amin in his swimming pool. Isolated now in his little metal womb
as it buzzed through the grassy plains and wooded hills of the Great
Rift Valley, he found his thoughts dwelling on the young man who
had been killed. Michael Hope must have been only a dozen years
older than his own daughters, and there he'd been, working in
Brixton, picking up the white man's burden by throwing in his lot
with another race, with the immigrants, the worst off in society. It
was like the attempts of the Victorians to lift up and 'civilise' the
black races, to make amends for slavery. How long was this guilt
going to last? It had hardly led to anything good for Michael Hope,
after all. On the face of it, his story seemed to confirm Delvers'
established suburban view on these matters: now that there was no
longer the work for blacks in Britain, it would be best for all
concerned, in the long run, to load them back into ships again and
send them back where they came from – simple. And yet today his
mind refused to be happy with that formula and to drop the subject,
and he hankered uncharacteristically after reasons as he sped through
the high, sunlit country, where ragged children herding goats shouted
at him from the roadside: why had Michael Hope gone to Brixton
like that, to live among the dispossessed – to prepare for the irony
of his death? Only when the car had entered the welcome shade of
the green trees leading into Kitale at about noon did he finally shake
himself clear of the question, for the time being.

In the town centre he leaned from the window to ask directions of
a white woman: she had stringy, brown-blotched arms and eyes
bleached of colour under the brim of her wide and tattered straw
hat. She seemed tired and uninterested. Five minutes later, he was
parking outside the police station, noting the convenience of the
hotel directly opposite and the post office within sight.

He sat and rubbed his sun-tired eyes for a minute, looked in the
driving mirror to pat his flat, grey-black hair, and resisted the impulse
to fish in the suitcase on the back seat for the bottle of whisky. He'd
get the measure of the police side of things first, then try the
Northrops on the phone again. He stepped out of the car, shaking

his legs and wriggling his shoulders to rid them of the stiffness of driving, and walked up the wooden steps which Juliet had mounted three nights before.

The sergeant looked up from the desk beyond the counter where he was writing something slowly, registered Delvers' presence, and looked down again.

'Good morning,' said Delvers, trying to be bouncy and friendly.

There was no reply. Oh Christ, he thought, not another one with a chip on his shoulder who's going to pretend he's too busy even to speak to me. He cleared his throat loudly, wondering if that might work instead. The man continued writing, so Delvers put one hand on the counter, leaned on it, and prepared to be patient. He looked round at whitewashed walls, plaited electric cables leading down to brass light switches mounted on wooden roundels. A notice board – much-pinned softboard crumbling away within a dark frame – held a few peeling notices in English and Swahili about stock theft, foot-and-mouth disease and the regulation of tribal areas. There was nothing, however, about the killing of Michael Hope. The place looked as if it had hardly changed since independence nineteen years ago; the parquet blocks on the floor were worn and uneven. Suddenly he realised the sergeant was now standing at the counter, looking at him impassively. He hauled an ingratiating smile on to his face.

'Ah, good day to you, officer, my name is Delvers, Robert Delvers, and I represent the *Daily Post* newspaper from London.'

His card, ready and waiting in his breast pocket, snapped crisply on the pitted wood of the counter. His own name was in flourishing italics, the name and address of the paper in bold capitals. The sergeant looked down at the card, then looked up at Delvers again with no discernible change of expression. Bastard can't read, sneered an angry little voice inside Delvers, but it was shouted down immediately by his self-interest: he needed, after all, to 'get-alongside' this man, as the slippery Fleet Street catch-phrase went. He cleared his throat again, fiddling with his belt buckle.

'I, er, wonder if I can speak to Mr Kariuke – er, Superintendent Kariuke, isn't it?'

'What is it about?' asked the officer coldly. 'Chief Inspector Kariuke is very busy.'

He stressed the rank slightly, to correct Delvers' mistake.

'I do appreciate that, naturally, but I have come a long way and I wouldn't take up much of his time. It's about the Hope case, actually.'

80

Delvers was studying the man: amazing, he thought, how they ranged from light brown to this sort of colour, almost blue in its blackness: then he quickly reminded himself not to stare so rudely, like a child at a stranger.

'What else?' said the sergeant, contemptuously unsurprised. 'A London newspaper does not send a man all the way to Africa on account of our normal business here, which concerns black people. Please wait here.'

Delvers had his mouth open to bring forth more soft soap, but the door at the back of the room closed on the sergeant, and he was obliged to return to the contemplation of his surroundings. He had seen police stations like this in other African countries, in India, Cyprus, Singapore. They had probably come off the same set of plans: official buildings, practical and cool, colonial officials, for the use of. The thought also stole into his mind that some buildings were a bit similar in parts of the south of Ireland.

He coughed: must be the dust from the journey, he thought, pushing his hands into his pockets and strolling up and down the office. He felt irritated as he thought about the disdainful black policeman. Christ, he told himself, if we hadn't been here these guys would be still charging round with spears and mud in their hair, performing barbaric rituals and killing each other for cattle. He stared again at the disintegrating notice board; yes, and they wouldn't have buildings like this, either.

On the other hand, he suddenly thought, would they really have been worse off to stay like that? Or to take on Western culture at their own pace? This mixture of tribal and technological living gave them the worst of both worlds, somehow. And maybe tribal society gave more rewards than, say, living in Dulwich with an increasingly unhappy wife and two daughters at costly private schools. He shook his head crossly: working on this story was bringing too many uncomfortable thoughts into his mind. The sergeant came back in.

'Chief Inspector Kariuke says I must inform you that all information about this case must come from the government information service in Nairobi.'

There seemed at last, thought Delvers, to be some animation in the man's face – triumph at being authorised to tell a white man to bugger off like this, no doubt. Well, he wasn't going to bugger off.

'Yes, of course,' he said, becoming a little brisker, but not too brisk. 'But you should have listened to me, Sergeant, before rushing off. Did I say that I wanted information?'

He stared hard, but tolerantly, at the sergeant, and was gratified to see the pantomime beginning to work: a little waver of doubt entered the man's eyes.

'You are from a newspaper, sir. Surely you want information?'

'That's as may be,' said Delvers, deliberately choosing a phrase which he was certain a man with limited English would not understand. 'But the important thing is that *I* have information to give to *him*.'

'You have information about this case?' The sergeant looked away and reflected for a moment, but came back with disbelief. 'What is this information? You have knowledge of the criminals?'

Delvers shook his head with a little smile which said he wasn't going to show his secrets to a subordinate. The man was just turning, and would soon be on the run.

'I'm afraid I can only discuss it with the senior officer in the case,' he said in his most serious tones. Now it was the sergeant who was fiddling indecisively with his belt; it was a thick, dark, polished job – again very colonial in style.

'Wait one moment, sir,' he muttered, and disappeared again. Delvers turned back to the notice board and a grin of self-satisfaction warmed his hard, compact features. He studied the details of the local foot-and-mouth outbreaks until he heard the door open again. As he turned round, the sergeant was raising the wooden leaf of the counter and motioning him through, his eyes remaining sceptical.

'Chief Inspector Kariuke will see you now, sir,' he said sullenly. He took Delvers through to a sunlit, dusty yard and pointed. 'Straight across, first door in next building.'

Delvers walked briskly over, trotted up the three steps, rapped on the door, and pushed it open. The first thing he thought about Kariuke was that the man was big enough to lift him bodily and chuck him back down the stairs again if he took a dislike to him. He switched on the smile again and stepped forward boldly, hand extended. The second thing he thought was that Kariuke looked unfortunately like Amin, and for a second his mind lurched back to his last job in East Africa, and the swimming pool. Kariuke moved round from behind the big desk to take his hand.

'Chief Inspector Kariuke? Pleased to meet you, a great honour. I'm Robert Delvers, *Daily Post*, London.'

Christ, he thought, the same big flat face as the madman. At the same time, though, he noticed a composure which told him to proceed with respect.

Kariuke nodded as he shook Delvers' hand: a hard little chunk in a big, firm paw. He motioned him to the chair in which Juliet had sat.

'I believe you have some information about the Hope case, Mr Delvers?' he said, settling back into his own chair and picking up a file from the desk; Delvers thought immediately that he would very much like to get his hands on that brown folder.

'In a manner of speaking, yes, I do,' said Delvers, shifting around uneasily, and trying to disguise the movements as the natural wrigglings and adjustments of anybody settling into a chair.

'In a manner of speaking,' Kariuke repeated slowly and flatly. Like Juliet before him, Delvers realised that Kariuke, despite his accent, had a good command of idiomatic English.

'Yes, well, I do have some information from the UK – probably only available in the UK – which could be useful to you in, er, completing the picture, as it were.'

Delvers' Ulster accent was becoming more pronounced, as it always did when he felt under stress – his colleagues used it to tell when he was lying. Kariuke raised his eyebrows a fraction, running his thumb over the open edge of the file, riffling the papers.

'The picture in relation to the dead man,' explained Delvers. It was slipping away from him, he thought: the man was not impressed.

Kariuke put the file down again, folded his hands over his waist, and looked hard at Delvers.

'We do not need information about the dead man,' he said. 'We need information about the three live men who killed him.'

'Of course, naturally, that's the most important thing.' Delvers was hurrying now, almost to the point of stammering, to play his only card. 'But you've heard of the riots in England last year?'

Kariuke nodded, a tiny motion of the head.

'Well, Hope took part in them – got himself arrested. He was sent down – put in prison – and had only just been released when he and his wife came out to this country for a holiday. Interesting, don't you think?'

Kariuke sighed, got up from his chair, and turned to look out of the window. He stayed there a good half-minute, immobile, and Delvers studied the width of his shoulders apprehensively.

His tight black curls were invaded here and there by wisps of grey: early fifties, Delvers guessed, and in very good shape for his age. Kariuke turned again, hands in pockets, and Delvers braced himself as if the policeman were about to demonstrate his obvious physical strength.

'Interesting, yes,' said Kariuke mildly. 'But helpful – I am not so sure.'

He sat down again, and Delvers' mind began spinning once more, working out how to consolidate this toehold. Kariuke continued.

'It might be useful if it indicated a motive for the murder, but I do not think you are suggesting that someone had a grudge against Mr Hope because of his part in the riots or his time in prison, and arranged for him to be killed in a foreign country. It is hardly likely, I think you will agree with me.'

It was a line of thinking which had not even entered Delvers' mind, and he was impressed that Kariuke had considered the possibilities of his piece of gossip, his little gamble, so punctiliously. He nodded judiciously to create the impression that he, too, had prospected this territory. But there was a faint twinkle in Kariuke's eye.

'The second possibility, Mr Delvers, is that you are telling me the man was himself a criminal, and therefore received his just reward when he was killed.'

Delvers opened his mouth to protest, but Kariuke held up his big brown-palmed hand. His amusement seemed to be growing.

'But I know, of course, that this cannot be what you are saying. It would be against British principles of fairness and justice. The third possibility is that the information could be useful in assessing the political importance of the case – and its impact on public opinion . . .'

That would do, thought Delvers. He hadn't actually considered that, but he cut in fast on Kariuke.

'Yes, indeed, sir. In the UK, for example, the fact that he was a rioter himself, had been involved in trouble, tends to make people in general less concerned about the case than if he had been, for example, a bank manager, or a respectable figure of some kind. It's rather a harsh fact, as I'm sure you know, but some deaths are more significant than others . . .'

He tailed off on the brink of the Fleet Street rule of thumb: 'a thousand wogs, ten frogs, one Brit.' He saw that Kariuke was grinning at him ironically.

'I am aware of that, Mr Delvers, and I accept that the fact that Mr Hope was a troublemaker will make the British public care less about his death. The fact that he took part in riots with black people, oppressed black people, some would say, might make the public in *this* country care even more, however. We will not go into that. Instead we will talk about the fourth possibility, which is the strongest, I think. This is that you used information which is only gossip to obtain an interview with me under false pretences.'

Kariuke got to his feet again and Delvers' spirits fell: he was going to be slung out. But the policeman turned again to the window, where the light gave a silvery profile to his half-turned face.

'You hoped I would be impressed by this gossip and its small amount of meaning. You hoped I would be flattered that a representative of a London newspaper would want to talk to me, a country policeman. And you hoped that I would give you details about the case so you could write a story full of sensation and human interest, which in this case would have a racial content, thus selling more newspapers than your competitors.'

Delvers felt hurt, knowing he had been rumbled but wanting to believe that his ploy had been more sophisticated, more noble, than Kariuke's brutally accurate summary. He was about to get up to leave when he noticed that the policeman was still smiling.

'It is nearly one o'clock,' Kariuke resumed in a lower voice, almost a stage whisper. 'And in the next office are two Nairobi Special Branch men working on this case with me. I suggest we meet in the bar of the Kitale Club in fifteen minutes? It is best not to go there together, I think.'

Something had struck home, then. A little voice deep in Delvers gave a whoop of delight; he rose, trying to keep his grin modest, stretched over the desk for another, quite unnecessary handshake, and trotted lightly down the steps outside. He glanced as glumly as he could at the sergeant in the front office, hoping to give the impression that he had got nowhere. That would satisfy the bugger, he thought – and the bugger would be wrong.

'Did you know that Mr Hope was also born and grew up in this country?'

Kariuke's question came casually, and Delvers continued carefully pouring his beer, keeping surprise off his face. More intriguing still, he thought.

'Yes, I did hear that,' he said lightly, craftily. 'But I haven't got much detail about it yet – cheers.'

Delvers drank and the cold, gassy beer soothed his dry mouth. Kariuke took longer to pour, as if deciding whether to volunteer any of that detail.

'His parents were here for ten years before independence, when they decided there was no future for them and went back to England.'

Kariuke's tone was light, almost amused. He drank, and put the glass down on the low, polished table. Then he leaned back and gazed speculatively around him, drumming his fingers on the arm of his chair.

They were in the bar of the Kitale Club. The gleaming wooden floor was covered with zebra-skin rugs, the walls with spears and the heads of waterbuck; barefoot waiters, wearing long white gowns and red fezzes, carried glasses and bottles on polished metal trays. Another indispensable colonial relic, Delvers thought cynically, following Kariuke's sweeping gaze. He too stretched back in his armchair, placing his glass on the wooden platform thoughtfully built into one of its upholstered arms. He was confident that something was going to come: what, he wasn't sure.

'I heard this from a man called Northrop, who knew Hope when he was a child here, and his parents, of course. A good man, Northrop, and a patriotic Kenyan citizen – but I would not be surprised if recent events have made him wish he had chosen differently in 1963 and joined the rest of them in Australia or South Africa or Brazil or one of the other places. But no doubt you have also heard about Northrop already?'

Delvers nodded smugly, unaware of the other man's irony, and took another pull of Tusker beer. He was beginning to relax after the strains of the early part of the day.

'The only thing Northrop did not tell me was your piece of information, about Hope's part in the riots and his prison sentence. I am puzzled by that, but perhaps he did not want to say anything which would convey a bad impression of the dead man to me. Out of loyalty, maybe, although it must be nineteen years since they met. I must confess, Mr Delvers, that I find myself very interested by this case – I do not mean the crime, in spite of its nastiness. In a way it was a very ordinary crime – the country has had several very like it already. But the crime puts an end to a very interesting life. A sad life perhaps, with many shocks and disappointments. It seems, in a way, to bind our two countries together, don't you think, Mr Delvers?'

Delvers shifted uneasily in his chair, cleared his throat. Surely Kariuke wasn't going to get all philosophical and sentimental about the victim, just because he'd had a session with Northrop about what a sweet little kid Hope had been? His own thoughts had provided him with enough of that sort of twaddle already today, and what he needed now was a bit of real progress on the story.

'I, er, suppose so,' he said, trying to show his reluctance to follow this road. 'There is a certain irony in the way he died, considering his past history. Part of the picture, certainly, but what I'm really looking for at the moment is, well . . .'

'Some hard information, eh?' Kariuke cut in, with a smile. 'I know, you are a journalist, you don't go for the soft stuff. Facts all the time — rather like a policeman. Only at the moment I do not feel much like a policeman.'

Delvers took up the offered scent. Snapping his fingers at the waiter to order two more Tuskers, he leaned back, narrowing his eyes slightly.

'Why don't we talk completely off the record?' he said conspiratorially. 'Both of us speak freely, and afterwards the conversation will never have taken place.'

Kariuke grinned and held up an admonitory finger. The beer seemed to be loosening him very quickly.

'A nice idea, Mr Delvers,' said Kariuke. 'One might say, an old trick. However' — his smile evaporated now — 'I am afraid that will not be possible. I am known in this club, and our conversation will be noticed. I might have to account for it to our two friends from Nairobi.'

'The Special Branch men?'

Kariuke nodded heavily, ironically.

'That is what they call themselves — special criminal investigators. But they are really here for political reasons, and they are prepared to use illegal violence. And if you were to write about what I am saying now, Mr Delvers, then, yes, you will please take care not to mention me in any way. They would probably not allow it to be distributed in this country, of course, but that would give me no immunity.'

Delvers nodded solemnly, with genuine feeling. He was impressed by this sudden intensity in a man whose behaviour, a minute before, had hinted at an alcoholic slide into flippancy. He also appreciated that Kariuke was taking a real risk; his own knowledge of the country was limited, but he was aware that the knock on the door in the night and the shot-up body in the bushes were no longer out of the question.

'They are beating people around unnecessarily, as I said. I think they enjoy it, they see it as something which goes with the job. But that is a common thing these days, I suppose. But there is also pressure to find a quick solution to this case. They want culprits, and preferably dead ones who cannot deny their guilt in a courtroom. It is becoming a favourite trick in this country, to achieve the desired result without any consideration for the law. As you probably know by now, Mr Delvers, I am not an entirely happy man. I do not like the way things have been going in my country, and I think there might be trouble soon. I am an old campaigner, I will be on the right side of things, I can assure you of that. But I think there will be trouble.'

He stopped talking while the waiter, an old, brown-skinned man with heavily drooping eyelids, laid the two fresh bottles of beer on the table, ceremoniously removing the tops with an opener, secured by a string round his neck which he fished forth from his white robe. Kariuke gave a little smile and leaned forward, his voice still lower. Delvers was thinking of the prophecies of Mike Schmidt.

'You will not believe this – or maybe you will, because I am sure there are similar tricks happening in your country too – but their latest little idea is to prove that the criminals came across the border from Uganda. This would be very tidy, you see, since it would let this country off the hook with an assurance that all that is necessary to protect tourists is an increase in border security. It would take advantage of the low reputation of our next-door neighbours and make them the scapegoats. Very convenient. Except there has never really been any trouble from the Uganda side of the border – Amin's men laid waste to it all, drove all the people out, soon after he came to power.'

'But they don't know that in London or Frankfurt, of course, and all the other places the tourists come from,' said Delvers, taking up the theme. 'Are you going along with it?'

Kariuke snorted with contempt and reached for his glass.

'Lip service is what you might call it. I know how to look after myself because I have had a lot of experience in that game, both under the British and under our own beloved rulers, who have made a nice little colony from the country as well. No, I am an old-fashioned policeman. I am prepared to crack a few heads occasionally, if I am sure they are the right heads and there is some evidence. But I am committed most of the time to straightforward police practice. That is something, along with many other things which were not so good, that we took over from you British, although there are people in this country who would rather die than say this . . .'

'And in our country.'

Delvers could not prevent himself from chipping in. His newspaper had been known to propound the argument that everything would now be much better in Africa if the British had never left, and Delvers tended to agree. Kariuke looked at him warily, read his thoughts, and gave a little laugh.

'Oh, yes, Mr Delvers,' he said. 'The temptation was too great, was it not? But we will not have a discussion about the British, I suspect it is an argument we have both had often before . . .'

'I apologise,' said Delvers quickly, anxious to regain any lost goodwill. 'And I quite agree, very difficult subject, best left alone.'

He poured some more beer to gain time, remembering what Schmidt had told him about Kariuke's history, and gave the policeman an unnatural little smile.

'Mr Kariuke, may I ask you a personal question?'

Kariuke was staring resentfully at the big buffalo head above the fireplace, as if challenging it to stay away from his case. He turned to Delvers, taking his time.

'Yes, Mr Delvers, but I am not sure I can answer it.'

'How come a man like you, with your talents, I mean, ends up running the CID in a provincial district like this? I mean, I hear a rumour that you were stationed in the capital once, destined for higher things, perhaps?'

Kariuke studied Delvers cautiously, trying to assess the fine line between using journalists for your own purposes and being sucked into compromising yourself.

'Something to do with being prevented from pursuing an investigation?'

Delvers' voice was thin and cajoling. Kariuke seemed to back off, as if he felt he were being asked to come and join the white men and poke fun at all the silly, corrupt niggers out there, just down from the trees.

'Mr Delvers,' he said severely. 'You have heard me talking about political pressures and interference in police investigations. Let us be clear about it – this was something I first came across under the British, in particular during the Mau Mau emergency, so-called, when the Kenya Police was under pressure from London, from the military authorities and others, to produce the culprits, if that is the right word – the men who were attacking farms, and killing the African people who would not join them. Eventually the authorities used the biggest form of political interference of them all and introduced detention without trial, and Kenya had concentration camps, just a few years after Hitler had shown the way. To my shame, I was part of the machinery which imposed that system on my country. What I do not like now is that the people who follow the example of the brave men who led the Mau Mau and brought us freedom, are now being victimised and imprisoned without trial by a ruling group which is behaving worse, in some ways, than the colonialists. If you go to Nairobi, listen to what people will tell you there about what is happening to the students, the academics, the opposition politicians, the politicians of the ruling party who are prepared to speak out. Then you will understand. As for my own case, yes, I was involved in an investigation where the government decided that it would be against the interests of certain powerful men – the *wabenzi*, we call them here, the owners of large Mercedes cars – for the truth to come out. It was made clear to me by the kind of men who are now occupying my police station calling themselves criminal investigators, that if I made public what I knew, my career prospects would be badly damaged. In other words, I would have no future at all. At all, you understand.'

Kariuke paused, wiped his face, and took a drink of beer. Delvers looked overwhelmed, his expression sagging as the intrigue sank in. Kariuke looked at his watch.

'I must go soon,' he said, calmer now. 'Well, we reached an understanding, my masters and I. I would come out here for a quiet life, and keep it all under my hat – one more of those phrases I learnt from my old British superintendent. And it will take more than two bottles of beer and some questions from a British newspaper reporter to persuade me to take those matters out from under my hat where

90

they belong. I have told you the other things because I now believe it will be to the long-term advantage of this country to have criticism abroad, especially in the West, of things that are happening here. The Hope case, I am worried, will end up as another shady business of which we have too many. You remember the death of Tom Mboya? Mama Ngina's diamonds? I have talked too much, Mr Delvers, and I will have to leave you.'

'You mentioned straightforward police work,' said Delvers hurriedly, casting around for the means to retain Kariuke, who began to drain his glass. 'Has that got you anywhere? Do you think you'll be able to outmanoeuvre the SB men, come up with the real culprits?'

Kariuke stopped drinking in mid-draught and laughed, his big face and teeth shining in the light from the window. Delvers felt miffed; he twitched his foot irritably and looked round the room, waiting for the gust to subside.

'I am sorry, Mr Delvers,' said Kariuke eventually, his voice spluttery, wiping his face with his hand again. 'But you journalists make very big jumps and require vision into the future, while I try to move forward slowly and carefully, one step at a time. But yes, I do have something. We have interviewed the villagers near the place of the attack, especially one old man who saw the murderers that night. He is very frightened, because he thinks they will return and kill him if he talks to us. But I persuaded him to talk, and now we have another set of descriptions and some other information.'

'That's very good progress,' said Delvers, suddenly animated and impressed: this was the kind of thing he could actually use for a news story. 'Are you making the descriptions public?'

'There is no reason why not – they have already gone to Nairobi by telex to be issued by the information department in the morning – if there is no interference, of course. Apparently the suspects spoke in Swahili, but our witness is convinced that at least one of them spoke like a local. He saw them on a path in the evening, when it was getting dark, so his descriptions were not very good. And unfortunately he did not remember something which stuck very strongly in Mrs Hope's mind. A scar on the face of one of the men. She called it tribal markings, but maybe that is more to do with prejudice than with fact. I do not know. But the only people who mark their faces are tribesmen from the north, not the town people who are involved in this sort of crime. All the same, she could be right. Also, she saw only three men, and this old man says there were four. It remains to be seen if the descriptions will help us – first they must be circulated and the criminal records checked in Nairobi. With a bit of luck they are on the files already and we can follow them up through their associates and past address. There were some markings and bloodstains on the road, and some information can be expected from the bullet about the gun that was used. Not very sensational, I'm afraid, Mr Delvers. Textbook stuff, as the same superintendent used to say in the old days, when I was a young constable.'

Kariuke stood up with a smile and held out his hand. Delvers got to his feet, feeling as if he were struggling out from beneath an avalanche of information and opinions which had just been precipitated over him by the policeman, and submitted his hand to the wringer again. He mumbled a goodbye, obtained a lukewarm permission to call at the station again, and watched the broad back recede.

He walked over and stared reflectively for a few minutes through the double glass doors at the green-brown golf course sweeping away from the clubhouse. A meaty African in a pale blue sports shirt was just driving off from one of the tees, watched by the boy in rags who carried his clubs. When he felt he had surfaced from the avalanche and might make some sense of it, he strolled over to the bar and ordered a sandwich; he needed food to steady him. He perched himself on a bar stool and studied the array of bottles on the glass shelves in front of him, laying a bet with himself that most of the exotically labelled ones had long ago been filled with coloured water. He breathed heavily in and out, looking ruminatively down into the yellow, lightly-frothed beer in the glass. What had he got?

His mind hung on to Kariuke: a remarkable man, he thought – many more like him and he was going to have to revise some of his racial prejudices. But now he was getting flippant, and he reminded himself of the dangers of alcohol in the hotter climate. Kariuke was, like the victim in his latest enquiry, one of the strange cases moulded by the pressures of decolonisation to be cast adrift somewhere between the past and present. Michael Hope's parents had certainly sat at this very bar. Unfortunately, however, the comparatively subtle interest provided by such cases was of no interest to his bosses or the commuters, suburban housewives and assorted Tory voters who read the *Daily Post*.

He was, he concluded, still very short of the kind of material he needed for the article the foreign editor had in mind: an account of the crime, in the fullest possible detail, and the feelings and reflections of the grieving widow. The barman came up with his sandwich, and his eyes widened slightly: you could actually get good ham in this country, unlike most parts of Africa.

'Thank you,' he said, reaching into his pocket and peering at the still-unfamiliar money. 'Tell me, how do I get to Twiga Farm?'

Eight

Christopher took a puff on his cigarette, breathed the smoke out through his nose and let his bombshell drop casually, as if it were an everyday remark.

'We're going to Rhodesia,' he said, flipping off his ash and gazing reflectively through a blue cloud: it was not dried leaves this time, but the real thing – filter-tipped du Maurier filched by Michael from his parents.

'Blimey,' said Michael, impressed by the news, but more immediately troubled by smarting eyes and a coughing fit. 'When are you going?'

Christopher, evidently feeling faint after his lavish inhalation, lay back carefully with his hands behind his head and stared upwards: they were sitting on a hillock overlooking the dam, and the sky was a vibrant blue with groups of cumulus forming behind the mountain. Nearly two years had passed since the Austins had moved to Mount View. Political events had brought the country to the brink of independence, and troubled family debates about the future had made both boys worldly-wise and precocious.

'Going? I dunno,' he said weakly. 'Quite soon, I think. As soon as they've found a manager for the farm.'

'Crikey,' said Michael, exhaling and stubbing out simultaneously in a gesture learnt from his father. 'That's really soon. I won't have anyone left to go shooting with.'

With a little moan of discomfort disguised as manly satisfaction, he also lay back, hands behind head, and the pair of them gazed skyward, the intoxication of their blood rolling the news around erratically in their minds. They had been seeing more of each other since Kimutei had gone away to the town where his father was said to be living. Michael's parents had wondered whether the move had been designed to take Kimutei away from a white family which had brought him down cut and injured from the mountain that Sunday; they certainly blamed Michael's scarred upper lip and broken tooth on Kimutei and were not sorry to see him go.

Then Christopher's parents, loosened by months of pleading, had bought him a second-hand .22 rifle like Michael's, and he had come running round to the Hopes' house one day to show it off. A new bond was created between them, the bond of outlaws which Michael had once shared with the now-forgotten Jan, and they set about roaming the locality in newly acquired bush hats and desert boots to murder small animals and birds.

Mr Austin and the farmer next door agreed to pay them for the carcass of a rat or a hawk, but at first they fired at almost anything that moved, from the big purple-bottomed baboons on distant rocks to the tiny brilliant hummingbirds in the bushes. It became a close friendship, but it was competitive and masculine, and brittle as a result. Christopher nearly always preserved a strong and unmoved exterior, but he often looked unhappy; Michael suspected the hose-pipe, but this was something about which he was frightened to ask. He also suspected that Christopher had joined forces with him to escape his parents and his loneliness, and did not care for him very much – he could as easily have been a dog. He turned his head now, and studied Christopher: the hard, closed face, the blond hair shaved tightly up the sides at his father's insistence, the wiry shoulders and long, bony arms. He was much taller than Michael, and still growing fast.

'Who *am* I going to go shooting with?' Michael repeated. Christopher twitched his elbows upwards, the nearest thing he could manage to a shrug in his present posture.

'We've got to go, and that's that,' he said, echoing his father's blunt attitudes. 'We can't stay here just because we like it. So you'll have to bring that wog friend of yours back and go shooting with him. 'Spect they wouldn't let him have a gun, though – probably wouldn't know which end to point.'

'Is that what your dad says?' asked Michael huffily.

'Dunno. It might be – why?'

'Sounds like the sort of thing your dad says.'

'Well, he only says what everyone else thinks,' replied Christopher. 'There'll be loads of trouble here when they get *Uhuru*, just wait and see. My dad says it'll never happen in Rhodesia because they've got a much more sensible attitude to the blacks there and keep them in their place. Anyway, what are your mum and dad going to do?'

'Dunno, really,' said Michael hesitantly, feeling insecure and frightened. The question prompted a conversation which he had overheard a few weeks before to slip stealthily back into his mind. He had been to the lavatory during the night and heard his parents talking animatedly as he passed the sitting-room door. The tone of anxiety and argument roused him suddenly from his shuffling sleepiness and made him put an ear to the door. His father was quieter, reasoning, but his mother interrupted, roused and emphatic.

'I *know* you want to stay, and I *know* the business is doing well, but how long do you think it's going to stay like that? There won't be the customers around, for one thing – you know how many of the farmers are planning to leave. Who d'you think'll be left in ten years? A few old diehards like Northrop, that's who, and a load of natives farming with nothing more than *jembes*.'

'Well, if things do eventually get worse, we would leave then,' his father cut in. 'If we stay through *Uhuru* it doesn't mean we'd have to stay for ever. I don't think there's any need to get panicky and pack our bags straight away. There's at least a year to go, anyway . . .'

'We've *got* to think about it now, darling. A year is not a long time. You're just trying to prolong everything and close your eyes to what's happening. The writing's on the wall, and it's been getting clearer for years. We don't know what'll happen – it might be like the Congo all over again . . .'

'No, it *won't* be like the Congo. Britain isn't going to pull out suddenly like the bloody Belgians, leaving everything in a blind panic. The whole thing's being much more carefully planned. You'll see, this country'll be much more dependent on Britain in ten years' time than it is now. Old Jomo knows a good thing when he sees one . . .'

'Yes, and you know as well as I do that *he* was involved in the whole Mau Mau business – why d'you think he was put inside? Cut a few throats in his time, I dare say. I just think we're foolish to take any risks, and Michael's still very young. Think of what happened to him in the township that time. What would you say if anything happened to him?'

'Darling, darling, calm down. Just answer me one question. What would we do if we went back to England? What sort of job would I get? Eh? Back in bloody Wolverhampton? You remember why we left – d'you really want to go back to all that?'

There was sudden silence in the frantic pace of their conversation. Michael, unsure of the time and trapped between the urge to listen and his reluctance to hear all this, began to shiver in his pyjamas. When his mother's voice returned it was quiet and doubtful.

'Well, there isn't a Labour government any more . . .'

His father laughed.

'That may be true, but it's only part of the story. Things have gone from bad to worse, you can tell as much from reading the papers and listening to the news. Seem to be nearly as many blacks over there these days as there are over here, from what I can tell. West Indians. And think of the bloody weather. Oh, my God . . .'

His father sighed and Michael heard footsteps followed by the clinking of ice cubes in a glass. He padded swiftly back to bed in fear of discovery. The sheets were cold again now, and his heart beat rapidly as he lay in the darkness, clenching his eyes closed and willing the sleep to return quickly and blot out his anxiety. What were they going to do?

He felt Christopher nudging his arm and opened his eyes to the blue brightness of the afternoon sky. He could hear one of the workmen calling loudly across the farm, and the reply from the other man on a deeper note. His limbs were heavy, his head fuzzy, and he wanted to stay here without thinking, sprawled on the red earth of his homeland, suffused in its scents and noises.

'Give us another fag, Mike,' said Christopher. 'If you can wake up, that is.'

Michael struggled to a sitting position and fought off the dizziness which attacked him. This smoking ritual had begun with clumsy experiments in setting light to rolled-up tubes of newspaper, which involved Michael having to explain some badly singed hair to his mother one night. But now it was a dedicated business, and he fumbled in his shorts pocket to bring out the cigarette tin, discarded by his father, in which he kept his supply. He gave a cigarette to Christopher, who lit it with pursed face behind elaborately cupped hands and lay back again.

'Well, come on then,' he prompted. 'What *are* you going to do? You're not going to just stay here, are you? My dad says it'll go to the dogs. Apparently the farms are much bigger and better in Rhodesia, and people get richer. The white people, anyway. The *munts* are just the same as here.'

'You shouldn't use that word,' said Michael, glad to have an excuse for stalling on the main question. The word was forbidden in his house, not because it was a derogatory term for Africans – there were plenty of those in regular use – but because it was a South African term, ruled out by snobbery.

'*Munt* – why not? We use it all the time.'

'Yes, you *would*,' said Michael, falling into his parents' contemptuous class-based patronisation of the Austins. A silence fell, save for Christopher, inhaling and exhaling noisily.

'I reckon you should come to Rhodesia and buy a farm like us,' he said eventually.

There was a plaintive note in his voice which immediately made Michael feel uneasy. It was one of those moments when Christopher's tightly controlled feelings, pale prisoners behind a high wall, were trying to peep out. Michael's instincts at such times were to withdraw, keep his distance. His experience suggested that anyone who came too close to Christopher would be rewarded only with Chinese burns and kicks on the shin, and he had the uneasy feeling now that the other boy wanted to hang on to him or pursue him. Would he ever be free of this hard-faced, hard-fisted, dog-eyed child? He wrapped his arms round his knees in a gesture of self-protection.

'Well, *I* hope we go to England if we don't stay here,' he said vehemently, asserting his independence, hoping to wound Christopher and warn him off. Christopher looked at him reproachfully, but Michael refused to meet his eye; they walked slowly home up the dusty track without speaking.

Some of the more recently arrived white families had already gone back to Britain, writing off a superficial investment of cash or commitment. More established families who could not stomach independence chose South Africa, or Australia, or Rhodesia. The Hopes, with their ten years' residence, seemed to fall between the two groups: they had developed a deep, almost physical, love for the country and the way of life it had given them, but felt it would no longer be lovable when it was governed by the majority of its people. Mr Hope wanted to stay, but his wife was frightened of what might happen to them, and there were more tears and arguments as they tried to reach agreement.

Michael came home from riding one Saturday to find that the car was there, but his father was not. He heard his mother crying in the bedroom, but did not go in to find out what was the matter – he already knew the outline, and could not bear the latest detail. Late in the afternoon a strange car drew up at the house and his father climbed out of the passenger seat. His glasses were askew, and he was so drunk he hardly seemed to recognise Michael as he weaved his way into the house.

'Hello, son!' he called unevenly, and directed an all-embracing clown-like wave at the farm, the mountain, and the gleaming African sky. 'We're leaving this fucking country, because your fucking mother says so. So get your bags packed.'

Michael could think of no words to reply to this threatening stranger, and wandered in confusion to the stable and sat in the hayloft. He felt tragically sorry for himself – no Christopher to go shooting with, no Kimutei to fall back on, and parents who had forgotten him in their struggles with each other. He sat on into the dusk, listening to his pony crunching hay and swishing its tail below him, determined to provoke his parents to come looking for him, to take anxious notice of him.

Just before complete darkness he heard his mother calling him, but he waited until she came and put her head over the stable door before he answered and climbed back down the ladder. Inside the house his father, eyes bloodshot, stood up from lighting the fire and hugged him silently, with a painful smile.

His parents seemed reconciled, but Michael felt they were gathering their resources, preparing for something they did not relish. After the houseboy had brought in the evening meal and left the room, Michael's father announced they had something to tell him. Michael sat with his eyes averted, not eating, throwing small, truculent queries into the pauses.

'Your mother and I have decided we're going back to live in England again.'

'Why?'

'Because this country's going to get *Uhuru* soon, and we don't think things will be the same for us here afterwards. The natives are going to start throwing their weight around – well, they've started already – and we just don't think the business is going to do very well. We might not be able to stay in this house or anything.'

'What will we do in England?'

Straight to the point; his mother stepped in firmly.

'Well, Daddy'll look for another job and we'll look for a nice house and a place for you to go to school. We'll find you a very good school, and you'll be getting a much better education in England anyway. Your school here will be full of black boys before long.'

Michael wanted to ask what difference that would make, but knew that it would only prolong the pain.

'I've never been to England,' he remarked instead, looking at the floor.

'I know, darling, but it's lovely,' said his mother, with a warmth he recognised as false. 'It'll be very different for you, I know, but you'll soon get used to it and make new friends and before long it'll be just like home. And you'll see snow and watch television and all sorts of things, and we'll be able to go to London and see all the museums . . .'

'But England's all cold and horrible,' he broke in with sudden passion. '*You* think so too – I've heard you say.'

His parents exchanged uncomfortable glances; then Mr Hope, who had been trying to continue eating in an unconcerned manner, put down his knife and fork. If Michael would not accept the gloss, he would have to look at the unvarnished article.

'Look,' he said. 'If we had the choice, we *would* stay here. We left England, before you were born, because we weren't happy there and I couldn't settle down properly after the war, after being in India and everything. But the way things are likely to go here, we couldn't stay on even if we wanted to, not for long, we're worried about what might happen . . .'

'*What* might happen?' Michael was stubborn and literal. His father sighed.

'Listen, all I'm trying to say is that the natives will have a completely different attitude after *Uhuru*, as if they owned the place . . . well, I mean, I suppose they do own the place, in a sense, from now on, but what I mean is that they won't run things in the same way as we do. They think they'll all be able to live like us, straight away, and that they'll all have a job and a big house and a farm, and of course it won't be like that, it'll take more time than they think . . .'

'What's going to happen, then?'

'They'll start fighting among themselves, that's what,' his mother broke in, her voice harsh and thick with fascinated disgust for the primitive tribal conflicts in her imagination. 'We're beginning to see already what's happened to some of the other countries which have got independence, going to the dogs . . .'

Mr Hope stretched over the table to take hold of his wife's arm as he broke in.

'We don't *know* what's going to happen, it isn't necessarily going to be all that bad, but we can't be sure, and it's better to be safe than sorry . . .'

'Oh, come on, let's not mislead the child.' Mrs Hope furiously shook off her husband's hand, her neck flushing with blood. 'We know very well the kind of thing that happened here during the Mau Mau – *he* knows about that as well, don't go thinking that kids don't get to know about these things, because they do – and there's nothing to prevent it from happening again, no matter how many assurances and guarantees they give to the white population and all this eyewash about a multi-racial society. The blacks are taking over from the whites, Michael, that's what's happening, and the boot is going to be on the other foot, no matter what your father wants to believe.'

Mr Hope was smiling deprecatingly, looking down and shaking his head.

'Oh, yes, they will, don't be so naive. What do you think all those demonstrations and rallies are all about at the KANU offices in town? They're not discussing how considerate they're going to be to the whites afterwards – they're talking about a takeover, and that doesn't just mean taking over the government, it means everything, the businesses, the land, the farms, everything.'

'I bet you that in ten years' – Mr Hope's voice and forefinger were raised now, and the downcast Michael was forgotten – 'life in this country will be much the same and there'll probably be as many whites of various kinds living here as ever.'

'All right, even if nothing happens in ten years, how long is it going to last? I grant you this is a more stable country than most, it isn't going to go Communist, at least not right away. But they can't run a modern country – they don't know how to.'

'They can learn – yes, why not? How d'you think the tribes in Britain were behaving, what, five hundred years ago? You talk about savages – they were hardly shining examples of civilisation, were they?'

'Oh, I see, you want this bunch of, yes, savages, to learn in ten years what it took us five hundred to learn? You're an optimist, my dear, that's your problem. You mark my words, in twenty years, if not ten, this place will be coming apart at the seams and it won't be a pretty sight.'

Mr Hope looked haggard now, worse than when he had staggered home three hours earlier. But he was determined to fight, and his mouth was open for the riposte when Michael cut in, unable to bear this tired argument any longer.

'Daddy?'

His father looked at him, as if surprised to be reminded he was there, and his tone softened.

'Yes, son?'

'When we go to England, will it be on a plane?'

His father grinned and leaned over to ruffle his hair. His mother was suddenly smiling and relaxing. The wrestlers retired gratefully to their corners.

'Yes,' said Mr Hope gently. 'A big Britannia – I'll show you a picture of one after supper.'

Michael did want to fly in a big aeroplane, and he knew from his own experience as well as adult conversation what racial conflict felt like. But going to England filled him with the dread of the unknown. He lay in bed listening to the familiar sounds which would soon be lost for ever – the steady sawing of the crickets, the occasional shout from the huts on the farm, the creak of the kitchen door, the houseboy's cough. They would be replaced by things he had only read about in books and seen in pictures: hard rain rattling at the windows, cold church bells chiming at midnight, fishing boats drowning in stormy seas, people in grey overcoats struggling through snowy streets. His father talked of sledging and snowballing, cinema and television; but he would have no pony, his gun would be sold, his new friends, if he had any, would know nothing about shooting and wild animals. He would have to wear long trousers, and some-times it would be dark at four in the afternoon and sometimes at ten o'clock at night. And now he had to pretend to look forward to it, or there would be more of these distressing family conflicts. He wanted to kick and scream like a baby; but only he, by silencing his feelings, could provide the peace the family needed for its imminent bereavement.

A week later, the Austins went. The parents had farewell drinks together one evening, and the next morning a truck loaded with packing cases stopped at the bottom of the Hopes' garden. Christopher climbed out and walked awkwardly and silently up to Michael, who was standing on the lawn. Christopher held his hand out, and Michael was embarrassed by the gesture. Maturity was being thrust upon him quickly enough without grown-up rituals like this.

102

'Goodbye,' said Christopher. 'P'raps we'll meet again.'

''Bye,' mumbled Michael, dropping the hand as quickly as he could and averting his eyes to avoid the requested significance and intimacy. He shuffled around the lawn, hands in pockets, watching the truck's dustcloud until it reached the main road and was safely off the farm.

Nine

Delvers loaded Juliet's borrowed suitcase into the boot of the Toyota, shook hands with Bill Northrop, and climbed into the driver's seat to wait for his passenger. Juliet appeared on the verandah, leaning against Marjorie Northrop, her arm round the older woman's waist. Her face was very pale in the sunlight, and as she came near Bill Northrop she put her arms around his neck and rested her head on his chest. Delvers looked away and fiddled with the knobs on the dashboard. He hoped that her calm would last, that she was not going to be tearful or incoherent during the journey – he had to draw her out, persuade her to talk. Northrop led her towards the car, and Delvers leaned over to push open the other door. Marjorie was now weeping, he noticed, and Bill was more red in the face than usual, but Juliet herself was impassive as she climbed in. Delvers watched the outline of her thigh under the thin cotton dress she was wearing – it was cream-coloured, slightly creased, with little blue flowers in the pattern. Marjorie put her blotched face through the window to kiss Juliet again, like a mother losing a child. Delvers started the engine.

'Goodbye,' called Northrop, hand raised solemnly. 'Drive carefully – and remember, I'll be taking care of everything else.'

''Bye, sir,' called Delvers, maintaining the deference which had won him such dividends over the last two and a half days. Juliet turned in her seat as the car pulled away, watching the house fall out of sight as they crossed the farmyard and turned into the main drive. A few of the farm workers stood, immobile and expressionless, to watch them pass.

As they thudded over the corrugations of the main road into town, it was Juliet who spoke first.

'You *do* think everything will be all right with the coffin and everything, don't you?'

'Of course,' he said soothingly, resisting an impulse to reach over and pat her on the knee. 'That pilot's a very sound bloke. Bill wouldn't have let Michael go with just anybody, you know that. And if there's any problem at the Nairobi end, you and I will be there to sort it out before the London flight tomorrow.'

It was by making all the arrangements for departure that Delvers had gained the confidence of Juliet and the Northrops, making them feel he was not just a vulture on the carcass. Within twenty-four hours he had made himself indispensable, first of all dealing with the hospital and police to make sure the post mortem had been completed and Michael's body could be released. Then he had spent hours in the tiny travel agency making sure of Juliet's reservation and arranging for Michael's coffin to be carried on the same plane. Fortunately, her ticket and passport had been left at the Northrops' during the trip to the coast, and so had not been taken on the robbery. In the arrangements for transport down to Nairobi he had, however, pulled a fast one: the pilot at the little airstrip had said both Juliet and the coffin could fit into his plane, but Delvers pretended to the others there was only room for the coffin and offered to drive Juliet down to the capital instead. She was nervous about flying in such a tiny plane and had quickly agreed. If the Northrops were to discover the subterfuge later, when they took the coffin to the airstrip in the farm pick-up, it would be too late, and too bad: Juliet was safely with him.

Delvers settled back in his seat, tucked his elbow on the ledge of the open window, and glanced across at his charge as he contemplated his first sally. He wanted a full and detailed description of the robbery and shooting, but he had to approach it obliquely.

'So you've seen quite a lot of the country, anyway?' he asked cheerfully. Juliet was staring out at a group of giraffe delicately nibbling the foliage from the flat-topped thorn trees on the surrounding plain, and for a while she said nothing. Delvers waited, slowing the car slightly so he could hear better. She sighed heavily.

'Oh yes, we saw plenty of the country all right. Michael took to it as if he'd never really been away. He seemed to remember everything so clearly, and I'd never seen him looking quite so alive. The country seemed to release all sorts of things he'd been keeping under wraps for years, in England. Like how, just before independence, he got involved in a fight with a black kid, really nasty, you know, both of them bleeding. He'd never mentioned that in all the years I knew him, but it was clear that the whole thing had gone very deep. And another time, in the middle of nowhere, he just stopped the car and led me up a path to a disused quarry where they used to play as kids, while their fathers were off shooting nearby. He knew exactly where it was, even after nineteen years – amazing.'

Delvers had taken his eyes off the road to look at Juliet. She had a firm profile, and her voice was strong, with confident, upper-class inflections. But her skin was milky and delicate, and he felt moved by the frail look of her right hand, lying in her lap, with fingers with bitten nails curled up to the palm.

'What else did he mention?' he asked, a new note of spontaneity in his voice. Juliet looked over at him, surprised, and their eyes met briefly. For the first time Delvers noticed the colour of hers – the blue-green of glaciers, with the flesh beneath them creased and darkened.

'All sorts of things – like how they went up Elgon one time, taking a black friend of Michael's, to see the caves up there. Apparently the two of them sneaked off and actually saw some elephants go into the caves, to lick the salt or something. He took me to see the caves – huge, and rather repulsive. It was only when he was actually back in this country that he felt able to talk about these things properly. As if in England, they'd all been dormant, or he felt he had to forget them, or they didn't count there.'

Silence fell again, and the car gained speed, seeming to skim over a plain shimmering with heat under a clear, pale blue sky. For the moment Delvers set aside his journalistic ploys and asked no more questions – they would only lead to more of these stories about the dead but dominant Michael, and while they remained silent he could dwell enjoyably on his closeness to Juliet; he felt almost as if they were teenagers on an outing, or lovers stealing time. As they slowed and entered the squat and ugly town of Eldoret, a clutch of skinny chickens ran, squawking and weaving ridiculously, out of their way. Juliet looked at him with an involuntary little laugh. It was a deep, rich sound which came incongruously from the almost elfin body, and it made Delvers even more cheerful. But when she spoke again it was, of course, about Michael: his parents had apparently tried to set up a branch of their business in this grim little town.

This led to an account of how Michael's parents, now running a small firm selling Japanese cars in Solihull, had taken the news of his death very badly, how she dreaded getting to England and confronting their grief. She felt angry with them for what they'd done to Michael – they must have known when they went out to Africa that it wouldn't last for long, that the boy would have had to be dragged away from the warm space and freedom of his childhood and incarcerated in a cramped and rainy island. The shock of the transition had made him retreat into himself, into his past, and given

106

him a constantly uneasy relationship with the present and the real world. For nine years he had been shunted around various minor boarding schools, surviving but never settling; then he had gone to study sociology and history at Exeter University, where Juliet had met him. She had been attracted by the unease and the mysteriousness which she did not immediately recognise as the marks of his unhappiness; it became her mission to draw out the secrets of this misfit, to reconcile and socialise him.

Juliet gave another long sigh and stared out of the window. They had left the plains and were climbing steadily now into the forest, where the air was thinner and cold clouds lurked around the hills. Then the veering, weaving road emerged into high, bare heathland and they passed through a scattered little township where groups of skinny children in ragged sweaters or grimy overcoats waved and shouted at the car. Delvers took a packet of cigarettes from his pocket and handed it to Juliet. She took it, lit two, and passed one to him in a gesture which he took as one of closeness, even intimacy. Then she resumed speaking, flatly, as if not even aware of his presence in the car.

For years after university, Michael, disillusioned and helpless, had done nothing in particular while Juliet became a civil servant specialising in statistics. Then at last he became animated by the idea of working to help poor and deprived people – in particular the black people. He got a job in a Brixton advice agency and they found a flat nearby. His uneasy courtship began of Everett Thompson, the street wise young Rastafarian, and this seemed to bring more interest and drive to his life than she had ever seen before. Then there were the riots, the court case, the prison sentence, the holiday . . .

Delvers, tapping a forefinger on the steering wheel, pulled the car up slowly at the roadside near a battered sign on which a black Africa on a yellow background was cut in two by a white line. It was the equator, at nine and a half thousand feet; the sky was low and grey with the threat of rain as they stepped out and breathed in the light, sharp air. Some wisps of cloud were below them now, lying on the creeper-tangled trees in a deep valley. Juliet gave an ironic little laugh.

'Michael said when he was a kid . . .'

'What about you, Juliet?' interrupted Delvers irritably. 'I haven't heard anything about you.'

He regretted saying it as he watched her stare at him in surprise, tears seeming to creep into her eyes, saying nothing. He suddenly realised how his feelings were leading him to jeopardise the calmness in her which he needed to preserve if he were to get the story out of her. He muttered apologies, rubbing his square brow between thumb and finger, and steered her gently by the elbow back to the car.

'I don't feel very interested in myself at the moment,' she said when they were moving again, the car heater running to warm them up. 'I sometimes wish they'd got me too. My parents will be awful about it all – my father's a really conventional small-town solicitor, and they never really liked Michael and didn't want us to get married. They thought he came from the wrong sort of background, so they'll have a hard time hiding their real feelings of relief that he's gone. And I'll see through them and lose my temper – and then feel guilty. All a bit of a strain. I'll go back to my job, of course, it's some sort of consolation to have that. But can you imagine, going back to government statistics after you've just been out to Africa and had your husband shot in front of you? They'll offer me compassionate leave for about three days, I suppose, but the best thing would probably be to get back to normal as quickly as possible. I sometimes feel I'll end up in a mental hospital, the way I'm going.'

Delvers could not prevent himself this time from reaching over and touching her hand, very lightly. She did not move or react, and he withdrew his fingers after a moment, as if he had touched something hot. There was something morbid, he thought, in the way he was stimulated by her tragedy and mourning. The journey continued in silence as they passed rapidly down from the hills into the rich agricultural plain which formed the floor of the Great Rift Valley. In Nakuru, enervated by the noise and vibration of the busy little car, they pulled up outside the Stag's Head Hotel and, stepping round the eager men and boys selling wood and soapstone carvings, went inside for lunch. On the terrace a group of well-fed men in suits with beer glasses in front of them were leaning forward to listen to a crackling transistor radio.

A lot of bustle and raised voices seemed to accompany their colonial-style meal – soup, fish with vegetables, a sponge pudding. Juliet, trying brightly to put aside her problems, asked Delvers about journalism, about how the system worked. He was flattered to be asked and wanted to talk, to show off, but did not give her too much of the truth: why tell a lamb how it's going to be slaughtered? he reminded himself.

As the car pulled away down the main street afterwards, a convoy of four army trucks passed them at speed, headlights on, their heavy tyres whistling on the tarmac. Delvers turned in his seat and noticed that they contained armed men in camouflage uniforms.

'Funny,' he murmured. 'Lot of activity for a Sunday. They must be on some sort of exercise.'

They left the town and its lake, shadowed pink in the distance by flocks of flamingos, and drove fast across the valley, past the conical volcano of Longonot. They had just started to wind their way up the green-forested wall of the Aberdare escarpment – the other side of the Rift – when Juliet asked Delvers to slow down.

'I want to stop at the church,' she said. 'D'you mind? Michael and I stopped here a few weeks ago.'

The small brick church, built by Italian prisoners of war while they constructed the escarpment road in the 1940s, seemed to press back against the steep wall of the forest, trying to hide. Their tyres crunched on the gravel of the little parking place; there were carefully tended beds of marigolds beside the path.

Delvers sat and watched Juliet, tiny against the hills, walk to the iron-studded door. He had run out of ideas for a tactful way of getting her to talk, and he got out and leaned against the car, smoking a cigarette and looking back across the valley. This was the Happy Valley of the prewar settlers; the white highlands of Africa, with their temperate climate, endless spaces for ranching cattle, for riding horses, flying planes, driving Chevrolets, drinking gin, committing adultery, abusing the natives. Lucky bastards, he thought: it may have ended, but at least they had a good long bite at it.

A thin child with imploring eyes materialised from the bushes and approached him tentatively, holding out highly coloured baskets. Delvers felt sorry for him and bought two or three items as presents for his daughters. The boy skipped off in delight, shouting to unseen friends. Delvers felt a prickling at the back of the neck: how many people were watching him from the forest? As he turned to get back in the car, he was startled to find that Juliet had already returned and was standing near him, looking out over the valley.

'You gave me a shock.' His laugh was edgy, and he noticed Juliet's face was wet.

'Apparently a man stopped here during the Mau Mau,' she said in a dull voice. 'There was a fighter with a rifle up in the trees, and he shot him, straight through the head. You can imagine it, can't you?'

Delvers nodded, and they stood silently for a moment, sharing the unease of interlopers. And then, unprompted, Juliet told the story of the hacking and shooting of Michael. She was telling it to him as another person, one she had begun to trust, not as a journalist. He felt moved and shocked by the detail of the violence and pain, but the journalist in him hung on every word, wishing he had a tape recorder running. He longed to be able to reproduce and communicate the reality of her speech, but knew that it would be condensed and titivated out of recognition by the production machine of the *Post*. At the end, she looked at him, drawn but dry-eyed.

'I hope you don't mind me telling you,' she said. 'I've been through it in my mind again and again, wondering how it could have been prevented. But it just seems to have been inevitable. I think they were so hyped up, they had to kill someone. And the racial thing, I'm sure that came into it too – revenge for all the wrongs the white man has done to their tribes. I see it again, all the time, in ghastly slow motion.'

Delvers put an arm around her shoulder, breathing a warm trace of her perfume, feeling the nearness of her bones to the skin. He said nothing: how could he tell her, in her naivety, that she had just crowned his mission with success? Within days, there it would be, in the centre spread of the *Post*. They continued their journey in silence again.

It was after they had reached the top of the escarpment and were approaching the capital city that Delvers began to feel that something was wrong. There was no traffic, and very few people – several days before, this stretch of road had been alive with cyclists, trucks, donkeys. He thought of the army lorries in Nakuru, the armed soldiers in the back, and suddenly remembered the huddle of wealthy-looking men around the transistor in the hotel. As they drove into the suburb of Kabete, he noticed a group of police gathered outside a large building which could have been an old colonial hotel. One of them turned in surprise and waved and shouted at them. Juliet came out of her torpor and looked at him enquiringly.

'There's something up,' he said. 'Feels to me like there's been some sort of emergency, someone's had a go at the President or something. A guy I talked to in Nairobi earlier, a journalist who lives here, was going on about how things were getting worse and something was going to happen.'

Juliet's pale eyes went wide with anxiety. Delvers took her hand, firmly this time.

'Don't worry,' he said. 'We'll be all right. It's not foreigners they're usually worried about when these things happen – it's an argument between themselves. We can always hole up in a hotel or something.'

As they came over the next rise, they saw the road block on the hill beyond: two blue Land-Rovers blocking the way, and a gaggle of uniformed men around them. As they came closer, slowing down carefully and gradually, Juliet covered her face in her hands; Delvers recalled her recent description of that other road block at the bridge. His heart was beating fast.

'Try to relax,' he said tensely. Juliet lowered her hands, and he saw that she was biting her lower lip and her face was almost green. The car came to a halt and a policeman strolled towards it. His big face and blue peaked cap filled the window as he leaned down to speak, and Delvers smelt the beer on his breath and saw little wedges of white at the sides of his mouth.

'Good afternoon, sir,' said the policeman.

Ten

Delvers was fishing in his breast pocket with clumsy fingers for his press card when he noticed the second policeman walking up, a brown leather holster empty at his waist and a pistol in his hand. This man's face was hard and aggressive and he shouted at them to get out of the car. Delvers clicked open the door to do what he was told and muttered to Juliet to do the same.

The policeman with the gun immediately grabbed her by the arm and steered her towards a ramshackle shop at the side of the road. She looked distractedly over her shoulder at Delvers: her face was corpse-white, her mouth half-open.

'What's going on?' Delvers asked the first policeman, as conversationally as he could. This man seemed more relaxed than his colleague.

'We are putting down rebellion,' he replied chattily, with a smile. Delvers was about to speak again when he too was grabbed violently by the arm by a third officer who had come up behind him unseen. He found himself pulled over to the shop's narrow verandah, his feet slipping on the sand which lay on the smooth cement. Juliet was beside him, trembling visibly. He reached out for her elbow, but his hand was knocked away by a powerful blow: he looked at the hand – no blood yet, or feeling, but the skin was scraped away, and the knuckle and thumb were white from the impact of the gun barrel.

'Hands up!' shouted the man who had led Juliet away. He was breathing heavily, and Delvers smelt the sweet fermentation on his breath too. As he obeyed, he was pushed violently forwards, and he braced his hands against the rough, whitewashed wall to stop himself falling. His nose was a foot away from a chipped enamel picture of a man with a delighted smile holding up a razor blade with an open-mouthed crocodile etched on it. He looked sideways and saw Juliet was now leaning in the same position. Then the search began.

The hands patted her briefly on the shoulders, then moved down under her arms and moved unhesitatingly to her breasts, where they lingered, squeezing and kneading. He could hear her trying to control her sobs, and began to push himself upwards to protest; he was shoved roughly down again. His blood was beating quickly now, and his mind clouding, and he was unable to discern the streak of envy

112

in his mounting anger. From the corner of his eye he saw the hands working and squeezing further down Juliet's body. He was a coward not to stop it, one voice told him; only a fool would try, said another.

He expected the hands to move to him, and braced himself for the contact. Then he realised that other hands had taken the place of the first and, screwing round his head, he saw the officer he had spoken to, the one he thought was reasonable, taking his turn. A big, wandering smile was on his face, and the other man was chatting to him, as if passing opinions or giving directions. Juliet was quite still now, her slender arms rigid against the wall.

The second search ended with the officer bending and running his hands up under Juliet's dress, lifting it above her buttocks, which he squeezed, laughing. Her legs looked very white.

'Stop that!' shouted Delvers suddenly, his voice hoarse. There was sudden silence, and he was grabbed by the shoulder and spun round to face the two men. They were both bigger than him, their eyes burning, their faces hot and damp. The one with the gun slapped him across the face with his open palm, softly and tauntingly.

'Shut up, white man,' he said in strongly accented English. 'Or I will shoot you like a dog.'

'You've been reading too many comics,' snapped Delvers. The blow to his face had swept away his caution and raised his brawling instinct; suddenly he wanted violence, to release the tension.

'Put your hands up,' said the officer softly. Delvers waited immobile, fists balled, for the first blow.

'Do as he says, Bob,' came Juliet's voice, small and dry. 'Don't resist, or they'll kill us.'

He looked round and saw her standing stiffly, arms crossed across her chest, eyes calm. It was as if she were no longer struggling in the surf but had been cast up exhausted on a firm beach. He raised his arms, and immediately felt hands going into his pockets, roughly pulling out his money – no body search for him, it seemed.

Another officer, a sergeant, was now walking towards them from the road block. He shouted a command in Swahili, and the rifling of Delvers' pockets stopped. The sergeant was a smaller man, with a serious, sober face.

'You must excuse the inconvenience, sir – and Madam,' he said in stilted English. 'But there has been a rebellion in our country and we have orders to check most thoroughly all traffic approaching the capital . . .'

113

'That's all very well,' interrupted Delvers, fiercely. 'But that's no reason for these louts of yours to start groping . . .'

'Shut up, Bob,' said Juliet in a low, firm voice. 'Just be grateful.'

The sergeant looked at her, gave a little nod, and continued.

'Please identify yourselves,' he said. The constables hovered, looking uncertainly at each other.

'We're both tourists,' he said quickly. 'British tourists. If you'll let us go back to our car, we can show you our passports and be on our way.'

'Please.' The officer gestured towards the green Toyota.

Its boot was open, and another two policemen were rummaging through the suitcases. Delvers fished under the steering wheel for the large wallet which held his passport, money and documents. He pulled out the passport and gave it to the sergeant, hoping that he would not notice the word 'journalist': there was a tendency for the authorities everywhere to try to limit the reporting of big stories like this, and pass them off as little local difficulties. The officer flicked through and handed the passport back without comment.

Juliet was already sitting quietly in the passenger seat; Delvers leaned in the window and asked her for her passport.

'My bag's missing,' she said flatly, looking straight ahead. 'It was here, in the footwell.'

Delvers faced the sergeant again. He was an older man than the others, and Delvers divined anxiety behind the serious eyes; he was almost certainly afraid now of his own men.

'The lady's handbag has been taken. It contains her passport.'

The sergeant looked blank for a moment, then he turned and went to the back of the car to exchange some brusque-sounding words with the officers there. One of them trotted off to the police vehicles, and the other closed the boot and brought the car keys back to Delvers, holding them out to him with resentment and aggression. Delvers noticed the flatness of the man's nose and allowed himself an inner moment of racial contempt. The other man came back with Juliet's bag – a small, brown leather sack, borrowed from Marjorie – and gave it to her. The sergeant hardly glanced at her passport.

'You may proceed,' he said, taking a step back and indicating a path around the police vehicles which blocked the road.

'Are there more road blocks between here and the centre?' asked Delvers, reluctant to abandon a source of information so soon. The sergeant shrugged.

'I do not know,' he said. 'There has been much trouble in the centre.'

'Who is behind the rebellion?'

'Please leave now,' said the sergeant brusquely, turning away.

Delvers climbed into the car where Juliet sat like a marble statue and drove slowly on to the dirt verge and around the road block. The road beyond looked empty and peaceful.

'I'm terribly sorry about that,' he said eventually, without looking at her. He felt weak and tired in his own relief, and felt he might lose his temper if she made any demands on him now.

'Don't worry,' she said dully. 'It's not your fault. And anyway, we got through it, which is more than happened last time.'

'Yes, of course,' muttered Delvers, wondering about the immediate future and what he should do to cover the story.

'They've taken all the money from my bag.'

'They've probably taken things from the cases as well – did you have anything valuable in there?'

'Not really. It all went the last time.'

'Don't worry – I've still got plenty of money.'

'What are we going to do? What about my plane?'

Delvers tried to reassure her as they drove on into the suburbs: they'd find a hotel, the airport would soon be reopened. Then, ahead of them, there was a crowd of people.

'Oh, Christ, not another road block,' murmured Juliet. Delvers slowed up, ready to turn round. But these people seemed to be carrying things, or balancing them on their heads, loading carts and cars.

'They're looting those shops,' said Delvers, suddenly realising. 'Westlands Shopping Centre, it says. God Almighty, look at that!'

A sturdy woman in a ragged yellow print dress was disappearing down an embankment with a large new sofa, upholstered in green velvet, on her head. Juliet glanced at Delvers and they laughed in a short burst. The shopping centre was swarming with people stepping through broken shop windows and carrying off boxes, food, blankets. Some men in khaki uniform were joining in the spree. Then the road was quiet again. They passed a bus parked oddly at the side of the road, with a knot of people sitting nearby. Some of them were holding up cards or papers towards a man in camouflage uniform standing over them with a rifle.

'There are bound to be more road blocks before we reach the

115

centre,' said Juliet suddenly. 'We could go to a hotel outside, near the museum, where Michael and I stayed once before. It's an old colonial place.'

Delvers nodded. It would allow him to leave her and try to find out what was happening.

A few minutes later they heard the first gunfire. They looked at each other, both pale; the roads were completely deserted.

'It's on the left, just a bit further up here,' directed Juliet. 'It's about half a mile from the centre, I think.'

Delvers swung the car off the main road up the drive to the hotel and came to a halt in the empty courtyard. On three sides of it were the rooms, the doors opening off a covered walkway; on the fourth was a hedge and gardens of bougainvillea and frangipani trees. Delvers went in and rang a bell at the reception desk. An old man's frightened face appeared for a moment in the doorway of an office. A minute later, after another impatient ring, a middle-aged man in a suit came and stood sullenly behind the desk. He had a little moustache.

'We'd like two rooms,' Delvers said irritably, feeling dominant again at last. 'And we'd like to know what's happening in this bloody town.'

'I know nothing, *bwana*,' said the man humbly, not raising his eyes. 'I am waiting for the guns to stop. I have done nothing wrong.'

'OK, don't take it personally,' said Delvers, cooling down. 'What about the rooms – have you got any free?'

'Yes, *bwana*, we have rooms,' said the man, swinging the hotel register round on the desk to face Delvers. 'Please sign here.'

They followed the manager down the wooden walkway to the far corner of the courtyard. The one-storey building had a dark cedar-tiled roof above grey stone walls which were splashed orange at the bottom where the rain had kicked up the soil. The windows on most rooms were shuttered and there was no sign of other guests. There was another burst of gunfire in the distance as they were let into their rooms – small, with iron-framed beds, wooden floors and washbasins in the corner. Delvers heaved his suitcase on to the bed, opened it, and took out two small notebooks and his map of Nairobi.

He knocked on Juliet's door and she opened it.

'Comfortable?' he asked, trying an ironic smile. She nodded.

'I'm off into town,' he said. 'Make sure they look after you. I'll see you later.'

116

'I asked him for some tea,' said Juliet. 'Won't you have some?'

Delvers looked at his watch.

''Fraid not. Four o'clock here, one o'clock in London. Gives me about five or six hours to get the story and file it.'

She shrugged, smiling, and watched him thud along the walkway to the car, a hard, square figure with a touch of waddle in his walk. He gave an awkward wave before reversing the car loudly and erratically back down the hotel drive. A man in a white robe and red fez appeared and bore down on her, carrying a tray.

Delvers soon saw the first bodies. Two young men, stripped to their underpants, were lying on their backs with arms outstretched at the side of the road near a sign reading Uhuru Highway. There were black puddles on the grass beside their heads.

'Jesus Christ,' muttered Delvers, his hands gripping the steering wheel as if to hold down his nausea. He could feel sweat starting out on his forehead. What had those poor bastards done? He heard more shooting in the city centre ahead of him – the tall round tower of the conference centre, the international hotels, the Parliament clock. There were the isolated, subdued whacks of rifle shots, and occasionally a burst of automatic fire.

He could see that the next road junction was occupied by the military. There were several sludge-coloured trucks and a dozen soldiers in camouflage uniforms and red berets were milling about, their stubby sub-machine guns dangling casually from their arms. His approach immediately aroused their interest: the weapons were raised to hip level and pointed towards him – six, seven, eight ugly little barrels. He slowed down, putting his arm out of the window and raising his hand, a kind of greeting to show he was no threat to them. He pulled up twenty yards away, took his press card out of his pocket, and walked towards the guns. The sun felt very hot on his neck, and he was desperately thirsty. He thought of tea at the hotel with Juliet, of her pale arms.

As he came closer, the aspect of the men in uniform reassured him. They looked disciplined, wary rather than wild, and their uniforms were spruce. Delvers chose the biggest of them and walked straight up to him, showing him his British press card.

'The army has taken over, then?' he asked, using his conversational tone and gesturing around them while the soldier studied the piece of laminated plastic. He had dark brown eyes and a thong of leopard skin tied around his wrist.

117

'We are General Service Unit,' said the soldier, handing it back and looking down at Delvers with a hint of amusement. 'You have not heard of us?'

Some sort of elite organisation, then. They looked hard, and evidently had a high regard for themselves.

'The GSU?' Delvers struck his forehead with his palm, mimicking laughter at his own stupidity. 'Of course, I should have known.'

The soldier smiled slightly; Delvers followed it up.

'You couldn't tell me what the latest position is?'

The soldier laughed.

'Don't worry, my friend,' he said patronisingly, patting Delvers rather hard on the shoulder. 'We have put down the rebellion. There is no coup for you to write about. Tell your newspaper that everything is quite as normal in Nairobi.'

Delvers suppressed his anger at the pat by rubbing his hand, where the bruise from the policeman's revolver still throbbed.

'Perhaps I could have a word with your senior officer?' he said, glancing around with an expression of enquiry. The soldier looked doubtfully at his colleagues, who were watching the conversation intently.

'He is down at the radio station. But it is not good for you to go down there.'

Of course, the radio station, the Voice of Kenya: it would have been one of the first goals – the radio station always was.

'Perhaps one of your men can take me down?' Delvers asked, making a slight move in the direction the soldier had indicated. 'All I need is a brief chat with him – find out how you did it, eh?'

The soldier could not keep a trace of self-importance out of his smile: this was evidently the productive approach. He slung his sub-machine gun on his shoulder, his mind made up.

'You come with me,' he said.

The soldier led the way down a track at the side of the main road, kicking a few stones away with his heavy boots. He walked fast and Delvers broke into a trot to come abreast of him.

'Who's behind this rebellion?' he asked. 'I mean, who are you fighting against?'

'The air force men,' said the soldier curtly. 'They are fools.'

A burst of automatic firing broke out ahead of them, loud and near.

'Is the fighting still going on, then?' Delvers felt weak in the legs

118

now. He was used to taking reasonable risks for his employer in return for his large salary and perks, but he could not claim a new life on expenses. The soldier just grinned.

'Oh no, my friend,' he said, with some heavy significance, looking straight ahead. 'Resistance stopped many hours ago. You will see.'

Delvers concentrated on walking steadily, his stomach slowly knotting up. They must be putting the poor sods who'd surrendered up against a wall. Could he detect the sweetish, sickly smell of blood in the air, like in a butcher's shop? They were now approaching the radio station, and two open trucks were standing by the gates. They had no army markings and looked as if they'd been commandeered from a building site. Two soldiers had just flung something inside one of the trucks and were walking back through the gates, looking at their hands and dusting them off. Delvers and his escort passed a car slewed to a clumsy halt at the side of the road: slumped backwards along the front seat was a woman in a bright dress, her eyes staring widely through the mass of blood and flies on her face.

'Who the hell's that?' Delvers asked the soldier, his voice weak in a face twisted with shock. The soldier just shrugged without slowing down.

The next body was dragged from the grounds just as they reached the gate. Two soldiers held the arms and legs of the corpse, which was also in uniform, and were dragging it along a well-worn trail in the dust, laughing and joking. They lifted it like a sack of grain, swung it twice, and heaved it into the heap of slumped and tangled bodies in the back of the truck. Delvers saw the dark fingers of blood sliding down the dirty tailgate.

'Wait here,' said his escort, studying him briefly. 'Do not move, or someone might shoot you too.'

With a huge laugh at Delvers' discomfiture, he strode in through the gates. Delvers walked to one side and sat down weakly on a large stone, relishing its cool touch through his clothes. He had seen bodies before, plenty of them, but never in such numbers, being manhandled and tossed about like the carcasses of animals. He lit a cigarette, hoping to steady his stomach and stifle the smell of blood, which was no longer just in his imagination. Another body was dragged out, head lolling backwards, staring upside down at Delvers. The eyes were astonished and appealing.

'Nothing I can do for you, mate,' Delvers muttered to himself stupidly as the body landed in the truck with a thud of bone on metal. He found himself drawing designs in the dust between his feet with the spent match: a column of ants was purposefully carrying husks of grain, and their activities were suddenly very absorbing and preferable to anything human. Then he felt a rough push on his shoulder and he dropped the match, looking up into the unnatural, excited brightness in his escort's face.

'You can see the senior officer,' he said. 'Come with me.'

Delvers stepped fastidiously over the bloodstained trail made by the dragging bodies. The building was pitted with bullets and most of its windows were smashed. Under one of the trees on the lawns a camouflaged long-wheel-base Land-Rover was parked. It had long antennae above the canvas canopy and a soldier with a headset was crouched inside with a microphone in his hand. To his surprise, Delvers saw a white officer walking towards him – a medium-sized, wiry man, in camouflage clothing, with sleeves rolled up over fore-arms covered in thick blond hair. He was about to smile, hold out his hand, make some remark of relief, when he realised the man's demeanour invited no such behaviour. His eyes were hard and green in a neat-featured face; his voice had the tones of Sandhurst, but was controlled and flat.

'Who the bloody hell are you, exactly?'

'Er, Bob Delvers, *Daily Post*, London.' Brevity and directness were evidently important to this man. 'And you, sir?'

'Never you mind. You shouldn't be here, you're putting yourself in a great deal of danger. This thing's far from over and there's no guarantee the chaps are behaving themselves. What do you want?'

'I've just reached here from Kitale and all I know is that some sort of coup attempt seems to have been put down. What's been going on?'

'Why should I tell you? You're just a nuisance to me.'

'People have got to know eventually – they might as well get the true story.'

It was amazing how the old ploys could work in the hardest cases. Hesitation entered the hard green eyes, and the officer looked round as if to check who was watching him. Then he took Delvers by the elbow and led him towards some trees. Delvers pulled out his cigarettes and the other man took one and exhaled a great gust.

'Right,' he said, jabbing towards Delvers' chest with the cigarette, causing little swirls of blue smoke to rise between them. 'First thing is, this conversation never took place, right?'

120

'OK,' said Delvers, on his mettle. This was no public relations person, selected to conceal anything of interest.

'Well, picture's getting a bit clearer. Seems a bunch of idiots in the air force regiment came into town from the airport side this morning and headed straight for this place. They made some damn fool broadcast about a People's Redemption Council taking over the country, and invited all the students to join them. They didn't seem to be making any serious attempt to take over other locations. We started into town about mid-morning, and gradually cleared them off Uhuru Highway and dealt with this lot here, what, about noon. Main problem now is they're still in control of Embakasi Airport, and we're off there shortly. Down town every Tom, Dick and Harry seems to have taken it all as a green light to loot everything in sight, and I'm afraid the Asians are going to have a bad time of it. The police are meant to be taking care of that side of things, but . . . how well do you know this country?'

Delvers shrugged, wagged his head.

'Been here several times, got a rough idea . . .'

'Well then, you can imagine how the police will be behaving. Still . . . the President's expected in town soon.'

'Where was he this morning?'

'Down on his farm in the Rift, near Nakuru. That's another of the bloody stupid things about this – if they'd waited a few days, he'd have been out of the country for a while. Anyway, he's going on the air at six, and one of the things he'll be doing is announcing a curfew, six p.m. to seven a.m., so I should bear that in mind for your future movements. If you want to see the nasty sights I should head for the university and the Kenyatta Hospital – the city morgue's full up already, I hear. OK?'

The indulgence was ending, turning to impatience: he might ask one more question. Delvers shook his head in disbelief, held both his palms up in enquiry.

'I just don't understand it,' he said. 'This is meant to be one of the most stable countries in Africa . . .'

'Not any more, it isn't. But that's the political side of things, which is not my job, so I'd go and find someone else to discuss that if I were you. But rest assured it's all over apart from the mopping up, and keep your head down for a day or two. Sergeant!'

Delvers' escort, standing by a tree, stood on his cigarette and hurried over.

'My chap will take you back to your car. Stay clear of this area from now on. And remember, you haven't been talking to me.'

The truck was grinding off as Delvers went out through the gates, thick red drips falling from its tailboard. He walked in silence with the soldier back to the main road. So there were still white officers in the Kenyan forces. He fought his tiredness and strained to fix every detail of the conversation in his mind. He asked the sergeant for a drink and was handed a military water bottle half full of warm, sour water. He took only one pull, suddenly imagining he could taste blood in it. Back in the Toyota, he made some hurried notes and worked out the way to the Kenyatta Hospital on the map.

He drove across Uhuru Park, past the casino and towards the suburbs. The police and army units he passed seemed to take no interest in him. He saw several knots of terrified people sitting outside buildings or at the side of the road, looking up gun barrels and holding out their identity documents. One abandoned bus had a line of bullet holes along its side, one every six inches or so. When he drew up outside the hospital – a huge, grey building with corner turrets, like a prison – he saw the reporters in the usual huddle at the main entrance. He joined them, and was eavesdropping to pick up the gist of things when he felt a touch on his arm – light and tentative for a change.

It was Schmidt. His fawning eyes were full of challenge and triumph, and he was fiddling with one end of his pale moustache. Delvers looked at him, tempted to pass a sarcasm about expecting to find him hiding under his bed. But he pushed a grin on to his lips instead, holding out his hand silently.

'Well, what did I tell you?' Schmidt's handshake felt damp and weak.

'Sure you didn't organise it? My office warned me you work for the CIA.'

'Shit.' Schmidt turned indignant and aggressive. 'If anyone organised this fuck-up, it would have been the goddam Soviets rather than our lot – you know, liberation for the Kenyan masses? That's the line those guys were plugging on the radio this morning.'

'Did you hear the broadcast?'

'Sure,' said Schmidt casually. 'Tuned into VOK as soon as I heard the shooting, about five a.m. Sure enough, some loon comes on the air and starts going on about the oppression of the people and the

122

corruption of the ruling elite. Fair enough points to make, you may say, but whoever these goons were, they sure fouled up.'

'The GSU seems to have taken them apart well and truly,' Delvers said. 'I've just been talking to one of their officers, a white guy.'

Schmidt's face darkened.

'You have? When d'you get back from up-country?'

'Two or three hours ago.'

'Sort out the Hope story, the one you were working on?'

'Brought Juliet Hope back down with me to put her on the plane.'

Schmidt was wholly sycophantic now.

'Jeez, that's not bad going. And now you stumble into this.'

'Any idea what's going on here?' asked Delvers, nodding at the fortress-like hospital. 'My officer said they were bringing the bodies here.'

'That's right. Couple of truckfuls came in about fifteen minutes ago from Kibera, just to the south of town. The army seems to be going round house by house looking for air force men, and just shooting anyone they take a dislike to. The opposite of what they call a surgical operation. The rebels seem to be in charge of Eastleigh and Embakasi, though, from what I've heard. One of the local reporters has been round the mortuary here and reckons the bodies are stacked ten high down there, and plenty of civilians, too. A couple of hundred, he reckons he saw . . .'

'There must have been fifty or sixty more down at the radio station.'

Schmidt shook his head and swallowed, looking at the ground.

'Yeah, what a mess. What a godforsaken, ghastly fucking mess.'

Delvers looked at his watch and put a friendly hand on Schmidt's shoulder.

'Mike,' he said, as chummily as he could manage, 'I reckon that between us we've got this story more or less sewn up for today. Is there any point in staying here any longer?'

Schmidt shrugged.

'Well, why don't we drive back to the New Stanley or the Intercon, maybe taking a look at the university on the way, and then we can listen to the President's broadcast and file in good time for London – providing we can get through, that is.'

Schmidt braced his shoulders and looked suddenly less hangdog, more purposeful.

'Sure,' he said cheerfully. 'Why not? I can feed you plenty of stuff on the political background, what they said on the radio . . . for the usual fee, of course.'

'For the usual fee, Mike,' said Delvers jovially, putting an arm round the American and taking him away to the dusty green Toyota like a battle trophy.

Delvers tapped on Juliet's door soon after eleven. He had filed a fulsomely adjectival report which had brought the editor on the line to congratulate him, drunk several beers with the other tense and voluble reporters in the hotel bar, and bribed a police patrol to give him a lift home through the curfew in their Land-Rover. He was anxious about her, especially since an American woman tourist in one of the city-centre hotels had been raped by soldiers. She came to the door quickly, wearing a blue sweater over her dress, looking pale and tired.

'Come in,' she said. 'You look shattered.'

'I am.' He walked uninvited into the bathroom to fetch a glass for the half-bottle of whisky he had brought with him. He paused a moment to look at her soap and toothbrush and to inhale the slight perfume. Back in the main room, he sat down heavily on the chair by the bed, holding the whisky bottle towards Juliet with eyebrows raised. She took a glass from the bedside table and held it out silently.

'What have you been doing?' he asked, feeling the whisky numb his mouth and exhaling its fumes slowly through his teeth. She shrugged and sat down on the bed, holding the glass with both hands on closed knees.

'Sitting here, reading. Reading P. G. Wodehouse, actually, which I found in the bookcase in their sitting room here, amazingly enough. It seemed ideal to take my mind off the surroundings.'

She picked up the old green hardback and turned the spine so he could read it: *Heavy Weather*. He grinned.

'Apart from that: got them to bring me some food, and kept the door locked. What about you though? What have you found out? The manager said the President's been on the radio and everything's meant to be calm.'

Delvers told her what he knew, omitting the story of the rape and the killing of other foreigners, one of them a Japanese tourist filming from his hotel window. He poured himself another tumbler of whisky before relating the scenes at the radio station.

'That was the worst bit of all. They'd simply gone in there shooting everyone they saw, and the ones who surrendered were just killed afterwards. Christ knows who that nutcase was in charge of them, but it certainly didn't seem to bother him that some of his chaps were misbehaving, as he so delicately put it. And then, there were just piles of corpses at the hospital – I didn't see them myself, thank God, but some of the others did. Thrown around like sides of bleeding meat. I wouldn't be surprised if they shoot the whole bloody air force after this.'

Juliet had been looking at the floor, not moving, but she raised her head now, and to his surprise Delvers saw bitter animation on her face, and a fierce new light in her eyes. He recalled for a second the face of the soldier who had guided him down to the radio station.

'To be quite honest, I couldn't care right now if they did – shoot the lot of them, I mean. I know it's wrong to be glad about death, but all the things you've been telling me make me feel . . . well, as if I've got some sort of revenge. For Michael, I mean, and for this morning . . . that was so horrible.'

She took a sip of her whisky and turned her head away, grimacing and shuddering. Delvers stared at her, not knowing what to make of this new Juliet, the outraged *pukka memsahib*. Her voice was resonant with revulsion and conviction.

'Their filthy hands all over me, and the smell of them . . . they were so drunk. If they behave like animals, I can't say I'm sorry when I hear about them being shot like animals.'

'Hang on a minute,' he broke in, trying to speak gently, surprised now at his own indignation and the way his desire for Juliet had given way to thoughts of laughing black women in smoky, earth-built huts. 'These were innocent people, many of them with wives and husbands and families like everyone else, just like you and me . . .'

'I haven't got a husband any more, remember?' There was violence in Juliet's voice. 'He was innocent too, and he was shot by three of those black bastards out there, those savages. I can't see any difference between them at the moment, quite honestly, and I can't find it in me to be sorry when I hear of people rampaging around this place shooting each other. I just want to get *out*, I want to go *home*, I never want to see another black face in my life . . .'

She put her face in her hands and her voice was strangled by a fit of crying. Delvers sat and looked at her bowed head: the pity and the horror of the day's events had struck him in human rather than racial terms, and yet he knew what she meant: it was like a random ritual of savagery, where it did not matter how many died, where individuals were irrelevant and expendable. And yes, there was a feeling of release, a wish for the soldiers to go on shooting, annihilating the hopeless poor who threatened the world from their terrible slums . . . He shook his head to clear the thoughts away and drained his whisky glass. Juliet took her hands from her face and looked coldly at him, her tears drying.

'So what's suddenly made you so liberal?' she asked flatly. 'You're the biggest racist out, but you've suddenly turned all humanitarian at the sight of a few bodies. I thought you hard men could take it.'

Delvers got to his feet, still sober enough to suppress his anger, telling himself that she was just escaping the guilt of her outburst of bloodlust. Now he wanted to go and finish his whisky in decent privacy. He placed a square, reddish hand on Juliet's head in an unconscious parody of absolution. Her hair felt very fine and soft, the skull too close to the skin.

''Night,' he said thickly. 'See you in the morning.'

PART TWO: ENGLAND

Eleven

Juliet stood on the ladder and reached into the attic, where little blades of light cut through the slates on to a jumble of gloomy shapes. She pulled the nearest box towards her and tilted it to peer inside: more bundles of papers and letters. She clasped it to her, its dust rising into her nostrils, and backed gingerly down the ladder.

She had been back in England for two weeks now, but this was only her second day in the flat. Her first task had been to spend five agonising days with Michael's parents, and then a calmer week with her own in their Northamptonshire village. Against her expectation, they had shown no sign of secret relief at Michael's death, and had soothed and consoled her. Now she was faced with clearing up the past here in her own home.

She felt exhausted as she pushed the box into line against the others, but made one last ascent to pull the trapdoor back into place; otherwise the black hole in the ceiling would prey on her mind as she lay awake at night, and threaten her when she crossed the landing to the kitchen or bathroom. Her legs trembled as she pulled the sharp-edged door into position, and dust fell into her face in lumps. The door cut one of her fingers, breaking the nail, and tears swelled out of her eyes as she clambered down. She sat hunched on the floor, grasping her injured finger and watching the dry brown carpet suck up the drops. Like Michael's blood falling on the African soil, she thought.

But immediately she stood up and pushed the thought from her mind. She was not going to dwell on the funeral, when Michael had been lowered into the hard, reddish earth of the churchyard just outside Nairobi. Briskly, she walked to the bathroom to clip the damaged nail and wash off the grime of the attic, and found herself thinking instead of Delvers. She used the anger he inspired in her to push aside the more dangerous and destructive emotions. She could not have managed without him during those three difficult days before the international airport reopened. He had helped her find and get possession of Michael's body while also coping with the demands of his newspaper; but each night he had called at her room, and his growing amorousness had culminated with him beating on her hotel door and pleading morosely on the eve of her departure.

There was also the article. Her mother had brought her the *Post* as she sat in the garden one morning, surrounded by English sunlight and birdsong.

'You'd better have a look at this, dear,' she said. 'Centre pages.'

'Victim of Hate,' the headline yelled; and underneath was Delvers' account of the shooting and the aftermath, told in the slick and sensational clichés of thriller fiction, propped up by pictures of her and Michael. It relied on half-truth, exaggeration and racial animosity. It implied subtly that all black people, simply because of their race, were bloodthirsty barbarians. What she disliked most, however, were Delvers' sentimental descriptions of her – 'palely beautiful' was one phrase; 'steely beneath the soft surface' was another. She felt he had taken advantage of the closeness and the friendship of sorts which had been forced on them by events. How was she to know, talking to him at the escarpment church, that he was noting every sad and cruel detail to reproduce it for the prurience of *Post* readers? She felt soiled and violated, as if he had surreptitiously succeeded on paper in taking what she had denied him in the flesh.

She dried her face and hands and carried the boxes to the living room, where she lined them up and sat confronting them: Michael's past. Another agonising chore. She had gathered all his clothes in one chest of drawers, and was unsure what to do with them; it hurt her to look at his books, his bicycle in the hallway. Now there were all these boxes she couldn't remember seeing before. They would be full of private things – old love letters, perhaps, attempts at poetry, or his adolescent diaries. Should she read them, burn them, keep them, give them to his parents? There had been parts of Michael he kept closed from her, and she hesitated to open them up in his absence, sniffing around corners he had shielded.

She went to the kitchen to make tea and stood staring at the sunlit street; the noise of the kettle swelled behind her, gradually overwhelming the enervating buzz of a bluebottle on the window. Everything looked faded in late-summer exhaustion: a gritty grey dust lay on the cars and was blown along by little gusts of tired wind. The browned, patchy grass in front of the flats at the other side of the road was littered with sweet papers, and two scruffy kids, one white, one black, were booting an orange plastic football up and down, shouting occasional obscenities at each other. The sunlight itself seemed lifeless, a flat, white heat without shadow or savour.

She thought of the small country town where she had grown up, in space and greenness, without conflicts. She would move soon, she decided; there was nothing to keep her in Brixton now that Michael had gone. His work, his preoccupations, had kept them there, and now she was going to make something new. She could live anywhere she chose; she could commute in tedious safety from Chalfont St Giles.

Back in the living room with her mug of tea, she pulled the first box towards her; if she found anything which she felt should remain private, she would leave it, seal it up, maybe destroy it in due course. She lifted out a red exercise book: in a rounder version of the well-known handwriting, it contained a history essay denouncing Napoleon for all the deaths he caused in war. She smiled slightly: he had never changed this way of seeing only one side of things. The other exercise books contained more history and English essays, with comments and exclamation marks in the margin in the master's bored, red scrawl. She put them aside and lifted out a packet of letters tied with string. The handwriting was Michael's mother's, and she quickly put the letters on the table to be sent back to their author.

The second box contained an assortment of cardboard- or cloth-backed books which were densely filled with Michael's small, earnest handwriting: journals of some kind. She pulled out a flat green book, blowing off the dust. The spine crackled as she opened it, the pages were brown with age at the edges, and she guessed that the writing dated from his time at university, when they had first met. She flipped through, reading here and there: descriptions of Michael's childhood experiences, mainly. There were many snippets she had already heard about – the earliest times in Africa, the Austin family, the rubber hose, the return to England and the first grim winter.

Then there were two thick, black-backed books which she recognised. She had bought them herself to take to Michael in prison, and as she opened them she saw they were written with the new fountain pen he had also asked for. More recent events were described here, she found – the start of his job in Brixton, ruminations about race and prejudice, the riots and the time in prison. Her eye was caught by the name of Everett Thompson, and she immediately pictured the vital, volatile young black she had once met at Michael's advice centre. It was while she was reading a passage where Michael described how he first encountered Everett at the door of a squat on the Front Line that she became aware that the telephone was ringing.

She gazed at it resentfully before sighing and getting up to answer it.

'Juliet?'

She recognised the voice and was immediately defensive.

'Bob Delvers here.'

'Yes, I know.'

'You don't sound very enthusiastic.'

'Don't I? Well, I suppose I'm not, to be honest.'

'Well, that's one of the things I was ringing about – to apologise.'

'What for?'

'The article, of course, the piece in the paper – if you've seen it, that is.'

'It was brought to my attention, as they say.'

'What did you think?'

'Awful. Really cheap and nasty and badly written.'

'I thought you'd say that. I thought so as well.'

'Oh, I see. D'you think that about everything you write? You took advantage of me, Bob Delvers.'

'Yes, I suppose I do think that about most things I write, in a way,' said Delvers, ignoring her final, essential remark. 'But the problem here was, I didn't really write it.'

How lame, thought Juliet angrily.

'Oh, I see. They took your fine prose and made a dog's breakfast of it, I suppose.'

'It sounds a bit feeble, but it's true. I actually wrote it fairly straight, which might have been a mistake, in fact. I mean, if I'd put in all the sentimental stuff, at least it would have been *my* sentimental stuff instead of the diseased fantasy of some sub-editor in the features department. Honestly, they'd have rewritten the bloody Ten Commandments to match the editor's prejudices.'

'Dear me.' Juliet was sarcastic. 'You do sound disillusioned. I'm nearly in tears.'

'Look, Juliet, I'm trying to tell you something serious. So will you stop being so bloody clever?'

She was surprised by the sudden anger, and recalled his square, pock-marked face.

'Sorry,' she said cautiously, after a silence.

'That's all right. I know I took advantage of the way things worked out, and you've got every reason to feel cross. But the main point about the article is that this time the victim, if that's the right word,

132

is someone I know and, well, like a lot. As you know. I'm looking at it from the other side, for the first time, I suppose, and I'm not very proud of it.'

'So you're leaving Fleet Street in a hair shirt and joining a silent order.'

'Oh, for heaven's sake, Juliet. Give us a break.'

'I just don't believe in the leopard changing his spots.'

'OK, OK. Let's just put all that on one side for the moment, then. The other thing is that there have been some important goings-on since you left Nairobi.'

'What?' Her voice rose slightly, her stomach muscles tightening.

'They reckon they've got the people who held you up and killed Michael.'

Her reactions were confused: visceral glee at the prospect of revenge, weariness at the thought of a trial, a trawling through it all again as if it could somehow be undone.

'Trouble is, all three of them are dead.'

'Dead? Oh, for Christ's sake, Bob, stop being so bloody melodramatic and tell me straight. What happened?'

'They stopped some guys in a car and shot them up. The police said they tried to jump a road block, and that their descriptions fitted the gang who attacked you and Michael. All just a bit too neat, especially when you think how worried they are about the tourist industry now they've had the coup attempt as well. I'm not happy with it – not at all. Nor, I might say, are some of the authorities out there. Anyway, I expect you'll be getting some sort of official communication from Nairobi soon, telling you the case has been solved and closed.'

'But when did this happen? Why hasn't it been in the papers?'

'It happened about five days ago – a couple of days before I left. I had yet another row with the paper about the story we carried – they only used about five paragraphs of the stuff I sent, which went into it all in detail – including the doubts. All the doubts were cut out, of course.'

'Why was that?'

'They gave me the usual old shit – it was an old story, I'd had a good run at it, no reason to cast doubt on the Kenyan authorities. They won't believe a thing the coons say most of the time, if you'll pardon their expression, but when it's convenient they swallow the lot.'

'Dear me, Bob, you *are* pissed off.' She gave an astonished little laugh at the vehemence in his voice. Where was the cynicism of their time in Africa together? A worm was turning.

'I certainly am. I've had to take a few days off.'

He too laughed, self-consciously, and seized the moment of relaxation for this next purpose.

'Anyway, that gives me plenty of time to see you. Are you busy?'

Juliet felt the armour shrinking tightly to her body. This was the man who had tried to jump on her a few hours after Michael had been dropped in a hole and weighted down with half a ton of African earth and stones.

'How are your wife and children, Bob?' she asked evenly.

'Oh, they're fine, fine. Very well. You must meet them some time.'

He sounded abashed; Juliet left the ball in his court.

'Look, don't be silly,' he said briskly. 'Surely you want to find out more about this road block? We can meet in a public place, I won't assault you.'

Juliet sighed indecisively.

'I suppose so. But I'm not sure what I'm doing over the next few days. Let me think about it and ring you back – why don't you give me your number?'

Juliet smiled as she took down his office number where she would be able to leave a message – evidently he didn't want his wife answering the phone to an unknown woman. She restrained her sarcasms and rang off.

Suddenly tired, she sat heavily on the sofa again and watched the dust which rose from the impact of her body and floated, glittering, in the sunlight. It mixed with an image of three dishevelled bodies lying on their backs on a dusty roadside, eyes open and covered in flies, blood going black in the nostrils. Just a few more of the random victims, she thought; there were so many, who could care? She clamped her eyes shut and shook her head to throw off the image.

She remembered the boxes in the attic, but recoiled from the idea of returning to them just now – it seemed there was nothing that would allow her to escape from Michael and the events of his life. She fumbled for her packet of cigarettes and lit one, feeling grateful in her self-destructive anger at the way the smoke cut into her lungs and fogged her mind.

Twelve

Michael knocked on the door and turned to look despondently at his surroundings while he waited. The sky was the colour and weight of lead, dropping a fine, cold drizzle on the London streets. Most of the low terraced houses on the other side of the road had windows blinded with corrugated iron. The colour of the bricks, he decided morosely, was that of the grey-and-ochre dog turds which dotted the uneven pavement. A red bus ploughed past, a sudden slab of bright colour against the November monochrome. It splashed up dirty water from the puddle over a blocked drain, and Michael dodged further into the doorway. It was cold, wet and miserable and he had a cough from too much smoking – how he hated this country. And yet here he was, poking around one of its drabbest and poorest corners, pursuing what he felt to be his duty or his fate. The little knot of men under the tattered awning of a nearby shop, where the pavement was slimy with trodden grease from take-away food, were still watching him suspiciously. Two of them were Rastafarians, one of them with his hair turned up and contained in a tall leather hat, the other with it dropping to his shoulders in coiled and tattered locks. They probably reckoned he was a copper, thought Michael – quite reasonable, given the number of plain-clothes men prowling around the area. Dimly, he could hear the crisp, relaxed beat of reggae from somewhere in the house: why the hell weren't they answering? He lifted his hand to knock again as the door was suddenly jerked open.

The young black man in the doorway confronted him with a look of such blank and intense hostility that for a few moments he was unable to speak. Then something happened inside his head – a tiny fizz of electricity, the present derailed on to an overgrown track – and he was back in the township delivering milk with Northrop, a white boy scorched by the hatred of a colonised people. The sunlight, the smell of the crowding bodies, suddenly whisked his senses away from this cold and colourless street. He stared back at the man, waiting for – almost wanting – the punches to start again. Nothing had changed except his need to make amends.

'You want something?' snapped the black man, voice as blank as his stare. One of his incisor teeth had a small silver star built on the front, a work of delicate craftsmanship. He, too, was a Rastafarian, but his locks were light, almost glossy, and he wore a smart black tracksuit with stripes down the arms and legs in the Ethiopian colours of red, gold and green. He had a long nose, wide lips, and a skin more brown than black; it crossed Michael's mind that he might be a half-caste.

'Er, yes,' he responded hesitantly, his voice soft and distant as his mind returned from the lost country. 'Sorry to disturb you, but I'm from the advice centre down the road.'

Advice centre – it sounded absurd, he thought. What place did advice have in the primitive feeling which dominated relations between black and white in this part of London?

'Oh yeah? Big deal. I'm impressed.' There was a sneering challenge in the reply, as if the man guessed Michael's doubts. He persevered with his prepared pitch, hands deep and immobile in the pockets of his duffel coat. It was his way of avoiding any movement which might be seen as threatening.

'We've got a steering committee which runs the centre, and we're trying to make sure it's representative of people who live round here, especially young people, and we were told we might find someone here who'd be interested in being on it . . .'

His voice petered out uncertainly as he noticed a smile spreading over the other man's features, reaching a strange radiance which he could not decipher. Delight? Some irony? Or a new twist to the hostility?

'Oh, I see, man. You want a token nigger on your steering committee? I get you. I'm with you.'

As soon as Michael began to smile uncertainly back, the man's face went stony again and his voice turned cold.

'I think you've come to the wrong place, man,' he said. 'What kind of a place you think this is, anyway? A fuckin' youth club? Who sent you here?'

Despite the hostility, he made no move to close the door. There was a thud of footsteps in the dimness behind him; the hallway had bare floorboards, peeling wallpaper, and an unshaded bulb showed another black youth on the half-landing, leaning down to see what was happening.

'Who's that, Ev?' It was a powerful voice, mixing Cockney and Caribbean. 'The pigs?'

'Nah,' said Ev, running his eye up and down Michael again. 'It's some jerk wants us to join some kind of committee.'

'Fuckin' hell,' said the other youth with feeling, and pounded back up the stairs. Michael was sure now that he could smell the warm, dry aroma of grass being smoked.

'It's not as stupid as it sounds, actually,' he said, a little indignation cracking his diplomacy. 'We're just trying to make sure the advice and services we provide are the right ones. Lots of people complain that the needs of black people aren't properly looked after, that the establishment refuses to understand the culture . . . look, d'you think I could come in for a while and talk about it?'

Wariness replaced mockery on Ev's face and he hesitated, glancing back over his shoulder as if to consult his friend. Then the defiance returned.

'Look, man, we don't want to join no committees, right? What good does that kind of thing do for us? Eh? Tell me that, clever clogs. There might be a few bleeding-heart white liberals like you who go around buttering up black people, but you can't kid me that this society wants too much to do with us. You think Margaret Thatcher's going to listen to black people? Do us a favour, mate.'

Michael opened his mouth, but Ev's forefinger was up and jabbing now as he warmed to his theme, his eyes narrowing and darkening. Michael stood and absorbed it, hands still deep in his pockets, holding the fierce stare. His mind felt paralysed as he tried to be neither intimidated nor provoked.

'You're probably educated and all that, been to university, and you think you know the lot, don't you, smart arse? But I tell you, man, you don't know nothing about *us*, all right? You don't know nothing about black people, you don't know nothing about Rastas, and you might not like it, but we can manage without all you white do-gooders sniffing round the place for Uncle Toms to adopt and take home. And this place isn't a youth club or a community centre or a this centre or a that centre, it's *ours*, man, we do what we like here, we come here to lick our wounds, and we don't want it taken over by clever dicks like you, see? And I'll tell you something, man. We know what you're after – the pigs and the magistrates and the Home Secretary and the rest of them. You want to get rid of us, send us back where we came from and all that shit. Get rid of the muggers and the rapists now we don't need them for the shit work any more, now we've got machines instead, isn't that right?'

Michael shook his head, tried to disagree, but Ev was not going to give way.

'And I'll tell you something else for free, man. We don't want to stay here either, man, this isn't our country, not even if we were born here. We want to leave too, you know that? We want to go, back to Jamaica, back to Africa, like the lost tribe. Guys like you think this place is so fuckin' wonderful that everyone in the world wants to be here, mother country and all that shit. Well, I'm telling you, my mother and father swallowed all that shit about freedom and justice and opportunity, and where did it get them? Twenty years of hard labour and then the dole, man, that's where. They can't even afford to go back to Jamaica to die. This is a racist society, man, no matter what you white liberals spout on about changing it. So what I'm trying to tell you is, we don't want to join no fucking committees, right?'

Michael stood nodding in acquiescence, like a spindly plant in a stiff breeze; it was a brand of feeling he was well aware of. You didn't get it from the older blacks, the ones you saw leaning heavily in bus shelters, holding tattered carrier bags, resignation and endurance bending their bodies to a stoop. Nor did you get much of it from younger blacks who were getting by, and were still close enough to their parents to inherit some of their values. But you got it increasingly from boys and girls without work in their late teens; there were tens of thousands of them, and Ev's fluent tirade was a growing philosophy. And most of all you got it from the young people who had adopted Rasta and the explanation and solace it brought to their predicament. Michael was glad there should be a creed for the dispossessed, but his social-work training made him worry that it would take them away for ever from the mainstream. He saw his task as bringing them back, with patience and effort. His nodding continued for some seconds after Ev had finished.

'What you nodding your head for, man? You should be hanging in the back window of someone's car, like them dogs.'

Michael stopped nodding.

'Well, I know what you mean . . .'

'No you fuckin' don't.' Ev glared at him, lip drawn back from the starry tooth.

'No, what I mean is, I understand the way you feel, and perhaps, well, maybe we could talk about it a bit more, I mean, our steering committee needs to understand your point of view, even if it does mean rejecting the system we're trying to make use of. After all, there's still plenty of common ground . . . Perhaps you and I could meet for a drink one evening.'

Ev smiled his biggest smile yet.

'We don't drink, man. We smoke ganja.'

He spoke the last word slowly and lovingly, chewing over its syllables, and quietly closing the door in Michael's face. Michael confronted the sludge-green paint on its panels; after a few seconds the volume of the reggae was turned up.

This was the first of the many encounters between Michael Hope and Everett Thompson. Usually their meetings produced a stalemate between Michael's intense and persistent idealism and Everett's streetwise blend of cunning, charm and aggression; but Michael was fascinated, envious of Everett's vitality, and Everett was prepared to play along with any game which might one day produce advantage. Michael was smiling slightly as he turned away from the squat and passed the group of men by the shop.

'What's he smiling for, you think?'

'Seen his own arse, man.'

'There goes Babylon.'

Michael turned off the Front Line towards Brixton Hill where he and Juliet lived. She would be home soon from the Central Statistical Office; later that evening they were going out drinking with friends from university days. He cringed at the prospect: they would go through the usual hoops, checking each other's progress in the Habitat lifestyle, joking about the lost ideals of their early friendship. He would rather be smoking ganja with Everett Thompson, listening for echoes of his childhood, picking gently and pleasurably at the scabs of unhealing wounds.

As he turned the next corner he saw two policemen approaching and moved to the inside of the pavement, making room for three abreast. But the officer on the inside held out his black-gloved hand to close the gap and prevent him passing.

'Excuse me, sir, we'd like a word with you.'

Michael froze his features into impassivity. This happened to most people round here sooner or later, and it was not the first time it had happened to him. The officer was about twenty, thin-faced, with a moustache and an accent that was not from London – East Anglia, perhaps.

'Where are you going, sir?'

'Home.'

'And where have you been?'

There was a crackle from the other policeman's radio and he moved away a few paces, talking intimately into it like the ear of a woman.

'I've been at work. At the advice centre down the road.'

'No, sir, I mean, where have you been *just* now? I mean, a few minutes ago?'

They were getting smarter all the time, with their observation cameras and helicopters and informers and God knows what else. And Ev's squat was evidently what they called 'suspect premises' – he was not surprised.

'I called to see a friend,' said Michael, taking his hands out of his pockets and raising them for the search.

'Precisely, sir. Suspect premises, as you probably know, and I'm afraid I must require you to submit to a search on my reasonable suspicion that you may be carrying prohibited substances.'

The policeman's voice was bantering and cynical, twisting the knife with these formal phrases. He patted Michael's sides, then asked him to take off his coat and turn out all his pockets.

'Take my coat off? It's bloody cold.'

'Yes, take your coat off,' repeated the officer, his voice hardening. Once he saw Michael was obeying, however, he seemed to lose interest; his companion had finished his radio conversation and was strolling back with mild amusement on his face. The two of them ignored the items Michael brought out of his pockets and laid on the low wall – money, a packet of chewing gum, his keys, a cinema membership card – and began talking and joking quietly about something else. He began stuffing the things back in his pockets, shivering, and by the time he was pulling his coat on again the two policemen were strolling away as if nothing had happened. The one with the moustache turned and raised a forefinger – it was the second black finger to be pointed up Michael's nose that afternoon.

'And another thing, sir,' said the policeman, his tone still bantering. 'Stay away from the coons, and you won't get stopped.'

Michael turned away, head hunched down, and thrust his cold hands impotently into his pockets again. At least they hadn't looked into his underpants, as they did with the black kids these days. He tried to numb his mind, prevent his feelings from rising, but failed.

'Fucking fascist little shitbag,' he muttered wildly to himself as the dirty orange street lights flickered into life around him.

Thirteen

For a couple of days Juliet went nowhere near the boxes of Michael's letters and diaries. But fingers always touch the wound in the end, testing the contours they dread, and she found herself on the sofa in the warm, quiet afternoon, holding another packet of letters, pulling apart the dirty knot in the string which held them together. The one at the back seemed to be the oldest, and she inserted two fingers to bring out the small sheets of cheap, lined paper, discoloured by time. The writing was in blotchy ball pen, but legible.

Mount View Farm,
Kitale,
27 July 1967

Dear Michael,

Thank you for your letter, I was very joyful to receive it from you, my old friend. After four years it was time to forget, and then I have this fine surprise. Your letter came directly to me, my friend, because my mother Mary and I have returned to Mount View Farm two years ago. All the people were most curious to see a letter arrive from England to me, and now I am hurrying to reply. You are right, it is very good to have a pen friend in a foreign country to give all the news and views. I am sorry to hear that you do not like England but I think it will be very good for you and you will get a best education for your life. I would also like to be at school in England. Here I am still at school but soon I must leave to try to find a job. My mother is poor and does not have a job now. The big man of this farm now is a businessman who comes here only sometimes in his Mercedes and shouts at people. The manager also is not a good man and wants people to work with no money. I shall look out for a job in town as a clerk because I can read and write in both Swahili and English but I am only thirteen years old and I do not know what will happen. It is sad that you and your mother and father do not stay in Kenya, there are many *wazungu* here and all is like before for them. Also there are still many people who want land to grow their food and animals. I wonder if we will meet again, my friend. I too remember the journey to see the elephants and I have the mark on my face from the wounds. I am happy you have not forgotten and I hope that maybe you will write to me again with more news from England. All best wishes from me and my mother.

Your old friend
Kimutei

Juliet's hand fell to her lap with the letter and she stared at the wall. This, then, was the black friend who went up to the caves with Michael and his family. Michael had never mentioned this correspondence, running to about fifteen letters. There must have been more to the friendship than Michael had ever acknowledged – but that was typical of the way he disguised and withheld himself. Perhaps it was only now, after his death and at second-hand, that she would discover new aspects of him and understand him better. And it would be too late to serve any purpose.

She glanced at the letter again, a question in her mind. Yes, that was it: 'I have the mark on my face from the wounds.' It sounded as if there had been some incident or accident, but even on their visit to the caves, Michael had mentioned no such thing. She thought of the scar on his upper lip, the faint white line which she had traced with her finger and kissed, and heard his voice, light and dismissive: 'Oh, I just fell over on the farm when I was a kid.' But he had been strangely elated, that day on Elgon when they had climbed through the damp and shadowy forest to those gaping, evil-smelling holes in the mountain. No doubt his full account of it would be found somewhere in one of the journals she had not yet studied; she would look for it later, she decided, opening a letter from the middle of the bundle.

Mount View Farm
12 March 1971

Dear Michael,

It is many months since your letter to me, but now at last I shall reply. Things are not well with me, my friend, and my life is very hard. I have only troubles, and I am sorry in my heart. My mother is ill and we have no money for the medicine. I think I am a bad son because I have been travelling many miles to find work and I did not know about her. She is ill in her chest and it is hard for her to breathe. I pray to God every day but I think maybe he has decided to end her life.

I have lost your letter in my travels, but I remember that you wrote you will be going to the university soon. I too would like to continue my education as a student at university, but for me it is not possible now. My job as junior clerk at Marshalls is finished last year when management give the sack to four people. It is harder to find work now. I have been to Eldoret and Kisumu and Kisii and I have no success. Some people tell me I should take work on a farm but I am most determined to get an educated job. My mother will be very sad and angry if I waste my education. I think also if my mother dies I will have to leave this farm because the big man who is the owner does not like me. Maybe I will go to Nakuru or Nairobi to find work there, but I am frightened of these big places where there are many bad

142

people. I will send you my new address if I move to another place. I would also entreat you, my friend, to send me information on how to come to England and find work there and perhaps continue with my education like you. I think England is a better place than Kenya and many people say life was better before *Uhuru*. Please write to me again, my friend, with your news. Send the letter here and if I have gone, people will send it forward to me. My mother too sends her love, and best wishes from your friend,

Kimutei

Juliet smoothed and folded the stiff paper and placed it thoughtfully on the pile. The correspondence had already changed. It had started as a boyish pen-friendship, prompted, most probably, by some internationally minded hobbies master, and become a serious and more mature business. The interval between letters, she saw, had lengthened to about six months, and there were only half a dozen more. She thought how painful it must have been for this African youth, with his poverty and shrinking horizons, to receive bulletins of success and plenty from his former friend.

Sliding the next letter from its envelope, she had a sudden conviction that it would end badly, that circumstances were turning Kimutei's life to a bad purpose. The letter was short and told of Mary's death and Kimutei's departure from the farm. His grief and fear for the future, expressed in the quaint phrases of some old-fashioned English textbook, made Juliet's eyes burn with tears. She remembered a mournful chanting one night near the hotel just after the attempted coup, a phrase shouted by one person and echoed by many voices. Just such an African lament would have sent Kimutei's mother on her journey to the ancestors, under the shadow of the mountain.

The next letters came from Mombasa and described how Kimutei had found a night job cleaning the holds of ships. The foreman came, like Kimutei, from the west of the country, and took pity on him. Juliet remembered the ragged young men hanging around the street corners of the port, watching the tourists intently, with blank eyes.

Then he lost the job because the foreman was sacked on suspicion of stealing and the man who took over was a Kikuyu who quickly turned out all the other tribes. 'One day we will kill the Kikuyus': it was the first violent phrase she had seen in this round, boyish hand. 'They believe that all this country belongs to them.' The final letter was dated October 1975. Although the postmark was clear – Nairobi, smeared over the leopard on the stamp – there was no address. Kimutei had finally come to the hungry, growing city.

Dear Michael,

I have not sent you a letter for many months, but please forgive this because I am too busy. I have travelled to many places to find work and food and I now have little time to write letters. I received your last letter in Malindi after great delay in forwarding from Mombasa. It is my biggest wish that I should study like you at the Exeter University and complete my education, but this is not possible for me. I envy you, my friend, to make your studies in this fine place.

I have now found work which brings me money, but it also gives me shame. In Malindi now there are many tourists, especially from Germany, with much money to spend. They like to buy carvings and souvenirs, and also they pay much money to take women to bed. Also the rich German women pay for men, and sometimes the men pay for little boys. I feel that it is a great shame for my country that these things happen, but it is better to do this than to have an empty belly. I was busy in selling carvings because I speak good English. The men who have the carvings have need of people who can speak easily with the tourists, and for many months I was working with a very big man. But he is also a bad man, and one day he sent me away and tells me he can now speak good English also and has no longer any need of me. I was angry and protested to him because I wanted to earn more money and take a wife. Then the man and his friends were angry too, and they beat me and throw me out. So I come instead to Nairobi.

At first I could find no work and soon I had no money. There are too many people in this place and they are all fighting for money. Then I find a kinsman who is selling belts with beads to the tourists, and I begin to work with him because I can speak English and he cannot. He has given me a small room in his house in Mathare. It is a bad place with many poor people and very dirty, but I have a bed there and in the day I go to city centre to sell belts. There are many other people trying to sell such things, and sometimes the other men warn us and say they will kill us if we do not go away. But there are many tourists in Nairobi now and there is business for all the people. If the tourists go away there will be much trouble for this country, I think. Uhuru is only good for some people, for the wabenzi and the big men and the MPs. Maybe one day you will be here as a tourist too and I will sell you a belt, a very fine belt with many beads.

It is very hard for me to write this letter because I think now you are becoming a very important man with full education and I am a poor man working every day on the street. I remember when we were little children and especially I remember our visit to the elephants, but many things have happened now. I do not think it will be possible for me to come to England because it costs too much in the aeroplane, and if you come to Nairobi you will stay in the Hilton Hotel and it will not be possible for me to visit you. When I think of such things I find I am very angry that my life is so poor. I think constantly of how I can become rich and have a wife and a house. Maybe you have some ideas for me, my friend, but I do not think so. Your last letter is very short and you are many, many miles away. Maybe you forget the country where you were born. I wish very much to leave this city and return to the place where I too was born, but I do not have work there and there is no place for me. Now I have to stop this letter and I must sleep and prepare for tomorrow, when I rise at 6.30 a.m. to take the bus to the city.

God bless you, my old friend
From Kimutei

Juliet stared, blinking, at the far wall. She remembered how she had wanted to buy a beaded belt from a street vendor in Nairobi and Michael had argued angrily that they were flashy rubbish, that bargaining for them had been demeaning to both parties. She had yielded, confused and hurt. And Mathare Valley – he had seen it as a symbol both of the country's past subjugation and its present prostitution. In revenge over the belt, she had refused to go there with him, and stayed in the hotel room reading a Western magazine. When he returned, she was asleep, and next day he refused to talk about it.

She remembered the vendors, the desperately importunate young men who trotted beside you with the decorative, beaded belts looped and buckled in dozens round waists, arms, and necks, asking, bargaining, pleading, pointing out the meaning the multicoloured designs. 'This is the finest belt in Nairobi, see, this means you have five cows, this means you have many wives. Best price, cheapest price.'

Juliet stood up and stretched her tense arms and shoulders. The tribesmen had taken the beads and trinkets of the white adventurers, and now they were grovelling to sell them back. What had happened to Kimutei now? Swallowed and drowned, most likely, in the tide of poverty and squalor which lapped at Nairobi's glass-and-concrete centre. For all she knew, this bundle of dog-eared letters, tied with a fraying piece of string, was the only part of him to be washed ashore.

Juliet started pacing across the room to the window. Brisk action was her involuntary defence nowadays against the feelings of sadness and waste which came at her constantly from many directions. A rib of dull gold, low in the gun-metal sky, reminded her it would soon be dark, and she must go now if she wanted to walk to the park and back without feeling frightened of attack. Swiftly she headed for the door: activity would prevent her distress turning to the stone of depression, keep it swilling bearably inside her, perhaps even spill a little of it.

Fourteen

Michael lay back among the lumps of horsehair exploding from the rips in the greasy sofa and took a drag from the cigar-sized joint, his ears buzzing in the pulse from the speakers. The walls of the room were adorned with posters of Marcus Garvey, Haile Selassie and Bob Marley, and part of the ceiling was missing. It had been a long process, but he was now warily accepted in the Front Line squat by Everett and the taciturn young blacks who drifted in and out.

'Has this place ever been busted?' he asked, self-conscious at the jargon.

'Don't worry, man,' said one of the youths sarcastically. 'If the pigs bust us now, they won't arrest you, they'll just arrest us. They'll pat you on the head and tell you to go home to Mummy.'

'That's not true.' Michael was indignant. 'I get stopped and hassled in the streets round here, just like you do.'

'Oh yeah?' The youth's voice and eyebrows rose. 'And I suppose they call you a nigger and a mugger and a coon and tell you to get back to the jungle? And then if you answer back they drag you off to the cells and work you over?'

'They're not supposed to call you nigger any more,' drawled a youth in the back corner of the room. 'So now they call you mugger instead. It's the same word really, 'cept it doesn't just mean you're black, it means you're a black criminal. They reckon all blacks are criminals.'

'Every nigger between six and sixty is a criminal,' said the first youth. 'That's what one copper told me. Twisting my arm at the time, he was.'

There was a gleam of intelligent and bitter irony on the speaker's face, and Michael could think of no reply. He drew again on the 'spliff' and passed it on. A lot of what they said was true – he had seen it happen. Searches on the street, jeering and truncheon-waving from vans. The room relapsed into music and ganja. Licking our wounds, Everett had called it.

Michael had succeeded in getting Everett on the steering committee, but he rarely turned up at meetings. When he did, he usually delivered an angry lecture; the other members smiled their discreet liberal smiles, but their eyes would dart nervously round the room.

They saw their real business as improving liaison with the Department of Health and Social Security, drawing up the grant application to the local council, plugging the gaps in the system; and when Everett told them the youth couldn't take any more pressure and there was going to be fighting in the streets, they nodded without believing. They thought he was posturing, and distrusted him because of his smart clothes and moneyed appearance. Michael once overheard his own boss and a youth worker anxiously discussing just how much that flashy piece of dentistry in Everett's front tooth had actually cost.

Michael, though, was dazzled by Everett, who belied all his experience of black people. He was neither a subservient colonial native, nor a sad creature who plodded to work at four in the morning and swept station platforms. Instead he was a mercurial, voluble, streetwise survivor, who needed no pity and flung back any contempt. Michael felt burdened with his own clumsy attitudes, and was grateful that Everett, with an air of slight amusement, accepted him as a friend.

And yet the question sneaked up on him too, prompted by a folk devil two centuries old: how *did* the black kids get the money for their gold chains and smart jeans and training shoes? How did they survive? Eventually he mustered the courage to ask the question. It was a sunny spring day and he and Everett were sitting on a bench by the taxi rank at the end of Coldharbour Lane. Brixton looked almost benign.

'What d'you reckon to this whole thing about black kids and, well, street crime?'

His tone was nonchalant, his eyes narrowed in apparent study of a passing bus, his hands deep in his trouser pockets.

Everett turned and studied him ironically for a while, deliberately increasing his embarrassment.

'You're going red, man,' he said eventually. 'What's the matter, you been talking to the pigs again?'

Michael glanced at him guiltily.

'No, course not. I wouldn't believe them, anyway – that's why I'm asking you.'

'Why you so bothered, man?'

'Well, you know the kind of thing people say, the kind of thing that's in the papers.'

'No I don't, man. You tell me.'

147

Everett's eyes were dark and hard; Michael decided to grasp the nettle.

'Well, they reckon most of the robberies and street crime are done by blacks. The pigs don't say so openly, they say they're just interested in crime, not colour, but that's what they think.'

'And what about you, Mike?' taunted Everett, lips drawn back from the starry tooth. 'What do *you* think?'

'Well, I think that with the kind of social and economic conditions . . .'

'Fuck the social and economic conditions! Don't start spouting all that crap, man, because I've heard it all before from liberal white pricks like you. Probation officers, social workers, youth workers, shit workers, you name it. I've grown up with it, man, I'm an expert. You don't actually say it, but it's written all over your faces. You're not even sure we're really human beings, man, that we come from the same planet. You reckon we came swinging down from the trees, basically, but if you're nice to us and throw us plenty of bananas, we won't jump up and down on your pretty little flowerbeds and rape your women. We're into all those things that aren't allowed, isn't that right? All that primitive stuff? All that screwing and fighting, all that fucking and stabbing with knives, eh, Mikey boy? P'raps you'd like to do it too, eh, man?'

Michael looked around nervously. A cabbie wearing a check cap on a head like a football was watching Everett with gimlet eyes. But he was not to be stopped.

'Smoking weed and shouting and fighting and fucking all over the place? Just like the niggers, eh? Maybe there's a little nigger inside you, man, fighting to get out, but you stamp on his head all the time. And when you see him walking around the street, you get a little panicky – he might creep up behind you in the dark and put a big smelly arm round your neck and stick a blade up your arse. And then he'll grab your woman and stick his black black cock in her and after that she won't be interested in *you*, man. So don't you rubbish the pigs, Mikey, they're all you've got. They know how to keep those big buck niggers down at the bottom of the shitheap where they belong. They'll drag him down the nick for you and put three on to one and kick him in the balls and bust his big fat lips for him. And guys like you will go' – Everett wrung his hands and mocked a middle-class voice – 'Oh, dear me, that sort of thing shouldn't really happen, but you know, we don't know what went on in there, maybe the police were provoked, I mean these coons, I *beg* your pardon, these black gents, they can be a little unruly sometimes, I mean, they shout and wave their arms around, don't they? It really *is* time they began to toe the line and be like us, otherwise we'll have to load them all up into ships and send them back to the jungles, *so* sorry, I mean the sunny Caribbean where everyone smiles big white nigger smiles and plays calypso.'

Michael felt a warm dew of sweat on his face and he nervously fingered his upper lip, tracing out his scar and its line of numbness.

'It isn't like that,' he muttered. 'And that wasn't what I asked about.'

'Shit!' Everett spat on the ground.

Perhaps he should tell him, thought Michael. About that episode at the caves twenty years ago. *That* was what it was really like, what it should be like. The flesh of both black and white bled when it was cut, and the blood made them brothers.

'You know, when I was a kid . . .'

Everett threw his arms round his head in mock defence.

'Oh no, man, not more of that colonial stuff. I can't take it.'

'All right, fuck off then.' Michael retreated into himself. Everett lowered his hands, softened.

'You know the trouble with you, Mike?'

'Go on, professor, tell me.' Michael stared at him bitterly.

'Your problem is you reckon you're responsible for it all. You reckon all the racism over here is your fault because you used to kick niggers' arses when you were a kid.'

'Well, the two things are connected, aren't they?' Michael could not resist a favourite theme. 'I mean, you're over here because we were over there. And because we can't kick you around over there any more, we bring a few of you in here so we can kick you around here instead. Well, isn't that it?'

'This is what I mean about you.' Everett shook his head, as if at an incorrigible child. 'You got it all worked out and you reckon you've got to do something to make it better. I tell you, man, you should stop feeling guilty and get on with things. We can look after ourselves, man, and if you're not careful you're gonna be dead before you've had a chance to enjoy yourself.'

'Thanks a lot.'

'Well, come on.' Everett spread a broad hand as if the plain truth were written on it. 'What d'you reckon you can do about it all? You going to grab all those politicians and make them understand? You going to find every racist copper and every racist housing officer and force them to be good boys? You should learn to face the facts, man. Wars ain't solved by having debates, they're solved by fighting. You'd be better off on your side of the struggle, 'specially since it's on top at the moment. And we're not like the blacks out in Africa that you used to kick around. We've been dragged around the world, man, we can take care of ourselves.'

Michael began talking about an integrated society, with the system flexing to produce racial justice, but Everett's attention had moved to the other side of the main road where a knot of young black people were gathering on the front steps of the town hall and chanting.

'I know those guys,' muttered Everett.

Michael followed him, dodging through the traffic, and they reached the demonstration at the same time as a pair of nervous-looking young policemen. Two of the demonstrators, a girl with beads in her braided hair and a boy in a leather jacket, struggled to fix a banner reading 'Housing Justice NOW' between the town hall's lamp standards. It caught and shattered one of the ornamental lights.

'Criminal damage,' said one of the young officers to his colleague, with the quiet satisfaction of an expectation fulfilled. But he stayed to one side, talking occasionally into his radio.

Everett had disappeared into the crush. A tall, skinny man with fiery eyes and dreadlocks in a Rastafarian tam pushed to the top of the steps and began haranguing the bystanders. His voice was raw and high, with a strong Caribbean musicality.

'We got nowhere to go in the society, we being pushed about by the authorities, out in the cold. Everywhere black people go there is ghetto and demolition and pressure. They are holding us down, pinning us down, telling us no, provoking us. And then we fight back and we violent and make our claim, and they drag us away so the prisons and police stations and mental hospitals are full of us. We won't survive if we no fight for our rights!'

Michael felt a touch on his arm and found Everett offering him a cigarette. As he lit it and looked up through the smoke Everett winked at him, as if he couldn't take this sort of demonstration seriously. Michael felt angry at such flippancy.

'Find it funny, do you?'

'No, 'course not,' muttered Everett, looking speculatively up and

150

down the street. 'Look, I gotta go somewhere, man. I'll see you around.'

Michael watched him saunter off down Coldharbour Lane, towards the railway bridge and the heart of the ghetto. He was almost dressed for a street war, he reflected – the green combat jacket with big pockets, the dark blue beret, the rubber-soled training shoes. He knew the police singled out black kids in army surplus gear, as if it reminded them too much of race wars in Rhodesia or Angola.

Michael drifted away from the demonstration, feeling dejected and comfortless; he had wanted someone to tell him he was a good man, that he was making atonement, but Everett had just reminded him that the black races outnumbered the whites and his efforts weren't needed. He rarely drank at lunchtime, but today he was going to. He stepped out of the sunshine into an interior rank with stale beer and tobacco, where unknown figures lounged in the shadows.

Fifteen

Juliet stared at the shapes cast on the ceiling by the orange street light cutting through the gap in the curtains. She lay on her back, arms flopped out, in the middle of the bed, dwelling upon the evening she had spent reading the journals packed with Michael's small, careful handwriting. She realised now that, half-buried beneath her grief, there were feelings of great anger towards him – not just because he had left her like this, but also because of his persistent concealment during their time together of things that mattered to him. The journals had received the confidences she felt she should have had.

She had found accounts of things he had never even told her about, or had mentioned only in a passing and secretive way – an incident in the playground where he humiliated a little South African boy, the bloody fight in the township with a skinny young African, a complete version of the visit to the caves, with the truth – at last – about his scar. There was a short and bitter description of how, homesick and lonely, he had arrived at his first school in England and tried to strike up a friendship with another boy by showing him his photographs of Africa; but they were sitting on a bench reserved for seniors, and a prefect came past, tipped them both on the floor, and tossed Michael's treasured album in a waste bin. Had this set the conviction that it was not worth giving his secrets?

There was also the extraordinary scene in the police station after the riots – a scene which, though it drew together his past and the present in a traumatic way, he had, again, never mentioned. As in the affair of Kimutei's letters, she was only now, after his death, beginning to form a full picture of his real preoccupations and personality. Her mind quailed at the complications and misunderstandings and lost opportunities of life, and she longed as she lay there for the calm simplicity of her protected childhood in the English countryside.

In this mood of drained resentment, she found herself drifting painlessly into recollections of the funeral. The main difficulty had been finding and getting possession of the body. When Delvers eventually found the pilot who had flown the coffin down from Kitale, it was to learn that he had been prevented at gunpoint from bringing it out of the domestic airport and forced to leave it in a

152

godown among crates of spare parts and military supplies. They finally secured it by passing a 500-shilling bribe to an army captain who asserted his authority by jabbing his gun barrel repeatedly into Juliet's stomach. That night, gunfire sounded somewhere in the city as she shouted down the phone to England, telling Michael's parents he had to be buried immediately, before he began to stink.

There were only four of them watching as the coffin was lowered into the dusty, stony hole that Tuesday afternoon by the pair of thin gravediggers in their patched shorts – Juliet, Delvers, the American reporter Schmidt, and the Rev. Josiah Ndovu. He was a big man, with kind eyes set deep in a shiny, impassive face, and Juliet felt comforted by him, and by the simplicity of the church by the road which led out of the city to the Ngong Hills. His voice, serious and deliberate, echoed round the stone walls as the African sun streamed through the two stained-glass windows above the altar, splashing violent colour on the floor of the nave. Delvers and Schmidt, who had borrowed a pick-up to serve as a hearse, were drunk – Delvers red and breathing heavily, Schmidt pale, as if about to faint. Ndovu marshalled them firmly to help him carry the coffin into the church, and later back out to the grave.

Juliet had behaved calmly. She had run out of grief, and the funeral felt almost like another of the chores holding up her escape from this country. She was pleased, though, that she was leaving Michael there, buried in the red earth of his homeland. She shook Ndovu's hand, thanked him and paid him; then the three whites drove back in silence to town, with Juliet cramped between the two pungent, heavily breathing men on the bench seat of the rattling pick-up. Dropping her at the hotel, Delvers embraced her, kissing her on the lips and holding on too long.

A car was driving down the street. Its headlights moved and changed the shapes on the ceiling, breaking Juliet's mood of contemplation and bringing her back to the present. She glanced at her alarm clock: three in the morning. There was a squeak of brakes, the engine fell to idling, and footsteps clipped across the pavement. She heard the metallic sound of the flap of a letter box falling back, bouncing; then footsteps again, the slamming of the car door, the sound of the engine dying away in the distant hum of night-time London. It sounded like her letter box. She lay motionless, thinking of the bleak, bare stairs and shadowy hallway; but curiosity won, and she dragged herself out of bed.

There was a large, buff envelope on the doormat, and she immediately guessed that it was from Bob Delvers. She had not yet phoned him back, and this could be another ploy of his to restore contact with her. She sighed and picked it up; it was bulky, and her name and address were typewritten on it by a machine with a smudgy ribbon. Back upstairs, she made herself tea, leaning against the fridge, yawning and staring speculatively at the package. Then, propped against pillows with her knees up, she ripped it open with her nailfile, using more violence than was strictly necessary.

Dulwich,
27 August

Dear Juliet,

I'm beginning to feel you aren't going to ring me, as you said you would, and I suppose in the circumstances I can more or less understand why. But as I mentioned on the phone, I think it's important that you should have a clearer idea of what happened at the road block than you're going to get from the authorities. Enclosed is my account of it all – written partly because I was so pissed off that the paper didn't use much of the story, and partly for your sake. And, of course, for my own sake, to test how involved I really am in the whole thing now. If there's anything more you want to know, just get in touch. I've some ideas about taking it further – and I won't make randy lunges; at least, not unless you want me to.

Yours,
Bob Delvers

The first sheet had a small newspaper cutting pasted on it below the written date: 12/8/82. It was the story about the road block, cut to almost nothing, which he had mentioned in his last phone call.

HOPE SUSPECTS KILLED
From our own correspondent, Nairobi

Three men wanted for the killing of British tourist Mr Michael Hope in Kenya three weeks ago have been shot dead at a police road block 100 miles from Nairobi, according to the authorities here.

The Ministry of Information said the men's car failed to stop, forcing police to open fire. The car was identified as the one stolen from Mr Hope, a statement said, and the dead men matched descriptions of the attackers.

Mr Hope was slashed and shot to death when he and his wife were ambushed by a gang at a river bridge in the west of the country. The killers made off with the car and luggage, leaving Mrs Hope unharmed.

154

A Ministry spokesman said the road-block incident was regrettable as the government would have preferred to bring the men before a court. But the tight security following the recent coup was ensuring the country would be safe for tourists.

The dead men were named as David wa Kataka, Josiah Oiro and Kimtai arap Koitalel, all said to be unemployed with no fixed abode. Two were said by police to have criminal records.

Juliet put the papers aside and stared straight ahead. As she listened to the ticking of the bedside clock and the gentle ebb and flow of breath in her own throat, she could think of only one thing: the name was, apart from the slight difference in spelling, the same as in the letters. The same forename, at any rate. If it was the same person, it would be the final, unbearable irony. She hoped it was just a coincidence – and either way, she felt she must try to find out. She climbed out of bed again and padded into the living room for her writing paper and address book: the Northrops would know Kimutei's full name, and she was going to write to them now.

Only when she had sealed the envelope, made herself more tea, and lain for some time twisting her hair and watching the dawn turn the windows grey, did she pick up the rest of Delvers' package and begin, yet again, to read.

Sixteen

The script which Delvers had delivered to Juliet at dead of night consisted of eight or ten pages of smudgy typewriting, with the round imprint of a wet whisky glass on the top one.

It was about ten days after the attempted coup and I'd arranged with my office to come back. For their purposes, the story had ended about four days after the events, as soon as they'd had a few descriptions of fuzzy-wuzzies killing each other and piles of black corpses. I'd filed stuff about the political aftermath, the arrests of the MPs, the purging of the air force, the way the police were behaving, but none of it was getting in the paper. They weren't even interested in a story about the police going through the university libraries taking out Marxist and left-wing books and trying to find out who ordered them. I had a row with the foreign editor about that, and his words were: 'We're not the fucking *Guardian*, you know.' I told him we ought to carry the story with an editorial saying what a good idea it was, but irony doesn't penetrate his thick hide. So I was looking forward to getting back to England, away from the smell of blood: the government figure of two or three hundred dead is probably about ten per cent of the real total. And now it looks like there could be real repression.

Anyway, I was having breakfast in the Thorn Tree that Wednesday when Mike Schmidt came over. I wasn't in the best of tempers, and he started all that stuff about 'Right, then, I *won't* tell you.' So I smoothed his feathers, and he told me he'd been speaking to some tame copper on his morning rounds. They'd got someone for the Hope killing, apparently. A police road block at a place called Kampi ya Moto, near the President's farm, had challenged a white 504 at around midnight, it failed to stop, so they filled it full of bullets. It's becoming standard practice out here these days, just like in my dear old native Ulster where the security forces cull a few Catholics every year like that.

Anyway, they dragged three corpses out of the 504, and managed to become certain even in the hours of darkness that they were the three who held up you and Michael. I imagine Schmidt was told because they were pretty keen for the world outside to hear that they'd sorted out the bandits who made life dangerous for tourists, whose money is going to be even harder to come by after the little local difficulties.

I don't want to sound too cynical about it, or say anything that upsets you. I know that Kenyans at the moment do not fill you with enthusiasm, and if there's even a chance these three were the ones who killed your husband, you're not going to have much sympathy for them. And let's face it, they might be the ones. It's just that there are doubts about it, and I don't want you to be hoodwinked by official lies. And I don't see you as someone who wants an eye for an eye.

I asked Schmidt if he was going to get down there to take a closer look, and he looked at me as if I was barmy. I was rude to him again, I'm afraid, and left straight away.

I had a 504 on hire by this time, and I got to the place in a couple of hours. Whenever I looked in the mirror, there'd be some old guy on a bike wobbling into a ditch or a donkey going berserk with a kid holding on for dear life; I haven't driven like that since I was about eighteen.

It was one of those days where that vivid blue sky was dotted with towering mounds of cumulus, gleaming in the sun. There was that light, thin, heady air of the African highlands, tinted faintly with dust and woodsmoke. Hot, but not too hot; faded yellow grassland on the floor of the Rift, the green smudge of the Aberdare Forest to the right. For a while I forgot about the attempted coup and imagined the Masai running the plains. I know why Michael felt the place was paradise.

The place I wanted was twenty miles beyond Nakuru. Kampi ya Moto means 'hot little valley' or something of the kind, and the place is more than a little flyblown, as you might imagine. There's a fork in the road and there, sure enough, was the road block: two or three white-painted oil drums, two police Land-Rovers, and a pole across the road. The first thing I noticed was the white 504 in the ditch, looking like a pepperpot. The bonnet and the doors had sprung open and were jammed at crazy angles – a real mess. I pulled up and went over to have a look; there were smooth marks on the ground where they had dragged away the bodies, and black gobs, like tar, studded in the dust. But almost immediately I had an unpleasant-looking plain-clothes man on my neck. He whistled up a man in uniform who shoved a little machine gun in the small of my back and before I knew where I was, I was up against a Land-Rover being patted and squeezed in a way you no doubt remember. They took no notice of my press card, put handcuffs on me, and shoved me in the vehicle to wait for Christ knows what. When this huge shadow blocked the window, I thought they'd sent some Goliath to beat the hell out of me for straying into private official business.

Then I realised it was your friend and mine, Chief Inspector Kariuke, peering in at me with a conspiratorial grin. He held up a key in his great meaty hand and took the cuffs off with it. He gave me a discreet handshake, and apologised, but not so loudly that the other cops could hear. Then he invited me to take a short walk in the bush. Coming from anyone else in that entourage, I would have been worried about a suggestion like that.

'I know why you are here, Mr Delvers,' said Kariuke, kicking up the white dust on the grass near the road. 'I admire your professional enthusiasm, but you are putting yourself in danger.'

On top of his smooth English, the bloke's also managed to acquire Anglo-Saxon understatement. It was like meeting Dixon of Dock Green among the Zulus. We stopped under the flat canopy of a thorn tree.

'I realise that and I'm very glad to see you. Who the hell are those other guys?'

'The gentlemen on the Hope case – the ones I described to you before. Plus a few colleagues of theirs from Nairobi. They are very excited about what has happened.'

'You don't need to tell me.' My wrists were still hurting from the handcuffs. 'The point is, *have* they killed the right men? They're putting it around in Nairobi that they have.'

Kariuke began picking bits of bark off the thorn tree. It was cool and quiet there, like in a house, and out of the shade the sun made everything look bleached. He spoke hesitantly.

'It looks like the right car, but I don't think it's the right people. Northrop told us the numbers stamped on the chassis and the glass, and they seem to match. Someone has tried to scratch the numbers off, but you still can make them out. But the three men – well, who knows? We have their names from papers they carried, but that proves nothing because we don't know the names of the criminals. We haven't found anything on them or in the car which definitely connects them with the crime – the stolen items, for example, which were in the luggage. And the car, that could have changed hands several times by now. These people could have bought it in good faith.'

'So why are your friends from Special Branch so sure?'

'Those fools? They are going only on one thing – one thing.'

He stuck his finger angrily in the air and stared at me. His head seemed to swell, he was so angry.

'Go on.'

He finally dropped the finger and ran it down the side of his face.

'One of the dead men has a long scar down here. And one of the best descriptions was of one of the men who tied up Mrs Hope. He also had a mark on his cheek.'

'I remember – she called it a tribal marking, though, didn't she? Not necessarily the same thing.'

Kariuke gave a twisted grin.

'Very good, Mr Delvers. You pick up the important details, I see. But there is nothing else from her descriptions of the men which fits these bodies. And the old man from the village who saw them noticed no scars at all. But one thing is enough for these so-called colleagues of mine. That is their method. Those dead men can no longer defend themselves, so the crime is hung around their necks. The political problem is solved, and the case can be closed. Tourists will be safe in Kenya now. And these' – he gestured aggressively towards the road with his big chin – 'these gangsters will get promotion.'

'Have *you* seen the bodies?'

Kariuke nodded.

'The men on the road block were very jumpy. After they had shot up the car, they gave the bodies more bullets from point-blank range. There are some very big holes, and one man is not recognisable because they shot into his face. Do you want to see them?'

I wasn't in any position to know whether the three poor bastards were the right ones, and I'd seen quite enough corpses recently. They'd be lying splay-footed on a dusty concrete floor in one of the nearby shacks, no doubt, their eyes milky, the blood going black as their skins, the flies swarming on the bits of sacking or blanket used to cover them. I shook my head.

'No thanks. What'll happen next?'

Kariuke shrugged and stirred his foot in the dusty grass. He looked furious and helpless at the same time. He'd been taking risks from the start of this case, not least in all the things he'd said to me, and it was unlikely that his reservations would have gone unnoticed. I was concerned about his future.

'I think the investigation will be closed. Adjustments will be made to the papers and the descriptions might be brought more in line with these very useful corpses. The Minister will make a statement in Parliament. Perhaps it will be said that the men in the car opened fire, thus obliging the police to pump twenty bullets into each of them. Easy enough to plant a gun on a corpse, after all. What else? Dramatic accounts of the incident and the bravery of the police will find themselves in the newspapers in this country and others. They might even say they knew these dangerous men would be coming down this road, and that they set up the road block specially for them. Anything is possible in times like these, Mr Delvers, when those in power are using every weapon to hold on to their position. And you will remember once again, I hope, that this conversation also has never taken place.'

I grinned at him. He looked back at the road, evidently feeling we'd been away long enough.

'Of course. But you – what are *you* going to do? You're not going to try to stand in the way of these people, I hope?'

He laughed and slung his arm around my shoulder, taking all the nape of my neck in one hand and steering me into the white sunlight again.

'Me, my friend? I am not so unwise. And sometimes I think people have a case when they tell me I am not patriotic enough, that I am just a sentimental old man. I shall survive, do not worry about me. I shall go back to my quiet provincial posting and keep my head down chasing cattle rustlers. I will devote myself to family life and stay clear of politics.'

The steering paw took me to the two plain-clothes men behind the Land-Rover. They both had electric-blue suits, bright shirts, puffy, drink-sodden faces, and slippery brown eyes. They looked like men who beat people to death in cells, and I was glad of the protection of Kariuke.

'This is my friend Mr Delvers.' His proprietorial pat on the back nearly made me spit my teeth out. 'We have had a little talk and now he understands that it is dangerous to stick his nose in things which are not his business, and he is about to get back in his car and drive back to Nairobi. Is that not so, Mr Delvers?'

He gave me an evil grin, and I wanted to congratulate him on his acting. The two gangsters responded to his speech with blood-chilling smiles, and Kariuke's grip on my arm relaxed as he steered me over to my car. I was suddenly sorry I wouldn't be seeing him again, and I've never been able to say that about a black person before. I wanted to say something, but he cut things short with a brisk handshake.

'Goodbye, Mr Delvers. And please write the truth.'

I mumbled goodbye, and he walked off. The cop with the machine gun eyed me speculatively as I drove off, and I was glad to see Kampi ya Moto fade in the dustcloud in my rear-view mirror.

I took the journey back more slowly, trying to get my thoughts straight. I felt indignant about the way they'd framed up these three corpses out of blatant political expediency; and I could feel the indignation was fuelled by white prejudice about blacks and their politics – you know, corrupt, violent, tribal, not fit for democratic institutions. But the confusing thing was that I had been encouraged to feel like that by Kariuke, a black man. He was playing the white man, backing me in my role as the racist. So was he an honorary white ingratiating himself with anti-African lobbies, or was our shared view of the Special Branch men not racism, but a sober judgment of the facts? Uninfluenced by colour? Are you still with me? I didn't know whether I was guilty of racism or not – I'd never really thought about it before, or cared, which is more significant.

Anyway, I wrote a story throwing all of Kariuke's scepticism on the official line, and then when I got back to London I found they'd boiled it down to about two paragraphs, leaving out all the doubts. And having now read the full account of things, you can probably see why I'm so frustrated about that. Once they'd used that interview with you, they'd milked all they wanted from the story – the sentiment, with a good squirt of violence and race to get the middle-class housewives nicely lubricated. They weren't interested in the real ramifications of the case. I've always known that about other stories, but this time it mattered to me. All they would carry was an official conclusion from an officialdom they normally hold in contempt.

Juliet put the script on the floor beside the bed and stared at the bright stream of sun now falling between the curtains. The bloody events Delvers described somehow seemed quite undramatic to her, as if she knew about them already or had never expected anything else. She found herself thinking not about the content, but the style of the writing, and how it was a complete contrast to the article printed about her under his name in the *Post*. Perhaps that piece had indeed started life in this sober, almost literary style; maybe his excuse about rewriting by editors was genuine. Maybe she should get in contact and arrange to see him, even if only to ridicule his new-found anxieties about racism. The Fleet Street heavy had become the sensitive flower, or so he seemed to wish her to believe. She picked up the papers again and looked at the letter. 'I've some ideas about taking it further.' What the hell was he up to now? She was not sure she could handle another sensitive flower with ideas – Michael had been one too, and it had only led to unhappiness and trouble. Why were men constantly driven to raise their puny standard everywhere, seeking out conflict, devising endless infelicitous, self-asserting projects? Exhaustion and irritation suddenly overcame her, and she pushed her head between the cool pillows to sleep.

Seventeen

'There's all hell broken out on the Front Line.' Michael, panting and excited, burst into the living room.

'I know,' said Juliet irritably. 'I can hear the sirens. And it's been on the news.'

'But it's really hairy – there are hundreds of kids down there, chucking stuff at the police. Petrol bombs, the lot.'

'Don't sound so pleased about it – or have you been joining in?'

Michael flopped on the sofa, blowing a weary sigh. He blamed things on the police, while Juliet was more sceptical. The police know who the villains are, she told him with middle-class assurance, and if the villains are black they have to take the consequences like everyone else.

'No, I haven't been joining in. I was up in Dulwich, and when I got back about seven, well, the place was more less alight. Apparently they've set the Windsor Castle on fire, you know, the place they won't serve blacks.'

'So it deserves to be burnt down, does it?'

'No, it doesn't *deserve* it, but you can see why it happens. It's called reaping what you sow.'

Juliet stared at him, fists on hips. He was tempted to taunt her about the fear of big black rapists; instead he stood up and took her hand.

'What d'you think's going to happen?' she asked, softened.

'Oh, I expect the police will get their act together and break a few heads open and suppress it.' Michael smiled at her resignedly.

'Sounds as if the police are getting *their* heads broken open at the moment.'

A new blast of sirens started up. Michael walked to the window and watched the flames and smoke half a mile away at the bottom of the hill.

'I'd better get back down there,' he said.

'What on earth for?'

'See what's going on – make sure the centre's all right.'

'Throw bricks at the police, you mean. You'll get hurt.'

'No, I won't.'

'Look, Michael, I know all about the grievances, but they don't really concern you. I don't want you to go back down there and get burnt alive by a petrol bomb.'

'Don't worry, I'm far too careful for anything like that.'

He kissed her and left her watching the flames and confusion at the beginning of the TV news. The light was fading from the warm April evening as he headed for the Front Line, sniffing the smoke in the air. At one street corner stood a knot of dishevelled policemen, helmets off to reveal short haircuts and worried expressions. They were watching a laden stretcher being loaded into an ambulance. One of the officers, sitting on a low wall, his face grainy in the black and white effect of the sodium lights, stared at Michael with a mixture of aggression and fear. Propped beside him were several long plastic shields, scorched and discoloured round the bottom.

The building burning ahead of him, he realised, was the junior school in Effra Parade. Flames were rushing and crackling twenty feet high and little gobs of soot were falling on the pavement. Further up the road was a noisy, moving mass of people. He nervously began to walk towards them, stubbing his toe on a half-brick in the gutter.

The whole road, he noticed, was littered with broken glass, tins, lumps of wood, stones, more bricks. Two figures emerged from an alleyway on the other side of the road, carrying a milk crate between them. Both of them – one black, one white – were wearing clumsy masks made of pieces of cloth tied behind their heads. They looked warily at Michael, and he caught sight of bits of rag spilling from the bottles in the crate. He thought he could smell the hazy, volatile fumes which rise into the nostrils at filling stations, and he noticed now that the night air was becoming chilly in spite of the roaring flames a hundred yards away.

He faltered, his anxiety growing. But there was the noise of feet, and someone was running towards him – into him; he threw up an arm in front of his face, elbow swinging out. There was a grunt as a pair of arms grabbed him round the waist and propelled him back into the school wall. His head crashed against the bricks, and as he put up a hand to rub it, his attacker took hold of his throat. A second person came running up, and he found himself staring at two black youths in T-shirts, faces streaked with sweat and eyes glittering in the lurid light from the flames.

'What the fuck's going on?' he asked weakly. The grip on his throat tightened. Warm breath and a spray of spittle hit his face as one of the youths yelled at him.

'You one of the pigs? Eh? You a fucking pig? Show him the blade, Rodney. Come on, you a pig?'

There was a flash of metal, and Michael felt the hand around his neck replaced by the prick of the knife point. He stopped rubbing his head, thinking that any movement would bring the blade through into his arteries. But he knew he must talk down the murderous excitement of his attackers.

''Course I'm not a cop. Do I look like a cop?' His voice was trembling.

'You're a fucking cop, they're all in plain clothes round here.'

'No, I'm not, I work at the advice centre, down the road. You know the advice centre.'

'No, I don't know any fucking advice centre,' shouted the one without the knife, pushing Michael harder against the wall. 'Who wants advice from a fucking pig?'

Surely the blade was going to pop through the skin, his flesh squirt out like sausage. They weren't going to listen, they were too worked up – all they wanted was blood, white blood. Michael felt a flicker of racial anger deep within him: he wasn't going to be sliced up by a couple of niggers. Could he duck free, kick them in the balls and run?

He was saved by a sudden shout from the crowd a hundred yards away at the corner of Railton Road: 'Here they come!'

The two youths were away as quickly as they had arrived, leaving Michael propped against the wall, gingerly fingering his throat to check for blood. In his sudden release from fear, he breathed deeply, unable to think. Juliet came into his mind; perhaps he should just go home.

'Are you all right, dear?'

The woman's voice was gentle, with a strong Caribbean lilt, and her hand was on his elbow. He looked round into a thin, anxious face, a black face which this time was puckered with sympathy and concern.

'Yes, yes, I think so.' He laughed nervously. 'Just a bit scared.'

The woman shook her head maternally and tutted.

'Shocking, those boys. I see what happen to you from my front window. You want to come in, have a cup of tea?'

'I don't know,' he mumbled, confused by the offer. 'They thought I was a copper.'

The woman shook her head sadly. She was wearing a loose, yellow cardigan.

'Well, there's plenty of policemen around here, that's for sure. Some would say too many.'

'That's right.' Michael could feel a lump on his head now, and was feeling sick and faint. The woman steered him slowly over the road.

'You come along with me, darlin', I got a pot of tea on the go.'

The bricks of the little terraced house were painted dark red, picked out in white. Michael followed the woman along the narrow hall to the kitchen. It was clean and ordered, with a slight smell of cooking and patches of damp on the yellow and purple walls. There was a crucifix above the sink, and a feeling of great calm after the violence in the street. He sat at the table and gazed at the huge scarlet flowers on the plastic tablecloth.

'What's been happening outside?' he muttered, sipping at the mug of strong, hot tea she gave him.

'Well.' The woman pulled the flaps of her cardigan across her chest and raised her eyebrows in a mixture of surprise and resignation. 'They chase the police out of *this* street, that's for sure.'

'What happened?'

'Well, the police bring forty, fifty men up that way' – she gestured the way Michael had come – 'and the youth come at them the other way. The police stop right here outside my window, and one of them takes my dustbin lid, I haven't seen it since. And they makes a wall with the big shields, the plastic ones, and the youth is throwing bricks and firebombs and shouting at them like they want to kill them . . .'

'They *do* want to kill them,' Michael interrupted with feeling.

'Well, maybe some of them *do* want to kill,' she said, meeting his eye defiantly. 'But thank God I don't think they kill nobody, but they make the police run back down the street. And the fire engine which come in behind the police, they go for that too. And when the police run, the firemen stop squirting the water and jump in their wagon and they off too, down the street. So then everyone outside here is laughing and rejoicing and smoking cigarettes and drinking cans of beer, you never seen nothing like it in your life . . .'

Her voice trailed off, as if she were unsure how to feel about it all. She was half-smiling, but hanging her head.

'So the youth controls the street?'

'That's right.' She looked up with sudden confidence. 'I don't hold with no violence and lawlessness, but the way those officers been behaving round these parts, well, I know why it has happened. And that's why they go for you, those boys, they don't want no police back on the streets again.'

'They'll be back, don't worry,' muttered Michael. 'They'll get their revenge.'

The woman sighed and silence fell between them. It was filled by a muffled roaring, chanting sound from outside, with sirens honking and wailing in the distance. There must be a counter-attack, thought Michael – there was nothing the police cared about more than controlling the streets. They'd bring the army in rather than let it last more than an hour or two. The woman started talking again, a quiet monologue, as if to herself.

'I got two grown-up boys, they live in Birmingham now, thank God, they taking no part in this, but now I wonder, you know, why I come to this country. We never get no thanks for saying yes when they ask us to come, run the buses, clean the hospitals. I been a nurse all my life, you know, I not been treated so badly, but I never get no promotion, and the young white girls, they come and I teach them and they get promotion and now I ordered around by the girls I teach. And maybe I prepared to take that sort of thing, I born in a colony, you know, but the youth now, they far too angry, they not ready to be second-class like that. They born here. Sure they get involved in thieving and stealing, but what choice they got, some of them, they got nothing, they have to survive in the society too.'

Her voice had become shriller, and she paused, not looking at him, shaking her head.

'I'm a Christian woman, you know. I believe in law and order and the punishment of sins, but the law has also got to be fair. Because they see one or two boys knock down old ladies, they think they can treat every black person like a criminal, like an animal. I never had no trouble with the law personally, you know, but I hear what my friends tell me, and they not liars. And I seen them beat up a boy on the street once, with them sticks, no reason I could see, and they shout "nigger" from the car windows. Many, many years I believe in British justice, Britain is the mother country to us, you know that? And everyone is dealt with fair under the law, but now I not so sure. British education, I believe the same once, best in the world. Both my boys go through school here, and they not stupid, you know, they bright boys, but they end up with no qualification, they have to start in life from the street. And I not so sure about British education now. I think, when I retire from work, maybe I can go back to Jamaica. The place is poor, that's why we leave it, but it's our own people and you treated like a human being there, and it's a warm island, warm, where no snow falls.'

Michael looked at the lines of hard work and sincerity in her face, thinking of Mary, whom he barely remembered. He was tempted to tell this motherly woman that he felt the truth of her complaints, that he too longed for a country 'where no snow falls'. But the sounds outside were swelling, and he was feeling revived, more courageous, and determined to see more of what was happening. He pushed the empty mug from him and stood up, his head pulsing slightly. She watched him, her face wistful and distant.

'Thank you for the tea.'

'OK, darlin'. Don't you go getting yourself into more troubles, that's all.'

Outside, Michael turned towards the shouting and noise from the Front Line and broke into a trot, worrying he had missed everything.

When he reached the junction the first thing he saw was a petrol bomb: the crash of glass, a sudden flash, a running, leaping line of blue and yellow flame. He watched it dance and sputter itself out, and then realised what its target had been: a plastic wall stretching almost across the road, with dark figures half-crouched behind it. Then suddenly the figures moved and the wall advanced, jolting and lurching but showing no gaps. After five or ten yards it stopped again, and the shadows behind it were still. The police were like Roman legionaries besieging some citadel.

Looking the other way, he saw the angry crowd, shouting, swarming, picking up missiles, pulling down a wall for the bricks. There was a sudden clattering as a volley of stones and bottles bounced off the shields and fell into the smoking roadway. Then another petrol bomb spun up, its cloth fuse glowing like tracer, and erupted against the plastic wall, which shrank away from the flames like a live thing. Michael dodged out of the side street and moved towards the rioters, but suddenly thought he was going to be trapped between the two sides and moved into a doorway for protection.

From the police lines there now came the chanting he had heard from inside the woman's house: the wall had parted, and a raiding party was running out through the gap. Only some were in uniform carrying truncheons, and the rest were in casual clothes carrying what looked like wooden staves and metal bars. Half a dozen of them were beating their weapons on the dustbin lids they carried, and Michael suddenly recognised what they were all chanting: the first verse of 'Rule, Britannia'. Cowering further into his doorway, Michael thought: it's the last colonial war.

The snatch squad ran into a volley of missiles and its momentum and chanting faltered. One or two police were now lying in the roadway. There was another volley from the crowd, and the police were now retreating towards the wall of shields, dragging a uniformed casualty along the ground.

Michael now realised there was a second wall of shields advancing from his right. Evidently police tactics were to put the rioters in a vice, squeezing them away down the side streets and making snatch arrests between advances. Already the police line on the left was much closer than when he had arrived, and as the gap gradually closed rioters ran off in twos or threes from the battleground. Behind it he could see dozens of blue and white vans, with dark, moving masses of uniformed police among them. Every copper in London must be here by now, he thought.

Frozen in his doorway, Michael began to realise that he was going to be lucky to escape. A police helicopter was now beating overhead, using its searchlight to cover the scene in a brilliant white light. On the right, the ordered wall of shields had disappeared and a mass charge had begun. Some of the running officers were banging on their makeshift shields again, and others were ululating like savages. The crowd was running, but the police seemed to be running faster, hitting out at the dodging, running rioters. Little clumps of bodies fell fighting to the ground. One black youth dodged into a doorway as the police charge swept by, then emerged with a half-brick and hurled it at close range into a policeman's back. The officer staggered and fell, and the youth leapt nimbly over his body and raced to join the retreat down the side roads.

The charge slowed as police managed to make arrests and drag people off, or bent to help injured colleagues. One man in plain clothes, carrying a stave, ran up to two uniformed men struggling with a black man on the ground. Carefully and deliberately, he kicked the prisoner's struggling lower body, choosing the right moment for the blows. Michael went hot with anger at this, but knew it was high time for him to leave; he peered round the doorway to calculate his retreat. Just then, a pain-filled bellow sounded a few yards away.

Two men were dragging a Rasta along by his hair, laughing at him vindictively. He stared, shocked, at the screaming face; he was sure it was Everett Thompson.

'Everett?' he called, hesitating, peering down. 'Everett – you OK?'

There was no reply from the contorted face – the man just continued to scream; but one of the officers looked up, directly at Michael. He was a big man with a small moustache and a face full of aggression.

Michael turned and ran, quickly reaching Effra Parade. But as he turned the corner, he could hear the footsteps closing behind him. Two policemen on the other side of the road moved towards him, spreading their arms to block his way. He ran harder and managed to squeeze through the gap, but seconds later he felt his legs suddenly stop moving, pinned together from behind. The pavement came up at his face, but he threw his arm up in time to take the impact. In a moment of clarity before pain and struggle for breath took over, he saw a pair of black-booted feet stop beside his face, and his head was jerked up by the hair.

He looked into a dirty young face grimacing in triumph. Then his nose and teeth were crushed down on the cold, gritty pavement and a constricted, salivary voice spoke harshly above him.

'Right, you nigger-loving little cunt – you're nicked.'

Eighteen

Michael lay on the floor of the van as it ground in low gear round the tight corners of central Brixton. It was overloaded with bodies, half of them prisoners like him, lying handcuffed on the wooden-slatted floor, the rest policemen slumped on the seats. Michael's face was a few inches away from another person's shins and feet, which lay immobile and slightly contorted, conveying hopelessness and defeat. He could not see through the forest of black boots and dark blue trousers to a window, but he was sure of the van's route: they would be pulling into the yard of the police station at any moment. He listened to the voices from the remote world above, the world of the victors; they sounded subdued and tired.

'We going back there after this lot?'

'Hope not – I reckon that last charge sorted them out, anyway.'

'Bastards – we'll never get home tonight, processing them.'

In the dusty gloom below, Michael studied the pair of legs in front of him: threadbare, greasy corduroy trousers, frayed at the ends; an inch or two of thin, brown leg, blue socks and battered training shoes. The uniform of the young street proletariat of today: he ought to feel proud, he thought, to share the floor of a police van with those legs. Their black owner would look him in the eye and accept him as a brother. But the pain where his face had been rammed into the pavement returned and pushed the thought aside; had he broken a tooth?

Then his thoughts slipped to Juliet and his parents, and a web of anxiety tightened. He would have to get word to them, and in due course he would have to explain, argue, apologise, reassure. He would end up disowning what had happened, his solidarity with the prisoner next to him. The van bucked suddenly, reminding him painfully of the bruises on his chest and arms. Then it pulled up and the back door was pulled open with a metallic squeal. Michael was confronted with a large, fleshy sergeant staring down into the van with distaste.

'Not another load of fucking slag,' he remarked coldly. 'That's all we need.'

The officers in the van climbed out of the side door and came round to pull out their prisoners. Michael was yanked by the legs,

170

then jerked upright by his jacket. His head struck the side of a seat, and he shouted in pain.

'Shut up and stand over there,' ordered the officer who had rugby-tackled him. His face was flushed, his black hair dishevelled. Then the man in corduroy trousers collided with Michael as he, too, was pushed away from the van; he was about forty, thin and bony, with a trickle of blood from a cut in his forehead. He looked drunk, feeble, bewildered, and quite unlike any modern hero of the streets. Michael stared for a moment into the confused brown eyes, and turned in disgust as a wave of foul breath played suddenly on his face. He felt weak and disappointed, and longed to be in the flat with Juliet, in a different world, watching this on television. He would just go over to the sergeant, explain things, come to an agreement, walk out of the yard and off down the street. But the coldness of the tight handcuffs reminded him that this game was entirely serious, and had to be played to the end.

There was a buzz of talk and harsh laughter, and he turned to see a dozen men walk jauntily into the yard. A few of them wore police trousers and shirts, but the rest wore jeans, training shoes, bomber jackets. In the murky light Michael could not quite see what they were carrying, but the nearest man to him had what looked like a pickaxe handle; or perhaps, he thought, it was some sort of special riot truncheon, like the night sticks of American policemen in films. Michael began to feel confused, as if all his knowledge of the world were no longer relevant and new rules now applied.

As the men moved past him to the back door of the station, one of them turned and stared at him. He had short blond hair and a moustache, and his body was tall and wiry. There was a certain simian turn of the shoulders and back of the neck as he climbed the steps and went through the door. For a moment Michael was in African sunshine, swimming across reddish water towards the crested cranes in the far shallows. Then there was a blow on his shoulder.

'Come on, let's have you monkeys inside.'

Michael and the black men who formed the rest of the group shuffled towards the door. There was the drunk whose legs he had studied, and three others; they looked about nineteen and wore jeans and T-shirts which were torn and stained by the battles of the night. One was limping, another had blood caking round his nostrils and lower lip. All looked sullen and furious. His instinct told him not to speak to them unless he wanted instant rejection.

171

They mounted the steps and passed through a lobby where a group of officers were leaning against the wall, smoking and talking. There was a sudden silence as they turned their attention to the new arrivals. The drunk, in front of Michael, staggered and nearly fell as one of the lounging constables stuck out a foot. Michael paused and stared at the policeman, feeling an angry pulse of blood in his neck. It was a boy, eight or ten years younger than him, with spiky, short-cropped hair, traces of acne round his nose, and eyes which looked back with a reptilian indifference. Michael felt an urge which rarely surfaced – to land a heavy blow on the thin, sneering lips, to see that expression of contempt dissolve in a mess of blood. But another push hit his shoulder and he staggered on into a corridor. His head was strangely light, and he found it hard to regain his balance with his hands pinioned behind his back.

Their names were written down, their shoes and belongings put in plastic bags, and they were taken to the cells. All four of them were pushed into one concrete box, hot and airless, with an acrid, hanging smell of urine. On the bench along one wall sat three bruised, listless men, two white and one black. The two youths with Michael took up the remaining bench space, leaving him and the drunk to the floor. The drunk quickly crumpled in an exhausted sprawl, leaving a small space for Michael at the far end. As he sat down on the concrete he realised he was next to a seatless lavatory bowl, screened from the rest of the cell by a low wall. It was full of piled excrement; he looked for the pipes and cistern and realised the flush was controlled from the corridor outside.

He thought about protesting, but fatigue and defeat were taking a grip on him, and he tried to concentrate instead on working out his own position. The police were obviously arresting so many people that none of them were likely to receive their proper rights: he doubted if he would get a phone call to Juliet. They would probably be kept down here for hours – overnight, even – before they were charged. He sighed and settled his shoulders as comfortably as possible against the wall. He rubbed his wrists and his face, realising for the first time that he had a graze on his cheekbone, sticky with drying blood. He took deep breaths, trying to relax into the restless silence of the fetid cell; gradually he fell into a torpor, eyes closed. Now and then one of the others would shift convulsively, mutter, and silence would return. It must have been midnight or later when he opened his eyes, suddenly alert, as one of the young blacks said, in a loud Cockney voice: 'I wish I'd killed the bastard. Next time I will, I swear it, next time I will.' He was looking down at his fists, clenched in his lap. Michael wanted to ask him what had happened, but did not trust his own voice or the response he might get.

A bunch of keys rattled and scraped as the door was unlocked, and Michael looked up blearily at the tall, blond officer who had stared at him in the yard. His eyes searched the cell and came to rest on Michael. This time he seemed confident in his recognition, and he pointed and crooked his finger. Who was he? Michael stood up stiffly and picked his way through the chaotic limbs of the drunk, into the brightly lit corridor, where he blinked and stared. The policeman was Christopher Austin.

'I thought I recognised you out the back.'

Austin spoke coolly with the flattened vowels of a Rhodesian accent still discernible, and his eyes flickered round Michael's face. 'Then I checked with the station officer and there it was: Michael Hope. Of Mount View Farm.'

'That's right.'

Michael's voice came out heavy and expressionless, and his throat was tight with thirst. 'And you're Chris Austin. Who went off to Rhodesia.'

'That's right. It's called Zimbabwe now – or so I'm told.'

Michael looked down for a mistaken moment as the other man moved slightly and he thought he was going to offer his hand. But the hand did not rise, and the movement proved to be a slight retreat by Austin's whole body. His manner was entirely hard and supercilious. Michael was offended for a second, then acknowledged to himself that there was no warmth on his side either. Yet he felt convention was being infringed, and hurried to say something.

'So you're in the police.' It came out foolishly.

'That's right. I'm in the police. And you're in the cells.'

Austin said it with heavy condescension and a pained smile, as if he were talking to an idiot. Now Michael felt outraged: this was the Chris Austin of his boyhood, tagging along, awkward, aggressive, a pest, his natural inferior. And here he suddenly was, lording it, emphasising his power. The tables were turned, and Austin seemed set to make the most of it.

'So you've come to let me go and drop all charges.'

Michael managed a grin, hoping that the irony would move them towards equal terms. But Austin did not smile in return; he shook his head firmly.

'No can do. It's a bit too serious for that.'

A wave of weary distaste struck Michael. It was so appropriate, even predictable, that Austin would show up in the police, using the violence which was his only language, producing phrases like 'no can do'. But the wave was engulfed in a larger flow of anxiety.

'Serious?'

'You're down for offensive weapons and assaulting police, far as I can tell. Can't just walk out of that.'

'You sure?'

'Just checked with your arresting officer. They'll be taking you up to charge you soon.'

Michael looked at the floor, as if to watch his spirits draining from him. He felt extremely tired, ready to fall over, and his mind was blurred.

'Offensive weapon? I wasn't carrying anything. As for assaulting the police, it was they who assaulted *me*. They just went for me and pushed my face into the ground. They've got it wrong.'

His voice was querulous, childish. Austin regarded him sceptically, speculatively, doing the mental equivalent of chewing gum: a policeman's way of looking at villains.

'Yeah?' he said eventually, noncommittal. 'Well, you'll have to tell all that to the magistrate. I can't see him taking much notice, though, not after tonight. A lot of coppers got hurt, and anyone out there on the streets was fair game.'

Michael stared at Austin, remembering this flinty constable as a boy of twelve, walking across the lawn at Mount View Farm to say goodbye. He had shaken hands then, craven and awkward. No doubt he could still turn sycophantic with superior officers, but otherwise it was the early playground bully who had flourished and taken over the adult man.

Suddenly, Austin took Michael by the upper arm. In a moment of confusion and panic, Michael felt something terrible was going to happen to him, that he was going to be interrogated or tortured; he tried to shrug the hand off but it held on tight.

'I could murder a cup of tea.' Austin's voice and eyes were amused at Michael's shrinking reaction. There was a good four inches in height between them. 'How about you?'

'Thanks.' Michael looked down, ashamed.

He followed Austin: the back of his neck seemed still to carry the tan of Africa. They went through a door marked 'interview room', and Michael sat in a moulded plastic chair at a bare table.

'Hang about while I go for the tea.'

There was the click of the lock after Austin shut the door. Michael stared at it, still amazed and resentful at the reversal of their roles. The officious, unpopular schoolboy whom he had so magnanimously befriended had become his jailer. He let his tiredness pull his head down to the table. It's the vicious bastards who do well in life, he thought, revelling in his position as victim; I always knew it.

The sound of the door woke him, disoriented. The light of the bare bulb was brilliant and harsh, and he rubbed his eyes.

'There you are.'

Austin pushed a cup of tea towards him, much of it slopped in the saucer. It was strong and refreshing. Michael decided again that he must make the effort at conversation.

'Well, what d'you make of it, then? Tonight, I mean? I expect they're calling it a riot, aren't they?'

Austin nodded.

'They caught us off our guard,' he said eventually, reluctantly. 'But we sorted them out in the end. And it won't happen again. Or if it does, we'll be ready.'

'Off your guard? It was pretty predictable, wasn't it? It's been building up for ages.'

Michael realised he was starting an argument, but could not stop himself. Austin looked at him coolly, sipping tea.

'What d'you do for a living, then?'

'I work in the advice centre, you probably know it, up the Front Line there.'

A hard gleam entered Austin's eye and he nodded slowly, putting down his teacup.

'I see. Now it all fits into place.'

'What does?'

'You out there, chucking bricks at us. You were obviously on the side of the coons from the start. D'you know, I'm surprised, quite honestly, that someone with your background in Africa should end up like that, as a nigger-lover. I'd have thought you'd know what they're like better than the average Britisher.'

Michael stared at Austin in disbelief: was the man taking a rise

175

out of him? There seemed to be no fissure in his expression to suggest he was anything but completely serious.

The pause lengthened while he tried to decide how to handle this conversation. He felt that Austin had brought him here to impress his views on him, and was not going to be thwarted; better to get it over with the minimum of fuss. He passed his hand wearily down his face.

'OK, what *are* they like?'

Again the cool look over the rim of the teacup. There was more banging of doors and harsh, nervous laughter in the yard outside: another delivery.

'Round here? They're a thieving, toe-ragging bunch of niggers round here, that's what they are.'

'Oh, so that's it.' Michael tried to put jollity in his sarcasm. 'I must have made a mistake. I thought they were just ordinary poor people trying to get along, like everyone else. You know, some-where to live, a job, schools for the kids, maybe a bit of money to spend.'

Austin did not seem to hear. He held his cup caressingly between his palms, and there was a filmed look to his eyes, as if his mind had locked into treasured memories which could not be interrupted. He continued in a calm, reflective voice.

'We gave one lot a good hiding tonight, though. Christ, did we give those bastards a hiding. Not that we had any choice. There were just too many of them coming in, it was ridiculous. No space in the cells, no transport to take them elsewhere. So we just offloaded a few vans in that cul-de-sac out the back and let them have it. Jesus, you should have heard those niggers screaming and carrying on. Took me right back to Rhodesia, I can tell you. You know what coons are like, they're the same everywhere. But that lot won't be chucking bricks at the police again in a hurry, I can guarantee that.'

Michael was gripped by the despair and exhaustion which falls in the deepest part of the night. He thought: this man could be talking of the slaughter of pigs. He remembered the biggest of the group of policemen coming into the backyard, a stave in his hand, his face gleaming with satisfied agitation.

'So you deliberately beat people up instead of bringing them in here and charging them? You people always blame the anti-police mob for saying things like that.'

Austin looked at Michael as if suddenly remembering his presence in the room.

'That's right, that's what we did. But don't try telling anyone because they won't believe you. You're lucky you didn't get the same treatment. If you'd arrived a bit earlier you would have.'

'You might have killed someone. Or injured them very badly.'

Austin shrugged his shoulders.

'If they didn't want to get hurt, they should have stayed off the streets instead of throwing petrol bombs at the police. You ever seen a petrol bomb go off?'

'Only tonight, for the first time.'

'Well, some of our blokes were quite badly burnt, earlier on. They had their clothes set on fire, and those bloody shields were melting. It makes you pretty bloody frightened, I don't mind admitting it – and pretty bloody angry, too. You want to get the bastards.'

'Yes, I suppose so.'

Michael's feelings were now at sea. He remembered the brick and its spine-cracking impact on the officer's back. Maybe it was a war – like it had been in Rhodesia.

'How long were you actually out there, then? In Rhodesia, I mean.'

'Until seventy-eight. Then we realised the politicos were going to sell us down the river. Parents and sister are back here too, of course. They've got a smallholding down in Kent, she's working in Maidstone as a secretary.'

'And you were involved in the war out there?' A new tack, but the course was inevitably the same.

'Sure. I did my army service like the rest. Kicked some shit out of the terrs, I can tell you.'

Austin's manner was nonchalant, but his fingers were now playing nervously with his saucer.

'Best of all was the 'copter units, out in the bush. We'd locate them, chase them for a bit, then go down and let them have it. They'd be running like fuck all over the place, and we'd just pick 'em off. Slotting floppies, that's what we called it. From the way they flopped over in the dirt. Killed dozens of the bastards. Never worked out where they all came from.'

Michael studied Austin's clipped moustache and pale lips, feeling cold and disgusted at this callousness over violence and death. His temper was rising, his self-control failing.

'You sound like a complete bloody barbarian.'

Austin sat up straight in his chair, his face darkening, his hands grasping the table edge firmly. His voice turned harsh.

'Ach, don't give me all that bleeding-heart stuff. They were the fucking barbarians, man. You should have seen what they did with their bayonets to some of the women and kids out in the bush who wouldn't support them. Bloody savages. And shooting down an airliner which wasn't even a military target – it was full of civilians, man. Tourists, even.'

'I don't see that either side was worse than the other. The blacks were in a war of liberation, and all the odds were against them. They had to be ruthless. But it was the whites who started the ruthlessness, when they walked into the country sixty years ago and shot anyone who stood in their way.'

Austin refused the broadening of the argument, folding his arms and sticking to details.

'So you'd justify killing innocent tourists in pursuit of a Marxist takeover?'

'What a loaded question. But sure, tourists who go to places where there's a struggle like that going on are bound to be fair game.'

'So you are a degenerate. A nice liberal English education, I'll bet, some sort of softy arts degree at uni, and now it's do-gooding with the *munts*. You always were a stuck-up little twerp, fuck knows why I bothered with you as a kid. You feel so guilty about living in an African colony that you've got to prove that blacks can be civilised human beings too.'

'That's right. Because that's what they would be, if they weren't denied the education, the opportunities, by racists like you.'

'Ah, come off it, Hope. Why don't you wake up? The Front Line out there tonight was just Britain's version of what was going on in Rhodesia – sorry, Zimbabwe' – he mouthed the word in a slow, insulting parody of an African voice. 'Same thing'll be going on down in South Africa before long. Blacks and whites will never be equal, don't you realise? You give them equality, they'd take it and do you down, man. They're not interested in equality, they're interested in winning – taking over. Those fucking Rastas actually think the black is superior, d'you know that? And there's more of them than us out there in the world, man, make no mistake. They reckon we've had our turn, and it's their turn next. They won't be happy until we're the slaves, I tell you. I'm surprised at someone with your background, going in for all that sentimental rubbish. But now I think about it, you've always been a nigger-lover.'

Austin's eyes were now glowing with fervour and contempt.

'What d'you mean?'

'You know what I mean, prick. When we were kids, that time you picked up that scar on your face. You went off up Elgon with that little nig-nog from the farm, the one who said he'd show you the elephants. Elephants, my foot. He led you over a fucking cliff instead. Typical.'

Michael's private world was being invaded, and he came angrily to its defence.

'As it happens, he didn't lead me over a cliff. We fell at the same time. And we *did* see the elephants – I never told *you* about them, because I knew it wasn't the kind of thing you'd understand or have any feeling for.'

'There's nothing to bloody understand, as far as I'm concerned.'

'Exactly. And since I'm a nigger-lover, there are a few things I remember which gave your game away, Austin, even then.'

The agitation of old and muddy waters had washed away Michael's fatigue, and the two men faced each other in an intimate conflict far from the events of this April night. They had branched off the same stem in different directions, and were both attached and opposed to each other. Austin's eyes turned cold and challenging. Michael did not care now how childish it became.

'Come on then, let's hear it.'

'That piece of garden hose your father kept on the wall. I actually watched through the window of your house one day when he gave you a thrashing with it. Not a pretty sight, I can tell you. You were cursing and screaming like a baby and he was hitting you all over the place, dragging you round the room. I'm not surprised that violence is the only language you understand. The real giveaway, though, was that you had a teddy bear under your pillow.'

Austin smiled but his eyes turned fearful.

'Spare me the psychological stuff, will you? That's like saying these black muggers knock down old ladies and kick their heads open because they had a deprived childhood. I don't go in for that shit. Sounds to me like *your* father should have given you a good hiding now and again, might have knocked some sense into you.'

'D'you know something, Austin? I'm a bit surprised they took on a racist like you in the police force, fresh from a civil war in Africa. I know they're bone-headed, but I didn't know they were *that* stupid. How did you slip through the net?'

'They don't want people who *like* niggers, fool, otherwise the force would be full of wankers like you. They want people who understand their disgusting habits, and there's nobody who understands niggers as well as me. And I know what authority is, and how to enforce it.'

'Christ, Austin, every word you say revolts me. For some reason, when we were kids, I was never quite honest enough, never quite sure enough, to tell you what a nasty, bullying little shit you were. I suppose in those days there were still some redeeming features, but I can't see any now.'

'You're making me wish I was your arresting officer, you know. You'd be facing a good deal more than assault if I was, I can tell you.'

'Oh, so you admit that what people get charged with bears no relation to what they've actually done?'

Austin's face suddenly closed, and he stood up, taking a grip on himself. His voice cooled to impassivity.

'I think you'd better go back to the cells where you belong, with your nigger friends. Perhaps it'll remind you of your wonderful experiences out in the caves, with your first-ever black chum. You can roll around on the floor together and work out how to create a multi-racial society. Swap stories about elephants.'

Michael stood too, still defiant and angry.

'Right. And you'd better get back to your racist pals. You can talk all night about beating them with rubber hoses to stop them taking over the world with their big black cocks. It's right, what they say about this country being the last British colony. That's why your sort brought the blacks over, wasn't it? To give you someone to feel superior to. If there weren't any black people to mistreat you'd all have to look each other in the eye and realise what a bunch of crawling white worms you are.'

Michael was aware of Austin's fists clenching, the muscle bunching between thumb and forefinger. He pulled the door open viciously and pointed. Michael walked through, the back of his neck braced for a blow, but it did not come.

The station was still busy with tired-looking officers in unbuttoned tunics and surly or dejected prisoners being led around the corridors.

Back at the cells, the atmosphere seemed fetid with the traffic of hot, angry bodies.

'You finished with him, Chris?' asked the jailer, opening the cell door.

'Yeah, I've had about as much as I can take.'

Michael was stepping round the snoring drunk when Austin stopped him with a hard grip on the upper arm. They came face to face, and Michael noticed for the first time that there were wrinkles of stress and gathering age in the blond skin around Austin's eyes. There was also a fleck of snot in the bristles of his moustache.

'You know,' said Austin. 'I reckon about six months inside will sort you out. You'll have had enough of coons by the time you come out.'

The door was slammed violently, and the sleeping drunk started up with a moan of fright. Seeing Michael above him, he threw up a thin arm in self-protection.

Nineteen

Juliet returned to work at the end of August, when the city lay exhausted under a gritty heat haze. Her colleagues ensured her comfort, made her coffee, took her out to lunch, encouraged her to go home early, and succeeded only in irritating her. She did not want to be the widow in weeds, and yet could find no tactful way to stop the clucking. She felt people would never let her find normality again, and began to avoid seeing her friends. She took evening walks up to Brockwell Park, trying to gain height, escape the cloying air of the streets. She sat looking over the grey jumble of Brixton to the tall buildings of the City, blending with the metallic evening sky. She studied the trees for the first tinge of brown, wanting the cool wind of a new season to come and clear her head, close the chapter. Afterwards she went slowly back to watch television, smoke cigarettes, leaf through the advertisement-packed Sunday magazines, which stirred no interest in her. The flat seemed populated by slow, fat flies.

One evening she encountered Everett Thompson strolling through the park; he recognised her too and stopped, shifting from foot to foot, hands thrust in pockets.

'Sorry to hear about Mike,' he said. 'Read it in the papers, and that.'

'I'm getting over it – life must go on.' She had repeated the hollow phrase endlessly, and her smile was mechanical.

'Mike was a good guy. I used to rip him off for being a white liberal, but he was a good guy. Took a lot of trouble over things.'

'Well . . . he thought a lot of you, too, I know.'

'Yeah, well . . . listen, I'm sorry I never got to see him when he was in prison. Trouble is, you've got to get permission, and I can't stand going near those places, know what I mean?'

'They're not the nicest places . . .'

'And he was fitted up something rotten, you know that? He wouldn't have got a sentence like that even if he'd been a black, that magistrate went over the top, if you ask me.'

Juliet smiled, wondering whether to tell him of the account of the riots she had just read in Michael's prison notebooks – how he'd thought he was going to Everett's aid just before he got arrested. But Everett was turning away to the hazy view, nodding at his own thoughts.

'Funny when people die, you know, they just disappear and no one knows any more what they were all about. People think they know, but everyone thinks something different. Then everyone sort of forgets, and there's nothing to remember them by. Anyway . . . I'd better get on my way.'

She studied his lean form as he sauntered off, jealous of his vitality and busyness while she felt so faded and played out. He was the future and she was the past, she felt; she was as finished as Michael and nothing could revive her.

Bob Delvers phoned her again that evening and in her loneliness and despondency she agreed to go out for dinner with him the following night. Their meeting was cautious and formal, and he took her to Covent Garden where they sat outside the restaurant in the cooling dusk, drinking wine.

Delvers looked younger and more good-natured after his break from work, and the pockmarks on his large hard face seemed less reddened than before. He was also less dogmatic and insistent, and paid her compliments without making her feel he was going to grope for her thigh under the table; she began to relax with the alcohol, and mentioned at last the midnight package.

'I wasn't surprised by what it described,' she said, repositioning her cutlery as she picked her words. 'I suppose I've become so cynical about African politics that people being shot at road blocks hardly seems out of the ordinary. What did surprise me, though, was the names.'

'Why the names?' He raised his lumpy eyebrows.

She explained about the letters from Kimutei to Michael, how he was the childhood friend who had taken him to see the elephants – and how his first name differed only in spelling from the one in the shooting.

'The letters do show that Kimutei was getting very disillusioned – living in Mathare Valley in Nairobi, selling stuff to tourists, getting frustrated and angry. It's conceivable that someone like that might get pulled into crime.'

Delvers took a swig of wine and stared at Juliet, his face seeming paler and smoother still, his stubby hands holding the edge of the table. He shook his head.

'I don't believe it – it's too much of a coincidence. Ironies as crude as that don't happen in real life.'

Juliet pulled a letter with a Kenyan stamp from her handbag and passed it to him. It was addressed to her in rounded, old-fashioned handwriting in fountain pen.

'It's from the Northrops. Michael told me that Kimutei's mother used to look after their children before the Hopes took her on, so I wrote to them and asked if they knew what his second name was. The reply arrived this morning.'

Delvers spread the letter on the table.

Twiga Farm,
23 August 1982

My dear Juliet,

Thank you for your letter which we received today. We are replying straight away because it seemed to us that you have been further upset by the business of the names and what it might mean, and we are anxious to do anything we can to reassure you. Unfortunately, however, that probably isn't very much. I'm afraid the plain fact is we don't know what Kimutei's second name was, and we didn't know what Mary's was either. It may have been remiss of us, but we just didn't enquire too closely into that sort of thing. Nobody ever did, very much. She was a very good *ayah*, almost a member of the family, but we didn't know all that much about her, although it was widely believed that Kimutei was illegitimate and that too many questions might hurt Mary's feelings and possibly give the impression we didn't approve of her, which was far from the truth. All rather unsatisfactory, I'm afraid.

The only thing we have been able to come up with tends to increase the uncertainty rather than do away with it, unfortunately. Something about the second name, Koitalel, rang a bell with Bill, and he wandered round with a frown on his face all day until he remembered where it came from. There's a book called *Kenya Diary*, written at the beginning of the century by an army officer who was out here – a bit of a nutcase called Meinertzhagen. Anyway, this chap was involved in an operation to pacify the Nandis, who wouldn't stay quietly in their reserve, and he tells the story of how he killed the *laibon*, or chief, thinking the bloke was luring him into a trap. The name of the chief was Koitalel, and since Mary and Kimutei were Nandis, it's quite possible he adopted the name when he grew up (arap, of course, means 'son of'). He might have done it to make a point, as it were – for all we know, Koitalel might have been a hero among the tribe, killed by the treacherous white man, and so on. On the other hand, it isn't such a rare name, and nor is Kimutei, so there's every chance it was someone else entirely. We'll make some more enquiries round the farm and put the word out, but we've already spoken to the two or three people we've got who still remember Mary, and they're no clearer than we are about the name.

I'm terribly sorry we can't put your mind at rest, Juliet, because it's a very cruel twist for you to come on this extra uncertainty just as you were probably beginning to get over things. It would be terribly ironic if all the men shot at the road block were innocent *and* one of them was Michael's boyhood friend. But even more ironic if they weren't innocent, although in a much more terrible way. Whichever way you look at it, though, there's no comfort in it for you, which is the worst thing. Chief Inspector Kariuke came out to see us about it all, actually, and asked us to send you his kind regards. He seemed to have taken to you, and he's not a bad sort of bloke, actually. Seems to be just looking forward to his retirement now . . .

Delvers slowly folded the letter and handed it back impassively. Their food arrived and they ate in silence. Eventually Juliet mentioned his package again.

'It was so different from that foul article you wrote. Much more thoughtful – apart from a few offensive phrases about culling Taigs and so on, which I suppose come from your primitive origins. But it could have been a short story or something, the way it was written.'

Delvers gave a pleased laugh and poured more wine.

'I know. It wasn't intended as a piece of journalism, you see. I was trying to convey the spirit of the occasion, and I've concluded recently that sticking too closely to the facts can actually prevent you from getting at the truth, in a way. I've begun to feel it's more honest just to make your beliefs clear and argue openly for your version of the truth, your interpretation of the facts. It's all rather new ground for me after twenty-odd years as a hack, strangely enough – but d'you see what I mean?'

Juliet was surprised to find his face red and anxious again. She began to feel uneasy and suspicious, and shifted in her seat, eyes down.

'Oh dear – is this what you meant by saying you had ideas for taking it further?'

'Well, I'm thinking of publishing something about this whole affair, from start to finish, from the time Michael was born out in Africa. The only thing is . . .'

'You'd need my help?'

'That's right. I've talked to a few people about it already, but I could never get the full picture without you. For example, those letters you mentioned earlier.'

'I see.'

185

Juliet stared around her at the garrulous diners. She had been relaxing, sharing the atmosphere, enjoying herself for the first time for weeks; but this made her very uneasy. What was Delvers after? If he were still pursuing her, she would prefer it to be straightforward; given the clenched loneliness of recent times, and tonight's unexpected return of conviviality, she might even comply. But getting inside her indirectly by writing, or pretending to write, about Michael – it struck her as sinister and obscene. The waiter brought their coffee and she fiddled with her spoon.

'What's the problem?'

'I don't know – I suppose I just wonder if I'm ever going to escape from what's happened. A dead person in your life is so powerful.'

He leaned forward, determined.

'But that's it, don't you see? This would be a way of escaping from what's happened – by making sense of it, tying it down. It would only be one version, of course, but it would be partly yours, and it would be something you could cope with, you could either keep it or forget it. Less uncertainty.'

Juliet remembered what Everett had said: no-one knows any more what they were all about . . . everyone sort of forgets, and there's nothing to remember them by. The things Michael had left behind had only confused her knowledge of him, made it more complicated.

'Well, yes. But the trouble is, you see, that Michael was trying to write something like this himself, although I didn't know about it until I started going through his papers. Bits of description from his childhood, his description of the riots, his time in prison . . .'

'But that's perfect! The ideal basis for the book.'

Delvers leaned back, smiling and spreading his palms as if the issue were settled. Juliet felt irritated by his hastiness, feeling she was being swept into something with no time to consider. The powerlessness reminded her of Michael in prison, standing at the high barred window and failing to see the trees in spring.

'Hang on a minute. You couldn't just do what you liked, you know. There are some bits Michael wrote that would have to stay unchanged. I'd insist on that.'

'Of course. A collaborative venture. It would all have your approval.'

'There's something particular I've got in mind – the last entry he made in his diary when he was in prison. I've read it again and again. It explains what was behind his character, really, why he wanted to write about what had happened. And why he wasn't going to write any more. You mustn't change a word of that.'

Delvers nodded, more thoughtfully than before.

'OK. Should be no problem.'

Juliet brushed back a sheaf of her pale blonde hair. The effectiveness of this gesture had become clear to her at the age of six, and she had never changed it. She smiled at Delvers, feeling suddenly excited by the project.

'Right. Let's get the bill and go, shall we?'

They drove across Waterloo Bridge, where bright lights on the water reflected her mood. She remembered her drive to Nairobi with Delvers, and was glad the feeling was now so different. Life would change, she could escape.

Then they were back among the dimmer landscapes of the south London hinterland, with its gloomy blocks of flats and groups of people waiting stoically for buses or walking the pavements with hunched, defensive shoulders. In Brixton, the railway bridge over the main road was decorated with bright and hopeful slogans.

'Everything's had a coat of paint,' remarked Delvers.

'Yes, but that's all it's had.'

'You don't sound too hopeful.'

'I'm not – but next time it happens, I won't be here. This rat's jumping overboard.'

By the time Juliet was making coffee in the little kitchen all the weight and complication of life had returned to her. She decided to tackle Delvers directly.

He was walking restlessly round the sitting room, picking up objects and putting them down again. She handed him his mug and told him irritably to sit. He did so, heavily.

'What's bothering you now?' he asked.

'This whole project – I suspect your motives. There's something unhealthy going on. You're using it as a complicated way of trying to, well, seduce me . . .'

Delvers, beginning to smile, raised a hand in dissent, but she forged on, pink in the face.

'. . . Well, come on, you've tried before, haven't you? In a really clumsy and tactless way, as it happens. And what the hell are you grinning at now?'

'Nothing. I'm relieved, I suppose. You're probably not aware of it, but your behaviour over the last couple of hours has been quite

187

seductive, in fact. I was beginning to worry that you were going to come across – or whatever the expression should be in the home counties.'

'Oh – I see. And was that such a repulsive prospect?'

'Not at all. Far from it. It's just that I've changed somewhat since we were out in Nairobi. I behaved very badly there, I know, and I've never been able to apologise properly for that. Now's a good opportunity, I suppose.'

She remained defiant, sitting with legs folded underneath her and staring at him darkly.

'So what's brought on this miraculous change? From sex fiend to little lamb in three easy stages?'

'Such a sharp tongue. The road block . . . leaving work . . . spending more time with my family . . . thinking about things. Thinking about this book idea. Kariuke asked me to write the truth.' He shrugged.

She continued to look at him impassively, wondering whether to question him further about this metamorphosis. He was hardly the most reliable witness to such changes in himself, and could people change like this, anyway? She wanted to change herself, and in a sudden act of faith she decided to accept what he said. It was enough for her that he should say the change had happened. She got up and fetched the bottle of whisky from the kitchen; it had last been touched by Michael, but she did not think of this.

When they were settled with half-full tumblers, she asked him what he considered to be the central theme of the planned book. He gazed into his glass for inspiration.

'The end of the Empire, I suppose. Variations on a familiar theme which, like it or not, is going to be heard for many years yet – decades. It's still woven into people, even into people who appear to be remote from it. Almost all the characters here, if you can call them that, are children of the Empire. The most obvious ones are the Northrops and Kariuke and Michael and Kimutei, but there's all their contemporaries and the kids who grew up with them . . .'

Juliet smiled, keeping to herself the surprise about Chris Austin's reappearance as a policeman in Brixton. That would win Delvers' enthusiasm.

'. . . and there's myself, of course, a product of the oldest colony, with attitudes to match. And there's you – you've never told me much about your background, but I can imagine your father having been in the Indian Army or something, facing up to rioting Congress wallahs in the forties.'

'I'll tell you all about it some time. Meanwhile, I suppose you'd better take those away with you tonight and start reading.'

His eyes followed the nod of her head towards the boxes from the attic, lined up like sentinels against the wall of the room.

Twenty

I was dozing on my bunk this afternoon when a pigeon began cooing, gently and rhythmically, in the trees outside. Spring is beginning, but you can see none of the greenness from this top-floor cell. The window lets you see other parts of the grey prison buildings, a sky which is occasionally blue, but no grass or trees. And yet the sound of that pigeon transported me miraculously from this stuffy, piss-reeking place to Mount View Farm and the home of my childhood. A vision, and all the sensations which went with it, was suddenly complete.

It was a hot, still afternoon, with great banks of cloud building up behind the mountain and throwing dark patches on the bright, brown-yellow land. I am lying on the lawn in front of the house, watching the big black ants plodding between the stalks of coarse grass in a dogged line. In the flowered bushes of the garden, the brightly coloured weaver birds are chattering and rustling; down on the farm there sounds the shout of an African, answered straight away by a still more distant call. Down near the river, leopards might be dozing, invisible in the trees, and up on Elgon the mysterious elephants will be standing silent and hidden in the bamboo forest. And then a pigeon, sitting in a red-flowered flame tree near the dam, starts calling, softly, lazily: cu coo-roo, cu coo-roo. Do not move! Keep your eyes closed and breathe lightly, and the world will stay like this for ever. The past has returned.

How can I communicate such longing? For much of the time since my sentence began, I have been scribbling away, trying to describe those childhood times which haunt me and those adult events which seem to flow from them; trying to recapture that bright-skied highland country, where the sun in the day gives a slight, delightful pinch to the skin and the cool, dust-stained evening air catches on the back of your mouth; trying to bring back colours and smells and sounds so intense they make you wince. But each time I read again what I have written, the focus has slipped, and the version composed so studiously only days before seems now to distort things, invent things, or leave too much out. It is as if none of these matters can be defined in, confined in, words. There is no release in the attempt at expression.

And so, like the country I am compelled to call mine, I am trapped: I cannot face the future and instead I glance constantly over my shoulder at past glories, making pathetic attempts to revive what used to be. I am crippled by the past, which cannot return to heal me. I am a man prevented by melancholy from living, who will only be real and come to life when he is dead. This is what depression is like – an unyielding gloom, so intense it sometimes gives pleasure, which stifles the desire to live.

I have sometimes believed I do not deserve to live because my cause, my predicament, is false. The exercise yard of the prison hospital can be seen from the window, and every day I watch a listless crocodile of men, half of them black, shuffling round the bare asphalt for fifteen minutes, observed by the stiff, blunt little prison officers. There is one man I watch in particular – he is black, huge and powerfully built, but with childishness in his movements and a fixed expression of inconsolable anguish. He walks slowly, alone, his eyes never changing their distant focus, his arms hugging his chest. What right do I have to my despair when faced with this man, who has lost his country and his birthright in a way I can never understand, and who has no prospects in life? I envy that man, because his despair is genuine and worthy. I want his suffering, and feel I could use it better than he.

Sometimes I hear two Rastafarians singing in the next cell, a mournful hymn for Sheshemane, their tract of land in Ethiopia. And when they fall silent I hear in my head a chanting which drifts up to our house at Mount View from the huts on the farm where the people are celebrating and feasting with a wild pig killed that day. I get out of bed, eight years old, and stand at the window where I can see the red glow of the fires and absorb those swelling, longing sounds. I go back to bed cold and lost and frightened, knowing my parents cannot help my distress, knowing that my thin and brittle voice could never follow songs like that.

And a few years ago, on television, I heard the same sound again in a film about the guerillas in Rhodesia. They sat in tattered combat uniforms, their bare and horny feet towards the fire, singing a chorus which ached with their love and fear: 'Long live Africa . . . aa, long live Africa.' Africa will live for ever, without me.

These were the men that Chris Austin used to kill with the enthusiasm and nonchalance of swatting flies: 'slotting floppies', he called it. Yet how did I behave as a child, what contribution did I make to black dignity and freedom? It was the same thing. A small boy, plump on food cooked by thin Africans, crisp in the clothes washed and ironed by them, would insult them and deride them. Men of fifty, with grave brown eyes, could not answer me back because they were powerless and wore rags. One who spoke English once said to me, with a brave and pitiful attempt at dignity: 'Do not abuse me.' And I danced round his bony, impotent body, mimicking his clumsy phrase and awkward diction.

No one is interested now in my repentance. Black people will not love me for it, and it leads me into trouble. It was not Everett Thompson I saw in the riot, when I paused to help him and was captured instead. I discovered later that he was in Birmingham that night, and he has never been to visit me here. We live in different worlds. He is a canny survivor, while I am moribund, lumbering clumsily into traps. He has no need or understanding of me and my bleeding heart. He has his own concerns and will make his fate without me, in the same way as Kimutei.

And perhaps, then, Austin is right. Warfare between black and white is the only true state of affairs; there may be truces, joining of forces, but never the same abiding interests. History, the sins of our fathers, maybe even our genes, bind us into conflict. And so the riots in Britain will be repeated, in a few years, and they will be more vicious on both sides, with deaths and shootings. The ghettoes will swell, we will create the miseries of America with none of its hope, and politicians will court votes by talking of repatriation for people who have known no other country.

In the moments when these clouds lift, I struggle to construct a plan for the future, a plan of escape. It is all people can do in prison if they are not to succumb. I have my programme, although it lacks conviction and lives only in my mind. I must put the past behind me, dismiss these things I have been writing about, change my life and become free. I must start feeling strong instead of guilty. Soon I will be out of here, and I will make our trip to Africa like an exorcism. Then, the old ghosts behind me, we will move away from the city, have children as a pledge of hope and trust, live and work far from the wastelands created in the death struggles of the Empire. The Empire was not my fault, and I will refuse to deal with its legacy any longer; for if I do not escape it, it will pull me down. This is the plan, this is the idea. I am determined to be optimistic. I must harden my heart, though it feels hollow, and we shall see what reality brings.